For Pascaline, obviously,
without whom, none of this would be . . .

SOPHIE

BLOOD WEDDING

Also by Pierre Lemaitre in English translation

THE BRIGADE CRIMINELLE TRILOGY
Irène
Alex
Camille

The Great Swindle
Three Days and a Life

Pierre Lemaitre

BLOOD WEDDING

Translated from the French by
Frank Wynne

MACLEHOSE PRESS
QUERCUS · LONDON

First published in the French language as *Robe de marié* by
Editions Calmann-Lévy in 2009
First published in Great Britain in 2016 by MacLehose Press
This paperback edition published in 2017 by

MacLehose Press
An imprint of Quercus Editions Limited
Carmelite House
50 Victoria Embankment
London EC4Y 0DZ

An Hachette UK company

A CIP catalogue record for this book is available
from the British Library.

ISBN (MMP) 978 1 848666 00 9
ISBN (OME) 978 0 857056 56 6
ISBN (E-book) 978 1 84866 599 6

10 9 8 7 6 5 4 3 2

Designed and typeset in Minion by James Nunn
Printed and bound in Great Britain by Clays Ltd, St Ives plc

Sitting on the ground, back against the wall, legs extended, struggling for breath.

Léo is lying across her, utterly still, his head resting in her lap. With one hand she strokes his hair, with the other she tries but cannot quite manage to wipe away tears. She is crying. The sobs rise to become a wail, she lets out a howl that comes from deep within her belly. Her head sways gently from side to side. At times her misery is so intense she pounds her head against the wall. Pain offers a temporary respite, but all too soon she breaks down again. Léo is perfectly behaved, he does not stir. She bows her head, looks at him, hugs him to her belly and weeps. No-one could imagine the depths of her misery.

1

This morning, like so many others, she woke with tears streaking her face and a hard lump in her throat though she had no particular reason to be upset. Tears are an everyday occurrence in her life: she has wept every night since she went mad. Were it not for the fact that her cheeks are damp every morning, she might think that her nights were spent in deep and peaceful sleep. But waking to find her face bathed in tears and a tightness in her throat is a simple fact of life. Since when? Since Vincent's accident? Since his death? Since the first death, so long ago?

She props herself on one elbow, wipes her eyes with a corner of the sheet, fumbles for her cigarettes but cannot find them, then suddenly she realises where she is. Everything comes flooding back, everything that happened yesterday afternoon, last night . . . Immediately she understands that she must go, she must leave this house. Get up and get out, but still she lies there, rooted to the bed, incapable of the slightest movement. Drained.

*

When at last she manages to drag herself from the bed and stumble to the living room, Mme Gervais is sitting on the sofa, calmly bent over her laptop.

"All good? Sleep well?"

"All good. Yes, thank you."

"You look a little peaky."

"I'm always like this in the morning."

Mme Gervais saves her file and closes the computer.

"Léo is still asleep," she says, walking over to the coat stand. "I didn't dare look in, I was afraid I might wake him. Since there's no school today, I though it best to let him sleep, give you a bit of peace…"

No school today. Sophie vaguely remembers something about an INSET day. Mme Gervais is standing by the door, she has already slipped on her coat.

"I'll leave you to it. . ."

She knows she does not have the courage to announce her decision. In fact, even if she had the courage, she would not have the time. Mme Gervais has already closed the door behind her.

Tonight . . .

Sophie hears footsteps on the stairs. Christine Gervais never takes the lift.

There is silence. For the first time since she has worked here, she lights a cigarette in the living room. She paces up and down. She feels like the survivor of a terrible disaster, everything seems futile. She has to leave. She feels less panicked now that she is alone, now that she is up, now that she has a cigarette. But she knows that, for Léo's sake, she has to get ready to leave. To give herself time to collect her thoughts, she wanders into the kitchen and switches on the kettle.

Léo. Six years old.

As soon as she saw him that first time, she thought he was beautiful. It was four months earlier, in this same living room on rue Molière. He raced into the room, stopped dead in front of her and stared up, his head tilted slightly. In him a sign of intense concentration. His mother simply said:

"Leó, this is Sophie – remember I told you about her."

He studied her for a long moment. Then he said "O.K.", stepped forward, and hugged her.

Léo is a gentle child, a little awkward at times but intelligent and full of life. Sophie's job entails taking him to school in the morning, collecting him at lunchtime and again in the evening, and looking after him until whichever random hour Mme Gervais or her husband finally return home. She can clock off work anytime between 5.00 p.m. and 2.00 in the morning. Her availability was a decisive factor in securing this job: she has no personal life, that much was obvious from the first interview. Mme Gervais did her best not to take advantage of Sophie's constant availability, but the day-to-day routine trumps all ethical principles and, in less than two months, Sophie has become an indispensible part of family life. Because she is always there, always willing.

Léo's father, a tall, lean, brusque man in his forties, is departmental head at the Ministère des Affaires Étrangères. As for Mme Gervais, an elegant, willowy woman with a captivating smile, she tries to balance her onerous responsibilities as statistician to a firm of auditors with those of mother to Léo and wife to a future secretary of state. Each of them earns a very comfortable living. Sophie was wise enough not to exploit this evident fact when it came to negotiating her salary. In fact it did not occur to her, since what she was offered was sufficient for her needs. Mme Gervais increased her salary at the end of the second month.

As for Léo, he is devoted to her. Only she can effortlessly get him to do something that would require hours of coaxing from his mother. He is not, as she feared, a spoiled child prone to tantrums, but a quiet little boy who listens. He has his moods, obviously, but Sophie ranks high in his hierarchy. At the very top, in fact.

Every evening at about 6.00 p.m., Mme Gervais telephones to get the day's news and in an embarrassed tone lets Sophie know what time she will be home. She always talks to her son for a few minutes before speaking to Sophie, with whom she does her best to be friendly. These attempts have met with scant success: Sophie confines her conversation to small talk and a resumé of what has happened during the day.

Léo is put to bed every night at 8.00 p.m. precisely. This is important. Sophie has no children of her own, but she has standards. After reading him a bedtime story, she spends the rest of the evening sitting in front of an enormous flat-screen television capable of receiving every available cable channel, a self-serving gift in the second month of her time there when, no matter what time she came home, Mme Gervais noticed that Sophie would be sitting in front of the television. More than once Mme Gervais has wondered how a woman in her thirties, who is clearly cultured, can be content in such a lowly job and spend her evenings staring at a small screen. During the first interview, Sophie explained that she studied communication. When Mme Gervais pressed her further, she said that she had completed a two-year technology diploma, that she had worked for a British-owned company – though she did not say what her role was – and that she had previously been married. Mme Gervais had been satisfied with this information. Sophie had come recommended by a childhood friend, now the director of a recruitment consultancy, who for some mysterious reason had been much taken by Sophie at her only interview. Besides, she needed someone immediately: Léo's nanny had left without warning, having given no notice. Sophie's calm, serious expression inspired confidence.

During the first weeks, Mme Gervais had probed her a little more about her life, but delicately gave up, sensing from Sophie's answers that some "terrible secret tragedy" had blighted her life, a vestige of the romanticism common to many people, even among the upper classes.

As often happens, by the time the kettle begins to boil, Sophie is lost in thought. With her, it is a state that can last for some time. It is as though she is absent. Her mind becomes fixated on a single idea, a single image, her thoughts slowly coil around it like an insect, she loses all sense of time. Then, by some force of gravity, she comes back to earth and to the present moment, and she picks up her life where she left off. This is how it is.

This time, curiously, it is the image of Doctor Brevet that comes into her mind. She has not thought about him in a long time. He was not at all as she had imagined him. On the telephone she had pictured a tall, overbearing figure, but in fact he is a short little man; he looks like a legal assistant overawed at being allowed to deal with less important clients. On one side of the consulting room is a bookshelf filled with knick-knacks. The moment she stepped into the psychologist's office, she told him she did not want to lie on a couch, preferring to sit instead. Doctor Brevet made a gesture to indicate that this presented no problem. "I don't have a couch here," he said. Sophie explained herself as best she could. "A notepad," the doctor finally declared. Sophie was to record everything she did. Perhaps she was making "a storm in a teacup" of these memory lapses of hers. One needed to try to see things objectively, said Doctor Brevet. That way, "You will be able to measure the extent of what you have forgotten, what you have missed." And so Sophie began to note down everything. She had done so for about three weeks . . . Until their next session. And during that time she had forgotten many things. She had missed several meetings and, two hours before her visit with Doctor Brevet, she realised she had mislaid the notebook. She could not find it. Would this be the day she stumbled finally on Vincent's birthday present? The one she had been unable to find when she had wanted to surprise him.

Everything is muddled, her whole life is a muddle . . .

She pours hot water into a bowl and finishes her cigarette. Friday. No school. Usually, she is required to look after Léo only during the day on Wednesdays, and sometimes at weekends. She takes him here and there, according to their whims and to the opportunities that present themselves. Until now they have had a lot of fun together, and a lot of arguments. To begin with everything was fine.

That is, until she began to have unsettling, and later disturbing feelings. She did not want to attach too much importance to them, tried to shoo them away like irritating flies, but they haunted her still. It began to affect her attitude to the child. Nothing alarming, not at first. Just something subterranean, silent. Something secret that involved them both.

Until the truth suddenly dawned on her, a day ago, on place Danremont.

That late summer in Paris was warm and sunny. Léo wanted an ice cream. She sat on a bench, she was not feeling well. At first, she put her unease down to the fact they were in the square, a place she hates more than any other since she spends her time avoiding having conversations with mothers. She has succeeded in warding off the incessant efforts of the regulars. They have learned not to strike up a conversation with her. But she still has to deal with the mothers who drop in occasionally, the newcomers, the passers-by, not to mention the pensioners. She hates this square.

She is leafing absentmindedly through a magazine when Léo comes and stands in front of her. He is eating his ice cream, looking at her fixedly for no particular reason. She looks back at him. And in that precise moment she knows that she cannot bury this thought that has suddenly dawned on her: inexplicably, she has begun to loathe the child. He continues to stare at her intently and she feels a rising panic at the thought that everything about him is hateful: his angelic face, his lips, his idiotic grin, his ridiculous clothes.

"We're leaving," she says, though given her tone she might just as well have said, "I'm leaving." The whirring contraption inside her head has started up again. With its lapses, its gaps, its holes, its babble . . . While she is hurrying back to the house (Léo whines when she walks too quickly), she is assailed by a jumble of images: Vincent's car wrapped around a tree strobed by flashing blue lights in the darkness, her watch at the bottom of a jewellery box, the body of Mme Duguet tumbling down the stairs, the burglar alarm howling in the middle of the night . . . The images flicker, forward and backward, new and old. The dizzying machine is once again in perpetual motion.

Sophie never measures the years since she first went mad. They go back too far. Perhaps because of the anguish involved, she feels they count double. It began as a gradual descent, but as the months passed she began to feel she was on a toboggan, hurtling downhill. Sophie was married then. It was a time before . . . all this. Vincent was a very patient man. Every time Sophie thinks of him, he appears in a series of slow dissolves: the face of the young man, smiling, serene, dissolving into the haggard, sallow face of those last months, the glazed eyes. In the early days of their marriage (she can still conjure their apartment in perfect detail and cannot help but wonder how a single mind can have so many memories and at the same time so many lacunae), Sophie was just a little scatter-brained. This was how he described it: "Sophie is scatter-brained." But she consoled herself because she had always been that way. Then her absentmindedness became strangeness. In a few short months, everything fell apart. She began to forget meetings, things, people; she began to lose things, keys, documents, only to find them weeks later in the most unlikely places. In spite of his natural calm, Vincent gradually became anxious. It was understandable. As time went on . . . she forgot to take the pill, mislaid birthday presents, Christmas decorations. It was enough to try the most patient of souls. At this point Sophie began to note everything down with the meticulous care of a junkie going cold turkey. She lost the notepads. She lost her car, her friends; she was arrested for theft, little by little her problems infected every area of her life and, like an alcoholic, she began to hide her lapses of memory, to lie, to cover up – so that neither Vincent nor anyone else was aware of anything. A therapist suggested a spell in hospital. She refused, until death arrived, uninvited, to join her madness.

As she walks, Sophie opens her bag, rummages inside, lights a cigarette with trembling fingers, inhales deeply. She closes her eyes. Despite the pulsing drone that fills her head and the physical malaise, she notices that Léo is no longer beside her. She turns and sees him in the distance, standing in the middle of the pavement, his arms folded, scowling, stubbornly refusing to move. The sight of this sulky child standing there suddenly fills her with rage. She retraces her steps, stops in front of him and lashes out, giving him a resounding smack.

It is the sound of the slap that brings her to herself. She is mortified, she turns to see whether anyone is watching. There is no-one, the street is quiet, a lone motorcycle passes by. She stares at the boy as he rubs his cheek. He stares back at her, he is not crying. It is as though he realises that this is not really about him.

"We're going home," she says in a decisive tone.

And that is that.

They did not say a word to each other all evening. They each had their reasons. She vaguely wondered whether the slap might not get her into trouble with Mme Gervais, though she realised she did not really care – now that she had decided to go, it was as if she had already left.

As though fate had willed it so, Christine Gervais arrived home especially late that night. Sophie was asleep on the sofa in front of the television where a basketball match was playing to cheers and applause. She was woken by the silence when Mme Gervais switched off the television.

"It's very late," she said apologetically.

Sophie looked up at the figure in a coat standing in front of her. She gave a muffled "No."

"Do you want to sleep over?"

When she comes home late, Mme Gervais always offers to let her stay the night, she says no and Mme Gervais pays for a taxi.

In an instant, Sophie replays the footage of her day, the evening they had spent in pained silence, the evasive looks, Léo gravely and patiently listening to the bedtime story, his mind obviously elsewhere. When he reluctantly allowed her to kiss him goodnight, she was surprised to find herself saying:

"It's alright, poppet, it's alright. I'm sorry . . ."

Léo gave a little nod. It was as if in that moment the adult world had burst into his little universe and he, too, was exhausted. He fell asleep straightaway.

Last night, Sophie was so exhausted that she accepted the offer to stay over.

She cradles the bowl of tea, now cold, in both hands, hardly noticing the tears that fall heavily on the wooden floor. She has a fleeting image of a cat nailed to a wooden door. A black and white cat. Other images bubble up. Corpses. Her past is littered with the dead.

It is time. A glance at the clock on the kitchen wall: 9.20. Without realising, she has lit another cigarette. She stubs it out nervously.

"Léo!"

The sound of her own voice makes her start. She can hear the fear in it, but she does not know where it comes from.

"Léo?"

She rushes into the boy's room. On the bed, the rumpled blankets look like a rollercoaster. She sighs with relief, even gives a vague smile. As her fear subsides, in spite of herself she feels a surge of grateful tenderness.

She moves to the bed.

"Oh dear me, where can my little man be . . .?"

She turns around.

"Is he in here?"

She gently taps the door of the pine wardrobe, still looking at the bed out of the corner of her eye.

"He's not in the wardrobe. Maybe in the drawers . . ."

She pulls out a drawer and pushes it home, once, twice, three times.

"Not this one . . . not that one . . . nope, not here. Where could he be?"

She walks to the door and says in a loud voice:

"Well, if he's not in his bedroom, maybe I should go . . ."

She clacks the door shut without leaving the room, staring at the shape under the blankets. Watching for a movement. Then she feels a knot in the pit of her stomach. The shape is all wrong. She stands frozen, tears start to well again, but they are different now, these are the tears of long ago, the ones that fell, shimmering, on the bloodied body of a man slumped over a steering wheel, the tears she felt as she pressed her hands into an old woman's back and pushed her down the stairs.

Unconsciously, she walks over to the bed and rips away the blankets.

Léo is there, but he is not asleep. He is naked, huddled, his wrists tied to his ankles, his head between his knees. In profile, his face is a disturbing colour. His pyjamas have been used to bind him. Around his throat, a shoelace is pulled so tightly that it has left a deep groove in the flesh.

She brings her hand to her mouth, but she cannot stop herself from vomiting. She lurches forward, managing at the last minute to avoid steadying herself on the child's body, then she has no choice but to lean on the bed. And the small body rolls towards her, Léo's head bumps against her knees. She clutches him so hard that nothing can prevent them falling on top of each other.

And now here she is, slumped on the floor, her back against the wall, hugging Léo's cold, lifeless body to her . . . Her own screams are so wrenching they might have come from someone else. Despite the tears blurring her vision she can see the extent of the tragedy. She strokes his hair instinctively. His face, pale and mottled, is turned towards her, but his wide eyes stare out at nothing.

2

How long? She does not know. She opens her eyes again. The first thing she notices is the smell of vomit on her T-shirt.

She is still sitting on the ground, her back against the bedroom wall, staring stubbornly at the floor as though willing nothing to move, not her head, not her hands, not her thoughts. Stay here, stock still, merge into the wall. When we stop, surely everything else must stop? But the smell makes her heave. She shakes her head. An infinitesimal movement to the right, towards the door. What time is it? The same small movement, this time to the left. She can see one leg of the bed. It is like a jigsaw: a single piece is enough to reconstruct the whole picture in her mind. Keeping her head still, she moves her fingers slightly, feels a wisp of hair; she feels like a diver coming to the surface knowing the horror that awaits her, but she is instantly paralysed by a jolt of electricity: the telephone has begun to howl.

This time she does not hesitate, her head turns to the door. The ringing is coming from the nearest telephone, the one on the cherrywood table in the hall. Her eyes flicker downward and she is transfixed by the sight of the child's body, lying on his side, his head in her lap. The scene has the stillness of a painting.

This is the tableau: a dead child lying in her lap, a telephone that refuses to stop ringing and Sophie, who is responsible for this child and for answering the telephone, slumped against the wall, her head nodding gently, breathing the stench of her own vomit. Her head is spinning, she feels another wave of dizziness, she is about to pass out. Her brain is melting, her hand helplessly reaches out like the hand of a drowning woman. It is an illusion brought on by panic, but the ringing seems to be getting louder. It is all she can hear now, it bores into her brain, overloading it, paralysing it. She stretches her hands in front of her, then out to her sides, blindly groping for some form of support. Eventually, on her right, she feels something solid, something to cling to so she will not founder. Still the ringing continues, it refuses to stop. Her hand grips the corner of the nightstand on which sits Léo's bedside lamp. She squeezes with all her strength, and this muscular reflex briefly causes her dizziness to subside. The ringing seems to have stopped. Long seconds tick past. She holds her breath. Mentally, she counts . . . four, five, six . . . the ringing has stopped.

She slips her arm under Léo's body. He weighs hardly anything. She manages to lay his head on the floor and, with a superhuman effort, struggles to her knees. The silence is almost palpable. She gasps and pants, like a woman giving birth. A long trail of spittle trickles from the corner of her lips. Without turning her head, she stares into space: she searches for a presence. She thinks: there is someone here, in the apartment, they have killed Léo, they are going to kill me too.

At that moment, another jolt of electricity shudders through her body, the telephone rings out again. Find something, anything, quickly. The bedside lamp. She grasps it and jerks hard.

The wire snaps and she gets to her feet and shuffles across the room towards the ringing, one foot in front of the other, holding the lamp like a firebrand, like a weapon, oblivious to the absurdity of the situation. But it is impossible to detect the slightest presence above the telephone, which howls, which shrieks endlessly, a ringing that cleaves the space, mechanical, maddening. She has just reached the door to the bedroom when silence is restored. She steps forward and, suddenly, without knowing why, she is certain that there is no-one in the apartment, that she is alone.

Without thinking, without wavering, she walks to the end of the hallway, to the other rooms, holding the lamp at half-mast, the flex trailing on the ground behind her. She goes back towards the living room, into the kitchen and comes out again, opens doors, all the doors.

Alone.

She collapses on the sofa and eventually drops the bedside lamp. The vomit on her T-shirt seems fresh. She is overcome by a wave of disgust. She pulls it off and throws it to the floor, gets to her feet and walks back to the child's bedroom. There she stands, leaning against the doorframe, staring at the tiny body, arms folded over her bare breasts, weeping softly . . . She has to call someone. It is too late, but she has to call someone. The police, the ambulance service, whom do you call in this sort of situation? Mme Gervais? Fear gnaws at her belly.

She wants to move, but she cannot. Jesus Christ, Sophie, what shit have you got yourself into this time? As though things weren't bad enough. You should leave now, right now, before the telephone rings again, before his mother panics, jumps into a taxi and turns up here screaming and sobbing, before the police, the questions, the interrogations.

Sophie does not know what to do. Call someone? Leave now? She has to choose between two evils. That has been the story of her life.

At last, she stands up straight. Something inside her has come to a decision. She starts running around the apartment, dashing from room to room, sobbing, but her movements are uncoordinated, the running is futile, she hears her own voice, she is whimpering like a child. She tries to steel herself: "Focus, Sophie, take a deep breath and try to think. You need to get dressed, wash your face, pack your things. Now. You need to get out of here. Get your things, pack your bag, hurry." She has been running in circles so long she is a little disorientated. As she passes Léo's room, she cannot help but stop once more. What she sees first is not the boy's lifeless, waxen face, but his neck, and the brown shoelace that snakes across the floor. She recognises it. It is one of the laces from her walking shoes.

3

There are things she no longer remembers about that day. The next thing she sees is the clock on the façade of église Sainte-Élisabeth reading 11.15 a.m.

The sun is beating down and her head is pounding fit to burst. And she is utterly shattered. The image of Léo's body surges up once more. It feels like waking up again. She steadies herself . . . against what? Her hand is pressed against a window. A shop. The glass is cold. She feels beads of sweat trickling from her armpits. Icy cold.

What is she doing here? And where exactly is she? She tries to check the time, but she does not have her watch. Yet she was so sure . . . No, maybe not. She cannot remember. Rue du Temple. Jesus Christ, it cannot have taken her an hour and a half to get here. What did she do with all that time? Where has she been? And more importantly, where are you going now, Sophie? Did you walk here from rue Molière? Or did you take the *métro*?

A black hole. She knows that she is crazy. No, she just needs time, that's all, a little time to pull herself together. She must have taken the *métro*, she decides. She cannot feel her body, only the sweat trickling from her armpits, an icy stream she tries to staunch, pressing her elbows tightly to her body. What is she wearing? Does she look like a madwoman? Her head is teeming, buzzing, whirling with random images. Think. Do something. But what?

She catches her reflection in the shop window and does not recognise herself. At first, she thinks it is not really her. But no, it is her, only there is something about her . . . Something about her, but what?

She looks down the street.

Keep walking, try to think. But her legs refuse to respond. Only her brain seems still to be functioning, somewhat, a whirling maelstrom of words and images she tries to calm by taking a deep breath. Her chest feels tight. As she leans against the window, she tries to collect her thoughts.

You ran away. That's it, you were scared and you ran. When they find Léo's body, they will come looking for you. You will be accused of . . . What do they call it? "*In loco*" something . . . Focus, for God's sake.

In fact, it is very simple. You were responsible for looking after the child and someone came and killed him. Léo . . .

Right now, she has no idea what is happening to her. She needs to think, but she simply cannot. Her every thought stumbles at the same frantic notion: this cannot be happening.

She looks up. She knows this area. It is close to where she lives. There, that explains it, you ran away and you are going home.

But to go home is surely madness. In her right mind, she would never have come here. They will soon come looking for her. They may already be searching for her. She feels a fresh wave of exhaustion. A café, over there on the right. She walks inside.

She finds a table right at the back. She struggles to think clearly. First, orient herself in the space. She is sitting at the back of the café, feverishly staring at the face of an approaching waiter, she glances around, planning an exit route in case she needs to bolt. But nothing happens. The waiter does not ask any questions, he simply looks at her apathetically. She orders a coffee. The waiter trudges back to the counter.

O.K., first she needs to get her bearings.

Rue du Temple. She is . . . let's see, three, no four *métro* stops from home. That's right, four stops, Temple, République, change trains, and then . . . What's the name of the fourth station? She gets off there every day, she has taken the same train hundreds of times. She can picture the entrance clearly, the stairs down and the metal ramps, the newspaper stand in the corner with the guy who always says "Fucking weather, eh?" . . . Shit!

The waiter brings her coffee, sets the bill down next to it: €1.10. Do I have any money with me? Her handbag is on the table in front of her. She was not even aware that she was carrying a handbag.

She is acting automatically, her mind a complete blank. That is how she came to be here, that is why she ran away. Something is stirring inside her, as though she were two people. I am two. One quivering with fear in front of a cup of coffee slowly getting cold and the other who walked here, clutching her handbag, forgetting her watch, blithely heading home as though nothing had happened.

She puts her head in her hands and feels tears running down her cheeks. The waiter looks at her as he polishes glasses, pretending to look blasé. I'm insane, and everyone can see it. I have to leave. I have to get up and leave.

She feels a sudden rush of adrenalin: If I am crazy, then maybe these images in my head are made up. Maybe this is simply a waking nightmare. One she is only now shaking off. That's it, just a nightmare. She dreamed that she killed the child. This morning, why did she panic and run? I was frightened by my own dream, that's all.

Bonne-Nouvelle! That's the name of the *métro* station, Bonne-Nouvelle. But there is another that comes before. This time she has no problem remembering: Strasbourg-Saint-Denis.

Her stop is Bonne-Nouvelle. She is sure of that, she can picture it.

The waiter is staring at her oddly. She is laughing. She was sobbing and suddenly she burst out laughing.

Is any of this real? She needs to know. To be clear in her own mind. She could telephone. Today is . . . Friday. Léo is not at school. He is at home. Léo must be at home.

Alone.

I ran away and left the child on his own.

I have to call.

She grabs her bag, rummages inside. The number is on her mobile. She wipes her eyes so that she can read the names. It rings. Once, twice, three times . . . It rings and no-one answers. Léo doesn't have school today, he is alone in the apartment, the telephone is ringing, but nobody is answering . . . She feels sweat begin to trickle again, this time down her back. "Pick up, for fuck sake!" She counts the rings: four, five, six. There is a click and finally she hears a voice she was not expecting. She wanted to speak to Léo, but it is his mother's voice that answers: "Hello. You've reached the voice-mail of Christine and Alain Gervais . . ." That calm, determined voice chills her to the marrow. What is she waiting for? Why has she not hung up? Every word nails her to her chair. "We're not here at the moment . . ." Sophie jabs at the "END CALL" button.

It is incredible, the effort it takes to string two simple thoughts together . . . Reflect. Understand. Léo knows how to answer the phone, in fact he loves racing to get there, picking up the phone, asking who it is. It is perfectly simple: if Léo were there, he would answer; if he does not answer, it means he is not there.

Shit, where can the little bastard be if he is not at home? He is not able to open the front door by himself. His mother had a childproof lock installed when he was starting to get around everywhere and into everything, and she was worried about him. He is not answering, he cannot have gone out: it is like squaring the circle. Where can the damn boy be?

Think. It is . . . what? 11.30 a.m.

The table is scattered with items from her handbag, there is even a tampon in the pile. What must she look like? At the bar counter, the waiter is talking to two men. Regulars, she guesses. They are probably talking about her. They glance over at her. She cannot stay here. She has to leave. She quickly scoops up everything on the table, shoves it into her bag and runs for the door.

"One euro ten!"

She turns back, the three men are looking at her strangely. She fumbles in her bag, takes out two coins, sets them on the counter and leaves.

The day is beautiful. Unthinkingly she notes the movement on the street, the strolling pedestrians, the passing cars, the roaring motorcycles. Walk. Keep walking and think. This time, the image of Léo is very precise. She can picture every tiny detail. It was not a dream. The boy is dead and she is on the run.

The cleaner will arrive at noon. There is no reason for anyone to be in the apartment before midday. But at that point, the child's body will be discovered.

So she has to get away. She must be vigilant. Danger could come from anywhere, at any moment. She cannot stand still, she has to keep moving, to keep walking. Collect her belongings and get away before they find her. Get away until she has had time to think. To understand. When she is calmer, she will be able to figure things out. Then she can come back and explain. Right now, she has to go. But where to?

She stops dead. Somebody bumps into her from behind. She stammers an apology. She is in the middle of the pavement, she looks around. There are a lot of people on the boulevard. The sun is sweltering. Life loses a little of its madness.

There is the florist, the furniture shop. She needs to move swiftly. She catches sight of a clock in the furniture shop: 11.35. She rushes into the entrance of her building, hunts for her keys. There are letters in her mailbox. No time to waste. Third floor. More keys, first the mortice lock, then the Yale. Her hands are trembling, she sets down her handbag, it takes her two attempts, she tries to calm her breathing, the second key turns, the door swings open.

She stands on the threshold, the door yawning wide: at no point did it occur to her she might have miscalculated. That the police might already be waiting for her. The hallway is silent. The familiar light from her apartment falls at her feet. She stands there petrified, but all she can hear is the beating of her heart. Suddenly she flinches, a key turns in another door. Along the landing on the right. Her neighbour. Without thinking, she hurries into her apartment. The door slams behind her before she has time to catch it. She freezes and listens intently. The empty silence, so often depressing, is reassuring now. She moves slowly about the only room. One eye on her alarm clock: 11.40. More or less. Her alarm has never been exactly accurate. But is it slow or fast? She seems to remember it runs fast. But she is not certain.

Everything happens at once. She pulls a suitcase from the wardrobe, opens the dresser drawers, stuffs clothes higgledy-piggledy into the case, then runs to the bathroom, sweeps her arm along the shelf and everything tumbles into a sponge-bag. A glance around. Her papers. She runs to the desk: passport, money. How much does she have? 200 euros. Her cheque book! Where is the damn chequebook? In my handbag. She makes sure. Another quick look around. Jacket. Handbag. The photos! She retraces her steps, opens the top drawer of the writing desk, snatches up the album. Her eyes fall on the framed wedding photograph on top of the dresser. She grabs it, tosses it into the suitcase and snaps it shut.

Frazzled, she presses her ear to the door. Once again the only sound is that of her heart beating. She presses both hands flat against the door. Concentrate. Still she can hear nothing. She grips the handle of the suitcase, throws the door wide: there is no-one on the landing. She shuts the door behind her, not bothering to lock it. She races down the stairs. There is a taxi passing. She hails it. The driver wants to put the suitcase in the boot. No time! She lifts it onto the back seat and gets in.

The driver says: "Where to?"

She has no idea. She thinks for a moment.

"Gare de Lyon."

As the taxi pulls away, she looks through the rear window. Nothing unusual, a few cars, pedestrians. She takes a breath. She must look like a lunatic. In the rear-view mirror, the driver is eyeing her suspiciously.

4

It is curious how, in emergency situations, one idea leads to another almost spontaneously. She cries out:

"Stop!"

Startled by the command, the driver brakes. They have not even gone a hundred metres. By the time the driver has turned around, she is already out of the car.

"I'll be right back. Can you wait here for me?"

"Actually, love, it's not exactly convenient . . ." mutters the driver.

He looks at the suitcase she tossed on the back seat. Neither it nor his customer inspire confidence. She hesitates. She needs him, and everything is already so complicated . . . She opens her bag, takes out a fifty-euro note and proffers it.

"Does this help?"

The driver looks at the banknote, but he does not take it.

"Oh, alright, go on then," he says. "But be quick . . ."

She dashes across the street and goes into the local branch of her bank. The place is almost empty. At the counter is a face she does not recognise, a woman. But she rarely comes in. She takes out her chequebook and sets it in front of her.

"I'd like know the balance of my account, please . . ."

The clerk pointedly looks up at the clock on the wall, takes the chequebook, keys numbers into the terminal and studies her nails while the printer clatters and whirrs. Her nails and her wristwatch. The printer seems to be performing a Herculean task, it takes almost a minute to spit out ten lines of text and numbers. The only number Sophie is interested in is the one at the bottom.

"And my savings account?"

The cashier heaves a sigh.

"You have the account number?"

"No, I'm sorry, I don't know it by heart."

She does look sorry. And she is. The clocks reads 11.56. She is now the only customer. The other cashier, a tall man, gets to his feet, walks out from behind the counter and begins to roll down the shutters. Gradually, daylight is replaced by the clinical glow of fluorescent tubes. With this dim, clammy light comes a throbbing, muffled silence. Sophie does not feel well. Not well at all. The printer clatters again. She scans the figures.

"I'd like to withdraw six hundred from the current account and . . . let's say . . . five thousand from the savings . . .?"

Her tone rises as she ends the sentence, as though asking for permission. She does this deliberately. It offers reassurance.

A breath of panic on the other side of the counter.

"You'd like to close your accounts?" the cashier says.

"Er, no . . . [No, you are the customer, you get to decide] I just need a little temporary liquidity." That's good. The word "liquidity" makes her sound serious, grown up.

"It's just that . . ."

The clerk glances in turn at Sophie, the chequebook she is

holding, the wall clock ticking remorselessly towards midday, the colleague crouching by the glass entrance doors to lock them, rolling down the last of the window shutters and staring at the two women with obvious impatience. Sophie hesitates.

The whole thing is more complicated than she expected. The branch is closing, it is noon, the taxi driver has probably seen the shutters being lowered.

Flashing a faint smile, she says:

"The thing is, I'm in a hurry myself."

"Just a minute, let me check."

There is no time to stop her, the clerk has already stepped from behind the counter and is knocking on the door of the office opposite. Behind her, Sophie feels the eyes of the other clerk who is standing idly by the door and would no doubt rather be sitting idly at a café table waiting for his lunch. It is unsettling, having someone behind you. But everything about this situation is unsettling, especially the man who now appears with the cashier.

This is someone she knows. She cannot remember his name, but it was he who dealt with her when she opened the account. Thirty-something, thickset, with a slightly brutish face, he looks the type to spend his holidays with the family, play *pétanque* with his mates and make off-colour jokes, wear socks with sandals, put on twenty kilos over the next five years, see his mistresses during his lunch break and make sure all his colleagues know, the sort of middle-management pick-up artist who wears a yellow shirt and lingers on the word "Mademoiselle". In other words, an arsehole.

The arsehole is now standing in front of her. Next to him, the small cashier seems even smaller. It is a mark of his authority. Sophie has a clear idea of what the man is like. She can smell his pheromones. She realises that she has stumbled into a hornet's nest.

"My colleague informs me that you wish to withdraw . . . [He leans towards the computer screen as though only now becoming aware of the details] . . . almost the entire balance of your accounts."

"Is there a law against that?"

As she says it, she realises she has adopted the wrong tactic. With a guy like this, a direct approach means all-out war.

"No, no, there's no law against it, it's just that . . ."

He turns and shoots a paternal look at the cashier who is standing by the coat rack:

"You can go to lunch, Juliette, I'll close up, don't worry."

The mis-named Juliette does not have to be told twice.

"Are you unhappy with the services offered by our branch, Madame Duguet?"

Doors bang at the far end of the bank, the silence is even more oppressive than before. Sophie tries to think fast.

"Oh, no . . . It's just that . . . I'm going away for a while. I need a little liquidity."

The word *liquidity* no longer seems as apt as it did earlier, it sounds rash, hasty, unsavoury, slightly suspicious.

"'Need a little liquidity'," the man repeats. "You should know that under normal circumstances, when dealing with sums of this magnitude, we prefer to meet with customers in private. During regular office hours . . . A matter of security, you understand."

The insinuation is so blatant, so in keeping with his character, that she feels like slapping him. But she reminds herself that she needs this money, needs it desperately, that the taxi will not wait all day, that she has to get out, that she has to get herself out of this.

37

"The trip became necessary at the last minute. The very last minute. I need to leave immediately, and I need to have the requisite funds."

She stares at the man and, inside her, something snaps, a little of her dignity. She sighs, she will do what she needs to do, she feels a little disgusted with herself, but only a little.

"I entirely understand your reservations, Monsieur Musain [The man's name has come to her in a flash, a small sign that her confidence has returned]. If I had had the time to phone you, to give you some notice, I would have done so. Had I been in a position to choose when to leave, I would not have come here at lunchtime. If I did not urgently need the money, I would not be troubling you. But I do need it. I need the full amount. Right now."

Musain flashes her a smug smile. She can tell the game is now on a more equal footing.

"There is also the matter of whether we have such a sum available in cash . . ." Sophie feels a wave of cold sweat. "But I can check," Musain says.

He disappears into his office. To telephone someone? Why should he need to go into his office to find out how much cash is available?

She looks helplessly at the entrance, the metal shutters now closed, then glances at the rear door through which the two clerks went to lunch and remembers the dull clack of reinforced steel. There is silence once again, but it feels slower, more menacing now. The guy is calling someone, she is convinced of it. But who? All of a sudden he reappears. He walks towards her but does not go behind the counter; he stops next to her and smiles winningly. He is standing close, very close.

"I think we should be able to accommodate you, Madame Duguet," he says in a breathy whisper.

She manages a tense smile. The man does not move. He smiles and stares into her eyes. She does not move either, she carries on smiling. This is what she needs to do. Smile. Respond in kind. He turns and walks away.

Alone again. 12.06 p.m. She hurries to the door, peers through the metal slats, her taxi is still waiting. She cannot see the driver. The taxi is there, that is all she can be sure of. But she needs to move quickly. Very quickly.

She has resumed her pose as a customer, leaning casually on the counter, by the time the man re-emerges from his lair. He counts out 5,600 euros. He settles himself in the cashier's chair, taps at the keyboard. The printer resumes its arduous task. In the meantime, Musain looks at her and smiles. She feels naked. Eventually she signs the withdrawal slip.

Musain feels the need to offer her a word of advice as he slips the money into a plain brown envelope and proffers it with a self-important air.

"A young woman like you, a slip of a girl, wandering the streets with all this money, I really shouldn't let you go alone . . . It's very dangerous . . ."

"A slip of a girl"! She cannot believe this man.

She takes the envelope. It is thick. She is not quite sure what to do with it, stuffs it into the inside pocket of her jacket. Musain looks at her doubtfully.

"The taxi," she stammers. "The driver will be waiting outside, he's probably worried . . . I'll put it somewhere safe later."

"Of course," Musain says.

She makes to leave.

39

"Wait!"

She turns back, prepared for anything, prepared to lash out, but she sees that he is still smiling.

"When we've locked up you have to go out this way." He gestures to the door behind him.

She follows him through the building, down a long narrow corridor to the exit at the end. He fiddles with the locks, the reinforced door slides sideways but does not open fully. Musain is standing in front of her. He's practically blocking the exit.

"There you go," he says.

"Thank you so much."

She does not know what she should do. He is still standing there, smiling.

"Where are you going, exactly? If you don't mind me asking."

Think of something, quickly, anything. She can tell she is taking too long, that she should have had an answer prepared, but nothing comes.

"The Midi . . ."

Her jacket is not quite closed. When she took the money, she zipped it half-way. Musain is staring at her neck.

"The south . . . Very nice."

As he says this, he reaches one hand towards her and gingerly pushes the corner of the envelope a little further inside her jacket. His hand grazes her breast. He says nothing, but his hand lingers. She feels an urge, an overpowering urge, to slap him, but something absolute, something terrible, prevents her. Fear. For a moment it occurs to her that the man could grope her as she stands here, paralysed, and she would say nothing. She desperately needs this money. Is it so obvious?

'Yeah . . .' Musain says, "I've always liked the Midi."

He has withdrawn his hand and is now smoothing the lapel of his jacket.

"I'm afraid I'm in rather a hurry . . ."

As she says this she side-steps, making for the door.

"I understand," Musain says, inching a fraction to one side.

She tries to slip past him.

"Well, have a nice trip, Madame Duguet." He shakes her hand, holding it a little too long. "See you soon, perhaps?"

"Thank you."

She bursts out onto the street.

This is the price of fear, being trapped there, unable to move, at the mercy of this slimy bank manager. She feels blind hatred coursing through her. Now that she is outside, now that it is all done with, she could gladly slam his head into a wall. As she runs to the taxi, she feels his fingers brush against her again and the almost physical relief of grabbing his ears and pounding his head against a wall. Because it is the ugly fucker's face she cannot bear. It triggers a blast of black fury . . . She can picture herself digging her nails into his ears, smashing his head against the wall. It makes an eerie noise, a deep, dull clang. The guy looks at her as though this was the most absurd thing in the world, but that look gives way to a rictus of pain. She goes on pounding, three, four, five, six times and gradually the rictus gives way to a frozen stare, his glazed eyes become blank, vacant. She stops, relieved, her hands covered in the blood that is streaming from his ears. His eyes are fixed, unmoving, like a dead body in a movie.

Suddenly the image of Léo rises up before her, but the child's eyes are truly dead. They are nothing like a movie.

Her head is spinning, a darkness descends.

5

"Hey, love, are we going or what?"

She looks up. She is standing, frozen, next to the taxi.

"You feeling O.K.? At least promise me you're not going to throw up?"

No, everything will be fine, Sophie. Just get into the taxi. Get the hell out of here. You need to calm down, everything is fine. You're just tired, this whole thing has been a terrible ordeal, that's all, you'll be fine, just focus.

As they drive to the station, the driver doesn't take his eyes off her in the rear-view mirror. She tries to calm herself, staring out at the landmarks she knows so well, République, the banks of the Seine, the pont d'Austerlitz in the distance. She concentrates on her breathing. Her heart begins to slow. The most important thing is to stay calm, get some distance, think.

The taxi draws up in front of Gare de Lyon. She gets out and pays the fare, standing at the driver's window. He looks at her again, worried, fascinated, afraid, perhaps a bit of everything, but he is also relieved. She lifts out her suitcase and goes towards the departures board.

She needs a cigarette. Feverishly, she delves into her pockets. She needs one badly. At the tobacconist's there are three people queuing. When it is her turn she asks for a pack of cigarettes, no two. The girl turns, takes two packs, sets them on the counter.

"Actually, make it three . . ."

"So how many do you want, one, two or three?"

"Give me a whole carton."

"Final answer?"

"Give me a fucking break. Oh, and a lighter."

"What kind?"

"I don't care, any lighter."

She grabs the carton of cigarettes, dips a hand into her pocket and takes out a fistful of notes. Her hands are shaking so much that the money scatters over the piles of magazines laid out in front of the kiosk. She looks behind her, then left and right as she gathers up the fifty-euro notes and crams them into various pockets. You're losing it, you're really starting to lose it, Sophie. A couple stares at her. They are standing a few feet away, obviously embarrassed for her; a fat man pretends to look elsewhere.

She re-emerges from the tobacconist's with the carton of cigarettes. Out of the corner of her eye she sees a red sign warning travellers to beware of pickpockets . . . What should she do now? She would scream if she could but, curiously, she feels something else, something she has often felt after these incidents, a strange, almost comforting feeling, like a child in the midst of a harrowing night terror who, at the height of her fear, feels a faint but unshakeable intuition that what she is experiencing is not entirely real, that in spite of the fear, something, somewhere, is protecting her. Some unknown force protects us all . . . The image of her father flickers for a moment, then vanishes.

Magical thinking.

Deep down, Sophie knows this is simply a child's way of feeling safe.

Find the toilets, comb her hair, compose herself, put the money in a safe place, decide where she is going to go, come up with a plan, this is what she needs to do. But before anything she has to smoke.

She rips the plastic film off the carton; three packs fall to the ground. She picks them up, piles her jacket, the carton and the loose packs on top of her suitcase, all but the one she opens. She takes out a cigarette, lights it. A cloud of well-being fills her lungs. The first moment of happiness in an eternity. And then, almost immediately, it makes her head spin. She closes her eyes to gather her thoughts and a few moments later she feels better. Two or three minutes smoking a cigarette, like a calm after the storm. She keeps her eyes closed and inhales. When she has finished, she stubs out the cigarette, jams the carton into her suitcase and heads for the café that faces the platforms.

On the mezzanine above her is Le Train Bleu with its sweeping double staircase and, behind the glass doors, the dining rooms, the dizzyingly high ceilings, the tables spread with crisp white linen, the bustle of the brasserie, the chink of silverware, the gilded mouldings and extravagant ceiling frescoes. Vincent took her here once upon a time, so long ago. All that seems so long ago.

She notices a free table on the covered terrace. She orders a coffee, asks where the toilets are. She does not want to leave her suitcase here. But she can hardly take it with her to the ladies. She looks around. A woman is sitting to her right, another woman to her left. Women are more reliable when it comes to such things. The woman on the right is about her age, she is leafing through a magazine and smoking a cigarette. Sophie chooses the one on the left, who looks older, more settled, more confident; she nods to her suitcase, her expression unambiguous and yet she is not sure the woman has understood. But the woman's face seems to say, "Go ahead, I'll be right here." A faint smile, the first in thousands of years. When it comes to smiles, too, women are better. She does not touch her coffee. She goes downstairs, resists the temptation to look at herself in the mirrors and immediately goes into a cubicle, locks the door, pulls down her jeans and her pants, sits down, her elbows on her knees, and sobs.

Coming out of the cubicle, she catches sight of her face in the mirror. Ravaged. She looks so old and worn out. She washes her hands, splashes water onto her face. She is so tired . . . She climbs back upstairs to drink her coffee, smoke a cigarette, think. No more panicking, she needs to be wary now, to think carefully. Easier said than done.

When she comes to the terrace she instantly realises the magnitude of the disaster. Her suitcase is gone, as is the woman. "Shit!" she screams, and she bangs her fist on the table. The coffee cup falls and shatters on the ground, everyone is looking at her. She turns to the other woman, the one sitting on the right. From some imperceptible expression, from a slight, furtive glance, she knows that this woman saw what happened and did not intervene, did not say a word, did not lift a finger.

"I don't suppose you saw anything . . ."

The woman is in her thirties, dressed from head to toe in grey. She has a mournful face. Sophie steps towards her, wiping tears from her face with her sleeve.

'You didn't see anything, did you, you fucking bitch!"

And she slaps the woman. There are screams, the waiter rushes over, the woman brings a hand to her cheek and sobs wordlessly. Everyone comes running, what the hell is going on? Sophie is in the eye of the storm, people are milling about, the waiter takes hold of her arms and shouts: "Calm down right now or I'm calling the police." She shrugs him off and runs, the waiter screams and runs after her, a group of bystanders follows them, ten metres, twenty, she has no idea which way to go, she feels the waiter's imperious hand on her shoulder

"You're not leaving without paying for that coffee," he roars.

She turns. He is staring at her furiously. Their eyes meet in a battle of wills. He is a man and Sophie senses it is important to him to win, his face is already red. So she takes out the envelope in which she has only large notes, her cigarettes fall on the floor, she picks them up, she is surrounded by people now, she takes a deep breath, snuffles, wipes away tears with the back of her hand, takes a note and presses it into the waiter's palm. They are in the middle of the station concourse, encircled by onlookers and commuters who have stopped to watch. The waiter dips his hand into the pocket of his apron to get her change and Sophie can feel, from the slow deliberateness of his gestures, that this is his moment of triumph. He takes his sweet time, he does not look around but concentrates, as though there were no crowd watching and this were his natural state, one of calm authority. Sophie knows her nerves are about to snap. Her hands are itching. The whole train station seems to have gathered around them. The waiter painstakingly counts out the change, setting each coin, each banknote into her trembling, outstretched hand. Sophie can see only the top of his head, the pale scalp, the beads of sweat between his thinning hair. She wants to throw up.

She takes the change, turns and pushes through the crowd, utterly distraught.

She keeps walking. She feels as though she is stumbling, but no, she is walking in a straight line, she is simply exhausted. A voice.

"Can I help?"

Hoarse, barely audible.

She turns around. God, this is depressing. The drunk standing in front of her seems to be carrying the whole weight of the world, he is homeless with a capital "H".

"No, I'll be fine, thanks . . ." she says.

And she moves away.

"Because it's no problem, yeah? We're all in the same b—"

"Fuck off and leave me alone!"

The man scuttles away, grunting something she pretends not to hear. Maybe you are wrong, Sophie. Maybe he is right, maybe in spite of your sense of superiority, you are in the same boat. Homeless.

What did you have in your suitcase? Clothes, rubbish. The most important thing is money.

She reaches into her pockets and breathes a sigh of relief: her papers are there, and her money. She has everything she needs. So, time to think again. She steps out of the station into dazzling sunshine. In front of her, a row of cafés and brasseries, there are people everywhere, taxis, cars, buses. And over there, a low wall by the taxi rank. A few people are sitting on it, a man chatting on his mobile seems engrossed, a diary open in his lap. She walks over, sits next to him, takes a cigarette, closes her eyes and smokes. Concentrates. Suddenly she remembers her own mobile. They will use it to track her. They will see that she phoned the Gervais' apartment. She opens it up, takes out the SIM card and drops it into a drain. Then she throws the telephone into a rubbish bin.

She came to Gare de Lyon instinctively. Why? Where was she heading? She has no idea . . . She racks her brain and then she remembers: Marseille, that's right, she went there once with Vincent a long time ago. They laughed as they checked into an ugly hotel near the old port because they could find nothing else and they desperately wanted to snuggle under the sheets. When the man at the reception desk asked for a name, Vincent told him "Stefan Zweig", because he was their favourite writer at the time. He had to spell the name. The man asked if they were Polish. Vincent said, "Austrian. Originally . . ." They had spent the night there, incognito, and that was why . . . She has a sudden realisation: her instinct is to go somewhere she has been before, whether it is Marseille or elsewhere does not matter, but somewhere she knows, even if only vaguely, because it is reassuring and that is what they will expect her to do. They will look for her in places she is likely to go, which is precisely why she should not go there. From now on, you have to leave behind all the familiar landmarks, Sophie, it's crucial. You have to use your imagination. Do things you have never done, go to places no-one would expect you to go. The thought of never being able to visit her father panics her. It has been six months since she has been to see him, and now she can never go there again. They will have his house under surveillance, they will have his telephone tapped too. She sees the figure of the old man in front of her, still tall and powerful as if carved out of an oak tree, just as old and just as strong. Sophie had chosen Vincent because he was carved from the same mould: tall, calm, serene. She will miss her father. When everything fell apart, when all that remained after Vincent's death were the ruins of her life, her father was the only person left, the last man standing. She can never go and see him again, can never talk to him. She is completely alone in the world, it is as though he too were dead. She cannot imagine a world in which her father is alive somewhere where she can no longer see him, no longer speak to him or hear his voice. It is though she herself is dead.

The thought makes her dizzy, as though she is stepping into another world from which she would never be able to return, a hostile world where everything is unfamiliar, everything is dangerous, where there is no place for spontaneity: everything she does must be new to her. She will never be in a place where she can feel safe, there will never be a place where she can give her name; Sophie no longer exists, she is just a fugitive, someone scared to death, living like an animal, focused only on surviving; the antithesis of what it means to live.

Another wave of tiredness: is it all worth it? What will her life be now? Forever moving, never staying in one place. Such a life is doomed to failure, she does not have the strength to fight. She does not have the temperament to be a fugitive, she is an ordinary criminal. She will never make it. They will catch you easily . . . She heaves a sigh of defeat: surrender, go to the police, tell them it is all true, but that she remembers nothing, that this was bound to happen some day, that there is such black bile in her, such a bitter hatred for the world. Better to end this thing now. She wants nothing to do with the life that awaits her. But what was her life like before? For a long time now she has not been herself. Now she is faced with a choice between two futile lives. She feels so tired. "I have to stop," she thinks. And, for the first time, this seems like a concrete solution. "I'll turn myself in," and she is not even surprised to find herself thinking as though she is a murderer. It has taken only two years for her to go insane, a single night for her to revert to being a criminal, and barely two hours for her to become a hunted woman with all the attendant fears, the suspicions, the ploys, the thwarted plans, the rising panic, and now even the vocabulary. This is the second time in her life she has realised that a normal life can tip over into madness, into death. It is over. It has to end here. She feels overwhelming relief. Even the terror of being locked up, which prompted her to run in the first place, has faded. A psychiatric hospital no longer seems like hell, but rather an equable solution. She stubs out her cigarette and lights another. After this one, I'll go. One last cigarette and then she will do it, she will dial 112. Is that even the right number these days? It hardly matters, she will manage to get through to the police, to explain. Anything is better than these last few hours. Anything is better than this madness.

She blows a long plume of smoke, exhaling forcefully, and it is at that moment that she hears the woman's voice.

6

"I'm so sorry . . ."

The woman in grey is standing next to her, nervously clutching a small handbag. She gives the ghost of a smile. Sophie is not even surprised.

She looks at her for a moment

"It's alright," she says. "Forget it. We all have bad days."

"I'm so sorry," the woman says again.

"It's not your fault. Forget it."

But still the woman stands there awkwardly. Sophie studies her for the first time. She is not really ugly, just sad. About thirty, a long face, fine features, keen eyes.

"Is there anything I can do?"

"Get my suitcase back! That would be a start, get me my suitcase back." Then Sophie stands up and pats the woman's arm. "I'm just a little angry. Don't worry about it. But now I have to go."

"Did you have anything valuable?"

Sophie turns.

"In the suitcase, I mean, did you have any valuable things?"

"Valuable enough to want to take them with me."

"What are you going to do?"

Good question. Anyone else would say: I'm going to go home. But Sophie is all out of ideas, she can think of nothing to say, nowhere to go.

"Can I buy you a coffee?"

The young woman looks at her imploringly. It is not a suggestion, it is almost a plea. Without knowing why, Sophie says simply:

"With the day I'm having . . ."

A brasserie opposite the train station.

The girl makes for the terrace, probably because it is in the sun, but Sophie wants to be inside. "Not by the window," she says. The girl returns her smile.

They do not know what to say to each other as they wait for their coffee.

"Arriving or departing?"

"Hmm? Oh, just arrived. From Lille."

"Into Gare de Lyon?"

Things are off to a bad start. Sophie feels like stalking off and leaving the girl with her belated scruples and her hangdog expression.

"I took the *métro* . . ." Sophie ad-libs, then immediately asks, "What about you?"

"Me? No, I'm not travelling." The girl hesitates about what to say next and decides to change the subject: "I live here. I'm Véronique."

"Me too," Sophie says.

"Your name is Véronique?"

Sophie realises this is going to be more tricky than she anticipated, she has not had time to prepare for this sort of question, she has to think on her feet. Get herself in a different frame of mind.

She gives a vague nod that could mean just about anything.

"Weird, huh?" the girl says.

"It happens."

Sophie lights a cigarette, holds out the pack. The girl accepts with a graceful gesture. It is extraordinary how this woman in her grey suit seems when seen close up.

"What do you do?" Sophie says. "For a living."

"I'm a translator. You?"

In a few short minutes of conversation, Sophie has invented a new life for herself. It is a little scary at first, but then it feels like a game – you just have to remember the rules. Unexpectedly, she can be anyone she chooses. Instead she behaves like those lottery winners who could completely transform their lives, but then buy a little suburban house like everyone else. Now she is Véronique, an art teacher at a secondary school in Lille, single, arriving in Paris for a few days to visit her parents who live in the suburbs.

"Has the Académie de Lille broken up for the holidays?" asks Véronique.

This is the problem: a follow-up question that could wrong-foot her . . .

"I took a few days' leave. My father is ill. Well, actually . . . [she smiles], between you and me, my father's not really ill: I fancied a couple of days in Paris. I should be ashamed of myself."

"Where do your parents live? I can drop you off. I've got a car."

"No, I'll be fine, honestly, but thank you."

"It's no trouble."

"That's very sweet of you, but it's really not necessary." She says this in a sharp tone and for a moment they are both silent.

"Are they expecting you? Maybe you should give them a call."

53

"Oh, no!"

She has answered too quickly: be calm, composed, take your time, Sophie, don't just say anything . . .

"The thing is, I wasn't supposed to arrive until tomorrow."

"Oh," Véronique says, stubbing out her cigarette. "Have you eaten?"

This is the last thing on her mind.

"No, not yet."

She glances at the clock on the wall: 1.40 p.m.

"Maybe I could invite you for lunch? My way of saying sorry. For the suitcase. I only live round the corner . . . I don't have much, but there's bound to be something in the fridge."

Remember, Sophie, do things you have never done before. Go where no-one will expect to find you.

"Why not?" she says.

They smile. Véronique pays for the coffees. On the way, Sophie stops to buy two packs of cigarettes and catches her up.

Boulevard Diderot. Elegant buildings. They have been walking side by side, making small talk. No sooner do they reach Véronique's building than Sophie is regretting her decision. She should have said no, she should have walked away. By now she should be a long way from Paris, heading in some unexpected direction. She accepted because she was weak, because she was tired. She follows Véronique automatically, stepping into the lobby of the building, allowing herself to be led like a casual guest. Into the lift. Véronique presses the button for the fourth floor, the lift jolts, creaks and sways, but it moves steadily upward and comes to a juddering halt. Véronique smiles.

"It's not exactly a palace," she says as she delves into her handbag for her keys.

It may not be a palace, but stepping inside, it reeks of the moneyed middle class. It is a huge apartment. The living room is vast, framed by two windows. To the right, a russet leather sofa and armchair, to the left a baby grand piano, on the back wall a floor-to-ceiling bookcase.

"Come in, please . . ."

Sophie steps across the threshold as though into a museum. The décor, she immediately thinks, is like a variation in a minor key of the Gervais' apartment on rue Molière, where at this very moment . . .

Instinctively, she looks around to find out the time and sees a small ormolu clock on the mantel of the fireplace in the corner: 1.50 p.m.

As soon as they arrived, Véronique hurried into the kitchen, suddenly animated. Sophie can hear her talking and answers distractedly as she studies the apartment. Her eyes flick back to the carriage clock. Time seems to have stood still. She takes a deep breath. Be wary in your answers, mumble the occasional "Yes, of course . . .", try to gather your thoughts. It is as though she has woken from a night of restless sleep to find herself in a place she does not recognise. Véronique busies herself, babbling excitedly, opening cupboards, programming the microwave, slamming the door of the fridge, laying the table.

"Can I help with anything?" Sophie says.

"No, no."

The perfect hostess. In a few short minutes, the table is laid with a salad, a bottle of wine, a fresh baguette ("Actually, it's yesterday's", "It'll be fine") which she carefully cuts with a bread knife.

"So, you're a translator . . ."

Sophie has been trying to think of a topic for conversation. She need not have bothered. Now that she is at home, Véronique is very chatty.

"English and Russian. My mother is Russian, which helps."

"So, what do you translate? Novels?"

"I wish. No, I do more technical stuff, letters, brochures, that sort of thing."

The conversation meanders, they talk about work, about family. Sophie invents relations, colleagues, a family, a beautiful, brand-new life, taking care to keep it as far from reality as possible.

"What about your parents, where did you say they lived?" Véronique says.

"Chilly-Mazarin."

She blurts out the name, she does not know where it came from.

"What do they do?"

"I persuaded them to retire."

Véronique has uncorked the wine, she serves a fricassée of vegetables with lardons.

"I should warn you: it's cooked from frozen."

Sophie realises that she is ravenous. She eats and eats. The wine gives her a woozy feeling of well-being. Thankfully, Véronique is very talkative. She sticks to small talk, mainly, but she has a talent for conversation, mixing everyday details with little anecdotes. As she eats, Sophie picks up information about her parents, her education, a younger brother, a recent trip to Scotland. After a while, the flow trickles, then stops.

"Married?" Véronique asks, gesturing to Sophie's right hand.

There is an uncomfortable silence.

"Past tense."

"But you still wear it?"

Remember to take off the ring.

"Habit, I suppose," Sophie improvises. "What about you?"

"I was all set to get the habit."

She says this with an awkward smile, hoping to forge a sisterly bond. In other circumstances, maybe, Sophie thinks. But not here.

"But?"

"It didn't work out, but who knows . . ."

Véronique brings out a platter of cheeses. For someone with nothing in the fridge . . .

"So you live on your own?"

Véronique hesitates.

"Yes." She bows her head over her plate, then raises it and looks Sophie in the eye almost defiantly. "Only since last Monday. It's still a bit raw."

"Oh."

All Sophie knows is that she does not want to know. Does not want to get involved. She wants to finish her lunch and go. She does not feel well. She needs to leave.

"These things happen," she says inanely.

"Yes."

They talk a little longer, but something in the conversation is broken. A small, private grief has come between them.

Then the telephone rings out in the hall.

Véronique turns towards the hall as though expecting someone to appear. She sighs. The telephone rings once, twice. She apologises, stands, and goes to answer it.

Sophie drains her glass of wine, pours another, stares out of the window. Although Véronique has closed the door behind her, her muted voice is still audible. An awkward situation. Were

Véronique not in the hallway, Sophie would grab her jacket and leave right now, without a word, like a thief. She can make out a few words and, without meaning to, pieces together the conversation.

Véronique's voice is grave and harsh.

Sophie gets up, takes a few steps away from the door but it makes no difference, Véronique's words are so clear now that she might as well be in the same room. The terrible words of a banal break-up. Sophie is not interested in this woman's life. ("It's over, I told you: I'm through with you.") Sophie does not care about this failed relationship. She moves to the window. ("We've been through this a hundred times, let's not rake over it again.") On her left, there is a little writing desk. An idea begins to form in her mind. She cocks her ear to listen to the conversation. It's got to the point of "For Christ's sake, just leave me alone", she still has a little time, she pulls down the central panel of the writing desk and finds two rows of drawers. "Save your breath. I don't fall for that kind of emotional blackmail." In the second drawer she finds a few 200-euro notes. Four of them. She stuffs them into her pocket and goes on searching. Her fingers ("I suppose you think that's going to upset me?") locate the stiff cover of a passport. She flicks it open but postpones examining it until later. She slips it into her pocket. She picks up a half-used chequebook and a driving licence. By the time she has reached the sofa and crammed everything into the inside pocket of her jacket, she hears: "Sad loser!" Then there is "A pathetic excuse for a man!" and finally "Scumbag".

The receiver is brutally slammed down. Silence. Véronique stays in the hall. Sophie tries to look suitably casual, laying one hand on her jacket.

Finally Véronique reappears. She apologises clumsily, tries to smile.

"I'm so sorry, you must have felt . . . I'm sorry."

"Don't worry about it," Sophie says, quickly adding, "I'll leave you to it."

"No, don't," Véronique says. "I'll make some coffee."

"I really ought to get going."

"It'll only take a minute, really."

Véronique wipes her eyes with the back of her hand, attempts another smile.

"It's so stupid . . ."

Sophie decides she will give herself fifteen minutes and then she will leave, regardless.

From the kitchen, Véronique says:

"He's been calling me non-stop for the past three days. I've tried everything. I even unplugged the telephone, but that's not very practical given that I work from home. And I can't bear just letting it ring. So, from time to time I go out for a coffee. He'll get bored in the end, but he's a weird guy. Clingy, you know the type . . ."

She sets the cups on the coffee table in the living room.

Sophie realises that she has had too much wine. Everything has started to spin slowly, the posh middle-class apartment, Véronique, everything starts to blur and then Léo's face, the carriage clock on the mantelpiece, the empty wine bottle on the table, the child's bedroom as she steps inside, the huddled figure under the duvet, the clack of drawers opening and closing and the silence as terror takes hold. Objects dance in front of her eyes, she sees the passport she stuffed into her jacket. A wave washes over her, everything gradually goes dim, fading to black. From far away she can just hear Véronique's voice asking: "Are you alright?" It seems to come from the bottom of a deep well, it echoes. Sophie feels her body go slack, then crumple and there is only darkness.

This is another scene she can remember perfectly. Even today, she could describe every last detail, even the wallpaper.

She wakes to find herself lying on the sofa, one foot dangling on the floor, she rubs her eyes, searching for a flicker of consciousness, now and then she tries to open them but feels something within her that resists, that wants to remain asleep, far from everything. She is so tired, so much has happened since this morning.

Eventually, she props herself up on one elbow, turns to face the room and slowly opens her eyes.

At the foot of the table Véronique's body lies in a pool of blood.

Her first reaction is to drop the kitchen knife in her hand, it clatters ominously on the floor.

It is like a dream. She gets to her feet and staggers. Instinctively she tries to wipe her hand on her trousers, but the blood has already dried. She slips on the crimson pool slowly spreading across the floor, but manages to steady herself on the table at the last minute. She reels for a moment. She is drunk. Without realising, she has picked up her jacket and is trailing it behind her like a leash. Like the wire from a bedside lamp. Hugging the walls, she makes it to the hallway. Her bag is there. Once more, her eyes blur with tears, she snuffles. She crumples and sits down heavily. She buries her face in the jacket now wrapped around her arms. She feels something on her face. Raising her head she notices that she trailed her jacket through the blood and has just smeared it on her face . . . Wash your face before you leave, Sophie. Get up.

But she does not have the energy. It is all too much. She lies back on the ground, her head close to the front door, desperate to drift back to sleep, desperate to do anything but have to face this reality. She closes her eyes. Then suddenly, as though a pair of hands has lifted her up by the shoulders . . . Even today she cannot say what happened, but she finds herself sitting up again, then standing. Staggering, but upright. She feels a brutal determination welling in her, something animal. She goes back into the living room. From where she is standing, she can see only Véronique's legs, sprawled half under the table. She moves closer. The body is lying on its side, the face obscured by the hunched shoulders. Sophie comes closer still and leans down: the blouse is black with blood. There is a deep wound in the middle of the belly where the knife went in. The apartment is silent. She goes to the bedroom. These ten paces took all the energy she could muster and she sits on the corner of the bed. One wall of the room is lined with wardrobes. Hands on her knees, Sophie painfully shuffles over and opens the first door. There is enough here to clothe an entire orphanage. She and Véronique are about the same size. She opens the second door, the third, and finally finds a suitcase which she tosses, open, onto the bed. She chooses dresses because she does not have time to find tops that would go well with the skirts. She takes three pairs of well-worn jeans. The effort of doing something brings her back to life. Without even thinking, she picks out things that are most unlike her own style. Behind the last door, she finds drawers full of underwear. She puts a handful into the case. As for shoes, at a glance she can see that they range from horrid to hideous. She takes two of the ugliest pairs and a pair of trainers. Then she sits on the suitcase so that she can snap it shut, drags it into the hall and leaves it next to her bag. In the bathroom, she washes her face without looking at herself. Looking in the mirror she notices that the sleeve of her jacket is stained with blood and rips it off as though it were on fire. Back in the bedroom, she opens the wardrobe again, spends four seconds choosing a jacket, opting for something bland in navy blue. In the time it takes to transfer the contents of her pockets to the jacket, she is standing in the hall, her ear pressed to the front door.

She can still picture herself clearly. Gingerly she opens the door, takes the suitcase in one hand, her handbag in the other, and leaves, taking the lift, her stomach heaving, her eyes now dry of tears, as though drained. Jesus, the suitcase feels heavy. Probably because she is so tired. A few steps and she is opening the door to the street, she is out on boulevard Diderot and turns left, away from the train station.

7

She has propped the passport on the washbasin, open at the photograph, and is studying herself in the mirror. Her eyes flick back and forth from her face to the photograph. She picks up the passport again and checks the issue date: 1993. It is old enough for her to pass. Véronique Fabre, born February 11, 1970 – not much of an age gap – in Chevreaux. She has not the faintest idea where Chevreaux might be. Somewhere in the middle of France? Not a clue. She will have to look it up.

Translator. Véronique said that she translated from English and Russian. Sophie, when it comes to languages . . . A little English, a few words of Spanish, and that was long ago. If she has to offer proof of her occupation, things will fall apart, but she cannot imagine any circumstances in which it might arise. Come up with more improbable languages: Lithuanian, Estonian?

The impersonal passport photograph shows an unremarkable woman with short hair and banal features. Sophie looks at herself in the mirror. Her forehead is higher, her nose broader, her eyes are very different. But she has to do something. She opens the plastic bag containing everything she has just bought at the nearby Monoprix: scissors, a make-up bag, dark glasses, hair dye. One last glance in the mirror. She sets to work.

8

She tries to read her fate. Standing beneath the departures board, her suitcase next to her, she scans the destinations, the times, the platform numbers. Choosing one destination rather than another might make all the difference. Avoid the T.G.V. for the time being, since she would be trapped inside. Decide on a densely populated city where she can easily melt into the crowd. Buy a ticket for the last station on the line, but get off at an earlier stop in case the person at the ticket desk remembers her. She picks up a handful of timetables and, at the table of a snack bar, works out a convoluted route which will take her from Paris to Grenoble, with six changes. It will be a long journey, it will give her time to rest.

The ticket machines are literally under siege. She will have to use one of the counters. She wants to choose. Not a woman, since they are supposed to be more observant. Not a young guy who might find her vaguely attractive and remember her. She finds the perfect person at the last counter and joins the line of people waiting. It is a single queue from which customers go to the next available ticket desk. She will have to manoeuvre subtly to end up with the one she wants.

She takes off the sunglasses. She should have done so earlier so as not to call attention to herself. She will have to think about these things now. It is a long queue, but her turn comes too soon for her liking, she moves forward, pretending not to notice a queue jumper slip past her and now finds herself in the perfect position. There is a God who watches over criminals. She tries to make her voice sound firm, pretends to rummage in her bag as she asks for a ticket to Grenoble on the train leaving at 6.30 p.m.

"I'll see whether there are any seats left," the man behind the counter says, and begins tapping into his terminal.

This possibility had not occurred to her. She cannot change her destination now, or decide not to buy a ticket since the man staring at the screen would surely remember that fact. She does not know what to do, thinks about turning and walking away, going to a different station, a different destination.

"I'm sorry," the man says after a moment, looking at her for the first time, "I'm afraid the 6.30 p.m. is booked out."

He types a little more.

"I still have seats on the 8.45."

"No, thanks."

She spoke too quickly. She tries to smile.

"I'll think about it."

She can feel it is going badly. What she is saying is implausible, it is not something a normal traveller would say in such a situation, but it was all she could think of. She picks up her bag. The next customer is already standing behind her, there is no time to lose. She turns and leaves.

Now she needs another counter, another destination, but also another strategy. She has to phrase the question differently so she can choose without needing to hesitate. Despite having carefully chosen the ticket seller, she is terrified that he will remember her. It is at this point that she notices the sign for Hertz Car Rentals on the station concourse. By now, her name will be public knowledge, people will be looking for her, but not for Véronique Fabre. She has the driving licence, and she can pay in cash, or by cheque. A car would offer her greater independence and freedom of movement. It is this thought that persuades her, she is already pushing open the glass doors to the rental office.

Twenty-five minutes later, a suspicious employee is walking her around a dark-blue Ford Fiesta, commenting on its perfect condition. She responds with a calculated smile. She has had time to think and, for the first time in hours, she feels resolute. People will be expecting her to get away from Paris as soon as possible. For the time being, her plan amounts to two things: check into a hotel in the suburbs for one night, and tomorrow buy a couple of number plates and the tools for changing them.

As she drives through the outer suburbs, she feels a little freer. "I'm alive," she thinks.

Immediately tears begin to well again.

9

WHERE IS SOPHIE DUGUET?

Police experts were all agreed and, depending on the sources, the predictions hardly varied: even in the worst case scenario, Sophie Duguet would be arrested within a fortnight.

Yet it is now eight months since the most wanted woman in France disappeared without trace.

In a series of high-profile press conferences, public statements and communiqués, the senior police detectives and officials at the Ministère de la Justice have been passing the buck.

This, then, is what we know:

On May 28 last, shortly before midday, a cleaner working for M. and Mme Gervais discovered the body of their son Léo, aged six. The child had been strangled in his bed with laces from a pair of hiking boots. Police were immediately called and suspicion rapidly centred on his nanny, Sophie Duguet (née Auverney), 28, who had been looking after the child and has not since been found. Early evidence seemed damning: there was no sign of forced entry to the apartment, Mme Gervais, Léo's mother, had left Sophie Duguet in the apartment at 9 a.m. that morning, supposing her son to be still asleep. The autopsy has revealed that by this time the child had been dead for several hours, most probably having been strangled in his sleep during the night.

The *police judiciaire* were all the more determined to make a quick arrest since, in the days that followed, the murder provoked a public outcry. The media circus around the case undoubtedly owes much to the fact that the victim's father was a close associate of the Ministère des Affaires Étrangères. Far-right parties, notably Pascal Mariani and several other organisations, some of which had notionally been disbanded, used the case to call for the reintroduction of the death penalty for "particularly heinous crimes", and in this they were vociferously supported by the right-wing member of parliament, Bernard Strauss.

According to the Ministère de l'Intérieur, the suspect would not be able to evade justice for long since rapid police response would have made it impossible for Sophie Duguet to leave the country. All airports and train stations were swiftly alerted. "Those few suspects who manage to stay on the run succeed only by virtue of experience and considerable preparation," commissaire Bertrand of the *police judiciaire* confidently assured the press. But this young woman had scant financial resources and no relatives or friends in a position to help her, with the exception of her father, Patrick Auverney, a retired architect who was immediately placed under police surveillance.

According to the Ministère de la Justice, apprehending the suspect would take "a matter of days". The Ministère de l'Intérieur went so far as to say "eight to ten days, maximum". The police were more prudent, suggesting "a few weeks at most"… Eight months have passed since then.

So what happened? No-one knows. But the fact remains that Sophie Duguet has literally vanished into thin air. With shocking audacity, the young woman left the apartment where the child lay dead, stopped at her apartment to pick up her passport and clothes, and went to the bank where she withdrew almost all the money she had. Police have confirmed that she was seen at the Gare de Lyon, but after that there has been no trace. Detectives are convinced that neither the murder of the child, nor the escape, were premeditated. If this is true, it gives a frightening insight into Sophie Duguet's ability to improvise.

Almost everything about the case is shrouded in mystery. No theories have been advanced as to Duguet's motive. The only inkling comes from the investigators' assertion that Duguet was suffering intense emotional trauma as a result of two bereavements. Her mother, Catherine Auverney, to whom she seems to have been very close, died of cancer in February 2000, and her husband, Vincent Duguet, a 31-year-old chemical engineer, paralysed in a road traffic accident, committed suicide the following year. Duguet's father – and her only surviving relative – is apparently sceptical about this line of thought, but has declined to talk to the media.

The case quickly became a headache for the authorities. On May 30, two days after the child's murder, Véronique Fabre, a 32-year-old translator, was found dead in her Paris apartment by her boyfriend Jacques Brusset. The woman had sustained multiple stab wounds to the stomach. The time of death established at the autopsy confirmed that the murder took place on the day Sophie Duguet disappeared, sometime in the early afternoon. Traces of D.N.A. found at the scene prove beyond doubt that Duguet had been in the apartment. A car was later rented by a young woman using a driving licence stolen from the victim's apartment. All evidence indicates that the woman who hired the car was Sophie Duguet.

Within two days of absconding, Sophie Duguet had been implicated in a second murder. The manhunt was intensified, but brought no results …

Despite repeated calls for witnesses, constant surveillance at all locations the suspect might use as a refuge and information from police informers, no new information has come to light. One cannot help but wonder whether Sophie Duguet has succeeded in fleeing the country. The police and the judiciary have half-heartedly attempted to shift the blame, but in fact it seems as though Duguet's success in so far evading capture is not due to any procedural errors in the investigation, but to her fierce determination, careful planning (contrary to police theory) or to an exceptional ability to improvise. The Préfecture denies reports that it has called in a crisis-management specialist.

We hear that the hunt goes on, and there is nothing to do but wait. Meanwhile, detectives at the *police judiciaire* can only keep their fingers crossed and hope that the next they hear of Sophie Duguet is not news of another murder. As for predictions, official sources are now more guarded. News may come today, tomorrow, or never.

10

Sophie walks stiffly, her hips do not sway. She walks in a straight line, like a wind-up toy. When she has walked for too long, her pace begins to slacken. At that point, no matter where she is, she stops, then starts again, with the same mechanical gait.

She has lost a lot of weight. She eats very little, mostly junk food. She smokes a lot and barely sleeps. In the morning she wakes with a start, sits bolt upright, her mind a blank, wiping tears from her face as she lights her first cigarette. For a long time now, this is how it has been. The morning of March 11 was no different from any other. Sophie is living in a furnished apartment outside the city centre. She has added no personal touch to the décor: the same dated wallpaper, the same threadbare carpet, the same battered sofa. As soon as she gets up, she turns on the television, an antiquated model where every channel comes with a blizzard of static. Whether or not she is actually watching (and she spends countless hours staring at it), the television is always on. She has got into the habit of leaving it on with the sound muted when she goes out. She often comes home late and, from the street, she can see the flickering blue glow of her apartment. The first thing she does when she comes in is to turn up the sound. Most nights, she leaves it on. At first she had hoped that even in her sleep the sound would keep her mind distracted and spare her the nightmares. To no avail. But at least when she wakes, every two hours, it is to the reassuring babble of early-morning weather reports, of tele-shopping programmes which she can be glued to for hours, sometimes the midday news if she has taken something to knock herself out.

Sophie mutes the sound and leaves. She goes down the stairs, lights a cigarette before pushing open the entrance door of the building and, as always, pushes her hands into her pockets to conceal their constant trembling.

"Are you going to shift your arse, or do I need to give it a kick?"

Rush hour. The fast-food joint is humming like a hive, whole families are queuing to be served, the smells from the kitchen fill the whole restaurant, the staff weave between the tables collecting trays left by customers, clearing away the polystyrene containers full of cigarette butts in the smoking area, wiping up the spilled drinks. Sophie is working with a mop. Customers balancing trays step over it, somewhere behind her a group of schoolchildren are making an infernal racket.

"Don't pay any attention to him," Jeanne says as she passes. "Stupid little bastard!"

Jeanne, a thin girl with a vaguely cubist face is the only person she gets on with. As for the "stupid little bastard", he is anything but little. He is about thirty, tall, dark-haired and clearly spends his evenings lifting weights. He wears a jacket and tie like a junior manager in a department store. He is particularly punctilious with three things: timekeeping, salaries and the arses of the female staff. During the lunchtime rush, he "marshals his team" like a legionnaire, and in the afternoon lull, he fondles the buttocks of any female staff members foolish enough to dawdle; the others have made a dash for the exit. His life is perfect. Everyone knows that he is running a scam with the franchise manager, that hygiene is a trivial consideration. And everyone knows why he loves his job: on average, he pockets 20,000 euros a year in backhanders and gets to fuck fifteen girls desperate to keep a job that scrapes the bottom of the employment barrel. As she mops the floor, Sophie can see he is watching her. In fact, he is not exactly watching her. He is sizing her up, with the air of someone who can have whatever he wants. His expression says it all. He treats his "girls" as objects. Sophie carries on working, telling herself she is bound to find another job soon.

She has been working here for six weeks. In her first interview, he was blunt and immediately offered a practical solution to her ongoing problem.

"On the books or cash in hand?"

"Cash in hand," Sophie said.

He said:

"What's your name?"

"Juliette."

"O.K., Juliette, you're hired."

She started the next day, with no contract, no payslip, no possibility of choosing her own hours, she is given breaks so short she has no time to go home, is allocated more night shifts than the others, and rarely gets home before midnight. She pretends to suffer, but actually it suits her perfectly. She has found somewhere to stay, at the far end of a boulevard that is thronged with prostitutes as soon as it gets dark. No-one in the neighbourhood knows her, she leaves early in the morning and by the time she gets back, her neighbours are slumped in front of the television or are already in bed. On nights when her shift ends after the last bus has left, she treats herself to a taxi. She makes the most of her breaks during the day to explore the city, look for another apartment, another job where no-one will ask any questions. This has been her strategy from the start: no sooner does she arrive somewhere than she starts looking for another place to stay, a different job. Never stay in the same place. Keep moving. In the beginning, she found getting by with no papers was reasonably easy, though exhausting. She slept very little, was careful to change the route she took at least twice a week, no matter where she was. As her hair grew out, it was easy to style it differently. She bought a pair of clear glasses. She is constantly on the alert. She moves regularly. She has already spent time in four different cities. And this one is not the worst. The worst thing about it is the work.

Monday is the most complicated: a sixteen-hour day with three breaks of varying lengths. At about 11.00 one morning, as she was walking along an avenue, she decided to stop for a few minutes ("Never again, Sophie, ten minutes maximum") and have a cup of coffee on the terrace of a café. She thought about the weeks ahead as she sipped her espresso. ("Always plan ahead. Always.") She leafed through the newspaper. Whole pages of advertisements for mobile phones, small ads selling second-hand cars. And suddenly she stopped, set down her cup, stubbed out her cigarette and nervously lit another. She closed her eyes. "It's too much to hope for, Sophie. You need to think carefully."

But however much she thought . . . It is complicated, but right here, before her eyes, she may have found a way out of her situation, a permanent solution. Expensive, granted, but absolutely dependable.

One last obstacle – a considerable one – and everything might be different.

Sophie spends a long moment mulling it over. Her mind is racing so fast that she is almost tempted to make notes, but that is not allowed. She decides to take a few days to think about it, and if at that point it still seems like a sensible solution, she will take the necessary steps.

This is the first time that she breaks her own rules: she spends fifteen minutes sitting in the same place.

Sophie cannot sleep. In her room, she allows herself the risk of jotting things down to get her thoughts in order. All the elements are in place. The plan can be summed up in five lines. She lights another cigarette, re-reads her notes, then burns them in the rubbish chute. Everything now depends on two conditions: finding the right person, and having enough money. Whenever she arrives somewhere new, her first precaution is to leave a suitcase at left luggage containing everything she might need if she has to vanish in a hurry. Aside from clothes and the various items she uses to change her appearance (hair dye, glasses, make-up, etc.), the case contains 11,000 euros. But she has no idea how much this might cost. What if she does not have enough?

How could she keep such a house of cards from collapsing? It is madness, there are too many conditions to meet. Thinking about it, she realises that, although her response to each individual obstacle is "It should be O.K.", the sheer number of her doubts and hesitations means that the plan is unrealistic.

She has learned to distrust herself. It is perhaps what she does best. She takes a deep breath, reaches for her cigarettes and notices that she has only one left. The alarm clock reads 7.30 a.m. Her shift does not start until 11.00.

At about 11 p.m. she leaves the restaurant. It rained during the afternoon, but the evening is cool and clear. At this time, she knows that with a little luck . . . She walks down the boulevard, takes a deep breath, asks herself one last time if there is any other way, knowing that she has already been through every possible solution open to her. And could think of nothing better than this. Everything will depend on her intuition. So much for intuition . . .

Cars prowl, stop, windows rolled down to enquire about prices and evaluate the merchandise. Some do a U-turn at the end of the boulevard and drive slowly back. At first, when she came home late, she was reluctant to take the boulevard, but the detour took her out of her way and, over time, she realised that she did not mind: she had reduced her contact with the outside world to a minimum and found something comforting about that, being a local, a familiar face, she was greeted with a nod or a wave by these women who, like her, were probably wondering whether they would ever get out of here.

The street is dotted with pools of light. The first section is known as the A.I.D.S. parade. Young girls, much too young, writhe and jitter, permanently anxious for their next fix. They are pretty enough to stand under the streetlights. Further along, others seek refuge in the half-light. Further still, almost cloaked in shadow, are the transvestites whose painted faces sometimes loom out of the darkness like carnival masks.

Sophie lives a little further along still, in an area that is calmer but sleazier. The woman she thought of is there. About fifty, bottle blonde, taller than Sophie, with an ample bosom that probably attracts a certain type of clientele. Their eyes meet and Sophie stops.

"Excuse me . . . I just want some information."

Sophie hears her voice ring loud and clear. She is surprised by her self-assurance. "I can pay," she adds before the woman has time to answer and flashes the fifty-euro note crumpled in her hand.

The woman stares at her for a moment, then glances around, smiles vaguely and says in a voice made hoarse by years of smoking: "Depends . . . What kind of information you looking for?"

"I need papers," Sophie says.

"What papers?"

"A birth certificate. The name doesn't matter, all I care about is the date. Well, the year. I thought maybe you might know someone . . ."

Playing out this scenario in her head, Sophie imagined that her request might be greeted with compassion, perhaps even complicity, but that was sheer fantasy. It was only ever going to be a business transaction.

"I really need it. And it has to be reasonable. All I'm asking for is a name, an address . . ."

"It don't work like that, love."

Before Sophie can react, the woman turns on her heel and stalks off. She is left standing there. Then the woman turns back and says simply:

"I'll have a quiet word. Come back next week."

The woman holds out her hand and waits, her eyes fixed on Sophie who hesitates, delves into her bag and takes out a second banknote which is snatched away.

Now that she has settled on a plan, and since she can think of none better, Sophie does not wait for the outcome of the first step before moving on to the second. Perhaps it is a secret desire to tempt fate. Two days later, during a break in the middle of the afternoon, she goes on a reconnaissance mission. She is careful to choose a target far from both the restaurant and her apartment, on the other side of the city.

She gets off the bus on boulevard Faidherbe and walks for some distance, using a map so she will not have to ask for directions. She goes straight past the agency, walking slowly to give herself time to look in the window, but all she can see is an empty desk, some filing cabinets and a number of posters on the wall. She crosses the street, turns back and goes into a café from which she can watch the office without being seen. From here it looks as disappointing as when she walked past: it is the sort of place where there is nothing to see, the sort of office that strives to be impersonal so as to discourage passers-by. A few minutes later, Sophie pays for her coffee, strides across the street and pushes open the door.

The agency is still deserted, but a bell jangles above the door and a moment later a woman appears. In her forties, with dyed red hair in desperate need of attention and too much jewellery, she thrusts out a hand enthusiastically as though she and Sophie had known each other since childhood.

"Myriam Desclées," she says.

Her name seems as fake as the colour of her hair. "Catherine

78

Guéral," Sophie says and, paradoxically, it sounds genuine.

It is clear that the manageress likes to think she knows a little about psychology. She props her elbows on the desk, cupping her chin in her hands, and is gazing at Sophie, her eyes filled with a mixture of sympathy and pain intended to demonstrate that she has spent long hours dealing with human suffering. Long, billable hours.

"You're lonely, aren't you?" she whispers gently.

"A little . . ." Sophie ventures.

"Tell me about yourself, Catherine."

Mentally, Sophie thinks through the notes she has patiently prepared, in which every element was weighed and considered.

"My name is Catherine, I'm thirty . . ." she begins.

The interview could have gone on for two hours. The manageress is using every trick of the trade to persuade Sophie that she is "understood", that she has finally found the patient, worldly mentor she has been seeking, that she is in good hands, the hands of a universal mother, a sensitive soul who can intuit what is left unspoken, a gift she communicates through small facial tics that signify "No need to say any more, I understand," or "I feel your pain."

Sophie's time is limited. As awkwardly as she can, she asks for some information about "the nature of the process", and makes it clear that soon she has to be back at work.

A situation such as this is always a race against time. One person wants to leave, the other wants her to stay. It is a struggle for dominance which involves all the phases of a small war: attacks, feints, redeployments, intimidation, tactical retreats, changes of strategy . . .

Eventually, Sophie has had enough. She has found out what

she wanted to know: the price, the type of clientele, the process of introductions, the guarantee. She stammers an embarrassed but convincing "Well, look . . . I'll think about it". She has done everything in her power not to leave an impression the woman will remember. Without a flicker of hesitation, she rattled off a false name, a false address and telephone number. As she walks back to the bus stop, Sophie knows that she will never come back here, but she has had the confirmation she was looking for: if everything works out, she will soon be able to have a brand-new, utterly flawless identity.

She can be laundered clean like dirty money.

Thanks to a genuine birth certificate issued under a false name. All she needs now is to find a husband to give her a married name that is untarnished and above suspicion.

It will be impossible to find her.

One Sophie the thief, the killer, will disappear. Farewell, Sophie the Psycho.

And out of the depths of the black hole.

Here comes Sophie the Saint.

11

Sophie has not seen many gangster movies, but she can conjure images: a backroom bar in a sleazy neighbourhood, full of repulsive men playing cards in a haze of smoke; instead she finds herself in a large white apartment with a picture window that offers sweeping views of the city, standing in front of a man of about forty who, although he is not smiling, is clearly civilised.

The place is a caricature of everything she despises: the glass-topped desk, the designer office chairs, the abstract painting on the wall, the work of an interior designer without one iota of personal style.

The man is sitting behind his desk. Sophie is standing. A note in her mailbox summoned her here at the most inconvenient possible time. She had to take an unscheduled break from work and is already in a hurry to get back.

"So, you need a birth certificate?" the man says, looking at her.

"It's not for me, it's . . ."

"Don't waste your breath, that's no concern of mine."

Sophie focuses on the man, trying to memorise his features.

More like fifty than forty, otherwise unremarkable. He could be anybody.

"Our reputation in the market is unrivalled. Our products are of the highest quality," the man goes on. "That is the secret of our success."

His voice is soothing and firm. It gives the impression of being in safe hands.

"We have a variety of good, solid identities we can offer. Obviously, they cannot be used indefinitely, but as a medium-term solution the product offers exceptional value for money."

"How much?" Sophie says.

"15,000 euros."

Sophie yelps, "But I don't have that much!"

The man is a negotiator. He thinks for a moment and then, in an authoritative tone, he says, "We cannot go below twelve thousand."

It is more than she has. And even if she could make up the difference, it would leave her without a cent. She is in a burning building, standing by an open window. Should she jump? She will not get a second chance. She tries to weigh the possibilities in the eyes of the man staring at her. He does not move.

"How does it work?" she says at last.

"It couldn't be simpler." The man smiles.

The restaurant is heaving when Sophie arrives back twenty minutes late. As she rushes in, she sees Jeanne pulling a face and jerking her thumb towards the far end of the counter. Sophie does not even have time to take off her coat.

"Are you taking the piss?"

The manager swoops down on her. To avoid customers

overhearing, he is standing very close as though about to hit her. His breath smells of beer. Through clenched teeth he growls:

"You pull this kind of shit again, and I'll fire you and personally kick you through that fucking door."

After that, the day is the usual hell of mopping floors, collecting trays, ketchup stains, the smell of hot cooking oil, the floor tiles sticky with spilled Coke, overflowing bins. Almost seven hours later, Sophie realises that she has been so engrossed in her thoughts that she did not notice her shift finished twenty minutes ago. She does not mind the unpaid overtime, she is mostly concerned about what is going to happen next. Because through all the turmoil, she has been thinking about her meeting and the fact that she has a deadline: now or never. The plan is sound. Everything now is just a matter of skill, and money. Since her visit to the agency, she feels sure she has the skill. As for money, she is still short. Not much. A little less than a thousand euros.

She goes into the small staff room, hangs up her uniform, changes her shoes and looks at herself in the mirror. She has the haggard face of those who work cash in hand. Lank, greasy hair falls into her eyes. As a child, she sometimes looked at herself in the mirror, stared deep into her own eyes and, after a while, she would feel a dizzying trance-like state and have to clutch the edge of the washbasin to stop herself from falling. It was like plunging into the unknown depths that lie dormant in each of us. She stares at her pupils until she can see nothing else, but before she can be swallowed up by her own gaze, she hears the manager behind her.

"Not bad."

She turns. He is standing in the doorway, arms folded, one shoulder resting casually against the frame. She pushes back her fringe and turns to face him. She does not have time to think, the words come unbidden.

"I need an advance on my salary."

A smile. An ineffable smile that hints at all the darkest triumphs of men.

"Well, well . . ."

Sophie leans back against the washbasin and folds her arms.

"A thousand."

"A grand? Really? Is that all?"

"It's more or less what I'm owed."

"What you will be owed at the end of the month. Can't you wait?"

"No, I can't."

"Oh?"

For a long moment they stand, staring at each other, and it is in this man's eyes that she finds what she was looking for in the mirror, that strange feeling of vertigo, but there is nothing intimate about it now. It is a dizzying nausea that assails her in the pit of the stomach.

"Well?" she says, trying to shrug it off.

"We'll see . . . we'll see . . ."

He fills the doorway, blocking her exit, and Sophie fleetingly remembers the man back at the bank several months ago. An unsettling sense of déjà vu. But there is something different too.

She moves to leave, but he grabs her wrist.

"It should be possible," he says, enunciating each syllable, "Come and see me tomorrow after your shift."

Then, jamming Sophie's fist against his crotch, he adds:

"I'm sure we can come to some arrangement."

This is the difference. The brash insolence. This is not an

attempt at seduction but a display of power, a crude deal between two people each of whom has something the other wants. It is very straightforward; Sophie is surprised at how simple it is. She has been on her feet for twenty hours straight, she has not had a day off in more than a week, she sleeps very little to avoid the nightmares, she is exhausted, drained, she wants it to be over, she has invested her last ounce of strength into this plan, she has to make it work, right now, whatever it costs it will be much less than the life she is living where everything is wasting away, even the very roots of her existence.

Without making a conscious decision, she unclenches her fist and grasps his hard cock through the fabric of his trousers. She is staring into his eyes, but she does not see him. She is simply holding his cock. This is a contract.

As she catches the bus, she realises that if she had had to give him a blow job, right there, right then, she would have done it. Without a flicker of hesitation. This thought stirs no emotion in her. It is a simple fact, nothing more.

Sophie spends the night sitting at the window smoking cigarettes. Down below, along the boulevard, she can see the halos of the streetlamps and she imagines the prostitutes in the shadows, sheltering under trees, kneeling at the feet of men who grip their heads hard and stare up at the sky.

By some strange association of ideas, this brings images of the "supermarket incident" flooding back. From her bag, the security guards are taking a series of things she did not pay for and laying them on a metal table. She is doing her best to answer their questions. The only thing that matters to her is that they do not contact Vincent.

If Vincent finds out that she is mad, he will have her committed.

He said as much, long ago, in a conversation with a group of friends. Said that if he "had a wife like that" he would have her locked up. He was laughing, it was obviously a joke, but it is something she has never been able to forget. This was the moment when fear took hold of her. Perhaps she was already too far gone by then to make allowances, to see the remark for what it was: a wind-up. For months afterwards, she found herself thinking: if Vincent sees that I am mad, he will have me committed.

In the morning, at about 6.00 a.m., she gets up from her chair, takes a shower and lies down for an hour before leaving for work. She stares at the ceiling and sobs.

It is like an anaesthetic. Something makes her act, she feels as though she is cowering deep inside her physical body, as though inside the Trojan horse. The horse does not need her in order to act, it knows what it has to do. All she need do is wait, and keep her hands pressed to her ears.

12

This morning, Jeanne looks as though she got out of bed on the wrong side, but when she sees Sophie arrive, she looks horrified.

"Jesus, what the hell happened?" she says.

"Nothing, why?"

"The face on you . . .!"

"Yeah," Sophie says as she goes into the staff room, "I didn't get much sleep last night."

Curiously, she does not feel tired. Perhaps it will come later. She sets to work at once, mopping the floors.

Mindless. You plunge the mop into the bucket, you do not think. You wring it out, swab the floor. When the mop goes cold, you plunge it back into the bucket and start over. You do not think.

You empty the ashtrays, wipe down the tables quickly, set the ashtrays down again. In a little while, Jeanne will come over and say: "You really don't look well . . ." But you will not say anything. You will not really have heard her. You will shrug ambiguously. You say nothing. Straining towards the escape you can feel crackling inside you, the necessary escape. Images will appear, more images, faces, you will shoo them like flies, pushing back the lank fringe that falls into your eyes every time you bend down. Automatic. When you are done you will go into the kitchen, into the haze of greasy smoke. Someone is circling you. You look up, it is the manager. You carry on with your work. Unthinking. You know what it is you want: to leave. Soon. So you work. You do whatever it takes. You will do whatever it takes to make it happen. Reflexive. A sleepwalker. You act, you wait. You will leave. You have to get away.

The end of the shift comes at 11 p.m. By then, everyone is shattered, and the manager has the hard task of galvanising his team so that everything is ready for the next morning. He strides around, through the kitchen, through the empty restaurant, shouting, "Get a fucking move on, we haven't got all night," or "Are you planning to do any work at all, you lazy bitch?" By 11.30, everything is done. It is a tribute to his managerial skill.

Everyone leaves quickly. There are always a few who stand, smoking a cigarette outside, chatting idly, before making for home. Then the boss does one last check, locks the doors and sets the alarm.

By now, everyone has left. Sophie goes into the staff room, hangs up her uniform, shuts her locker, walks through the kitchen. There is a corridor that leads to an alley behind the restaurant and, on the right, the door to the manager's office. She knocks and goes in without waiting.

It is a cramped concrete room, the breezeblocks have been painted white; it is furnished with cast-offs, a desk piled with papers, invoices, a telephone, a calculator. Behind the desk is a metal filing cabinet and above it a grimy window that looks out onto the yard behind the restaurant. The boss is at the desk, talking on the telephone. When she appears, he smiles and gestures for her to sit as he goes on with his call. Sophie remains standing, leaning against the door.

He says simply "O.K., later . . ." and hangs up. Then he stands and comes over to her.

"You come for your advance?" he says in a low voice. "How much was it again?"

"A thousand."

"I should be able to sort you out." He grabs her hand and presses it to his flies.

Sophie no longer remembers the details now. He said something like, "We understand each other, yeah?" Sophie must have nodded, she understood, but in fact she was not really listening, she was overcome by a kind of vertigo, something that came from deep within her and left her mind a blank. She might easily have collapsed like a dead weight, right there, melted away, swallowed up by the earth. He must have put his hands on her shoulders and pushed, hard, and Sophie felt herself sink to her knees in front of him, but this is something else she cannot really remember. Then she saw his stiff penis moving towards her mouth. Perhaps she clung to him, she cannot remember what she was doing with her hands. No, her hands hung limp, she was reduced to a mouth wrapped around this man's cock. What did she do? Nothing, she did nothing, she let the man pump in and out for a long time. A long time? Maybe not. Time is difficult to measure. It passes eventually. There is one thing she does remember: he got angry. Probably because she was not enthusiastic, he pushed deep into her throat and she recoiled, banging her head against the door. He must have taken her head in his hands, yes, that must be right, because his hip movements became jerkier, more feverish. One more thing. She remembers him saying, "Tighter, for fuck's sake." Angrily. Sophie tried to make herself tighter, she did what she had to do. She pressed her lips tighter. She had her eyes closed, though she cannot really remember. And afterwards? Afterwards, nothing – almost nothing. The guy's cock stopped for a moment, he gave a hoarse grunt, she tasted his sperm in her mouth, it was thick and bitter and tasted like bleach, she let him come in her mouth while she wiped tears from her eyes, and that was all. She waited and, eventually, he stepped back, she spat on the ground, once, twice, and when he saw her spit he yelled "Slut!", yes, that is what he said, Sophie spat one last time, doubled over, one hand on the cold concrete floor. And then . . . what? He was standing in front of her again, furious. She was still in the same position, her knees ached so she got up, but it was difficult to get to her feet. When she was finally standing, she noticed for the first time that he was not as tall as she had thought. He was having trouble getting his dick back into his trousers, he looked as though he did not know how to go about it, squirming and swaying his hips. Then he turned around, went to the desk, came back and pressed money into her hand. He was staring at the floor, at what Sophie had spat up, he said, "Go on, piss off." Sophie turned, she must have opened the door and walked down the corridor, she must have gone into the staff room. No, she went to the toilets, she needed to rinse out her mouth, but she did not get a chance. Hardly had she taken three steps than she raced for the toilet bowl and vomited. This much she remembers. She vomited everything up. The pain in her belly was so excruciating, the wracking heaves so powerful that she had to kneel and cling to the porcelain. She clutched the crumpled notes in her hand. Threads of saliva hung from her lips, she wiped them with the back of her hand. She did not even have the strength to flush the toilet and the whole room stank of vomit. She pressed her forehead against the cool porcelain and tried to regain her composure. She saw herself get to her feet, but did she actually get up? No, at first she lay down on the wooden bench people used to change their shoes. She brought a hand to her forehead as though trying to stop her teeming thoughts from engulfing her. She rests her head in one hand while the other rubs the back of her neck. Using the locker for support, she struggles to stand. This simple act requires superhuman effort. Her head is spinning, she has to close her eyes for a moment to steady herself and the dizziness passes. Gradually, she comes round.

Sophie opens the locker, takes out her jacket but does not put it on, she slings it over one shoulder as she leaves. She gropes about in her bag. It is not easy with one hand. She sets the bag down on the ground and carries on searching. She finds a crumpled piece of paper – a receipt, an old supermarket receipt. She rummages a little more and finds a ballpoint pen. She scratches hard on the paper until the pen finally begins to work, scribbles a few words and slips the note under the door of one of the lockers. Now what? She turns left, no, she needs to turn right. After closing, staff leave by the rear door. Like they do in banks. The corridor is still lit. He will lock up. Sophie pads down the hall, passes the door to the office, places her hand on the metal bar and begins to push. A breath of cool night air buffets her face for an instant, but she does not step outside. Instead, she turns and looks down the corridor. She does not want it to end like this. So she retraces her steps, her jacket still slung over her shoulder. She is standing in front of the office door. She feels calm. She transfers her jacket to her other hand and gently opens the door.

*

The following morning, Jeanne found a little note pushed under the door of her locker: "We'll meet again in another life. Much love." The note was not signed. Jeanne stuffed it into her pocket. The staff on duty are already in the restaurant, but the metal shutters have not been rolled up. Forensics technicians from *identité judiciaire* are hard at work at the far end of the corridor. Police officers have already taken names and are carrying out the initial interviews.

13

The heat is stifling. Sophie is half-dead with exhaustion and yet sleep will not come. Close by, she can hear dance music. Electric music. Electric nights. Her mind cannot help but pick out the titles of some of the songs. Golden oldies from the seventies. She never liked dancing. She always felt too awkward. She would dance to rock music now and then, but always the same four steps.

A gunshot makes her flinch: it is a firework, the first of the display. She gets out of bed.

She thinks about the documents she is paying for. This is the only possible solution. It cannot fail.

Sophie throws the window wide, lights a cigarette and watches another firework streak across the sky. She is chain-smoking. She does not cry.

My God, what has she set in motion?

14

The office is just as impersonal. The supplier watches her as she comes in. They both remain standing. Sophie takes a thick envelope from her bag, takes out a wad of notes and begins to count them.

"That won't be necessary."

She looks up. Immediately she realises that something is wrong.

"You have to understand, mademoiselle, our business is subject to market forces."

The man's tone is measured, he does not move.

"The laws of supply and demand are as old as time. Our prices are based not on the intrinsic value of our products, but on each client's *need*."

Sophie feels a lump in her throat. She swallows hard.

"And since we last met," the man goes on, "circumstances have changed somewhat . . . Madame Duguet."

She feels her legs give, the room begins to spin, she clings to a corner of the desk.

"Perhaps you would prefer to sit?"

Sophie slumps into a chair.

"Don't worry, you are in no danger. But we need to know who we are dealing with. We always conduct background checks. In your case, it was no easy matter. You are a very resourceful woman, Madame Duguet, as the police have discovered to their embarrassment. But we know our business. We now know who you are, but I can assure you that we will keep your identity confidential. In this business, we cannot afford the slightest indiscretion."

Sophie has regained a little of her composure, but his words are slow to penetrate, as though they had first to pierce a dense layer of fog. She manages to say a few words.

"Which means . . .?"

This is all she can say.

"Which means that the price is no longer the same."

"How much?"

"Double."

Sophie's panic is clearly visible in her face.

"I do apologise," the man says. "Would you like a glass of water?"

Sophie does not answer. Here all her hopes come to an end.

"I can't," she whispers, as though talking to herself.

"I am quite sure you can. You have proved yourself to be enormously resourceful. Otherwise, you would not be here. Let's meet again a week from now, if that suits. After that . . ."

"But what guarantee do I have that . . .?"

"Sadly, Madame Duguet, none. Other than my word. But trust me, that is worth more than any guarantee."

*

M. Auverney is a tall man, the sort people describe as "sprightly" by which they mean that, though old, he has aged well. Summer and winter he invariably wears a hat. This one is unbleached linen. Since it is a little hot in the post office, he holds it in one hand. When the man behind the counter beckons, he steps forward, sets his hat on the counter and hands over the delivery note. He has his identity card ready. Since Sophie has been on the run, he has learned never to look behind him, he knows that he has been under surveillance. He may still be. Just in case, as he leaves the post office, he ducks into the café next door, orders a coffee and asks for the toilets. The message is brief: "green_mouse@msn. fr". M. Auverney, who gave up smoking almost twenty years ago, takes out the lighter he was careful to bring and burns the message in the toilet bowl. Then he calmly drinks his coffee standing at the bar. He props his elbows on the counter, rests his chin on his clasped hands, the very image of a man who is taking his time. In fact, he does so to stop his hands from trembling.

Two days later, M. Auverney is in Bordeaux. He steps inside an old building with an entrance as imposing as that of a prison. He knows the building intimately, it was he who oversaw its renovation some years ago. He has made this journey especially, just so that he can go in and come out again. As though playing cat and mouse. He came here because he knows that when you enter 28 rue d'Estienne-d'Orves and take the long, winding route through its cellars, you emerge from 76 impasse Maliveau. Here, the alley is deserted. There is a painted green door that leads to a courtyard which offers access to the toilets of Le Balto, a bar that opens onto boulevard Mariani.

M. Auverney walks slowly up the boulevard to the taxi rank

and asks to be driven to the bus station.

Sophie stubs out her cigarette, the last in the pack. Since morning, it has been overcast. The sky is fleecy. There is a bracing wind. The waiter, having nothing to do at this hour, loiters by the door next to the terrace table where Sophie has just ordered a coffee.

"It's a westerly, that . . . Not a chance of rain."

Sophie responds with a low-key smile. Do not engage in conversation, but do nothing that might make you stand out. After a last glance at the sky to confirm his prognosis, the waiter goes back to the counter. Sophie checks her watch. In the months that she has been on the run, she has trained herself to an implacable self-discipline. She will leave at 2.25 p.m. Not before. It is a five-minute walk, no more. She aimlessly thumbs through the pages of a women's magazine: "*Ten Things You Need to Know if You're a Scorpio!*", "*Are You Cool Enough to be a Hipster?*", "*Tease Him and Please Him!*", "*Brit's Playlist!*", "*Lose 5 Kilos in Just 5 Days!*"

It is 2.25, at last. Sophie leaves some coins on the table and gets up.

It may be a westerly wind, but it is bitterly cold. She turns up the collar of her jacket and crosses the boulevard. At this time, the coach station is almost deserted. Sophie has only one concern: that her father will not have had the same self-discipline. That he will still be there, waiting to see her. Her relief is tempered when she sees that he has obeyed her instructions to the letter. There is no familiar face among the few customers in the snack bar. She crosses the room, goes down a short flight of steps to the toilets and takes the plain brown envelope from behind the cistern. As she emerges onto the street, the first fat raindrops are pounding the pavement. Westerly wind indeed.

The taxi driver is patient.

"Look, as long as the meter is running, I don't care," he said.

He has been parked here for almost a quarter of an hour, his customer in the back staring distractedly out of the window. "I'm waiting for someone," he tells the driver. He has just wiped the misted window. He is elderly, but seems fit for his age. A young woman who has been waiting for the traffic lights to change now crosses the street, turning up the collar of her jacket because it has started to rain. She glances briefly at the taxi, continues on her way and disappears.

"Never mind," the customer says with a sigh. "I can't wait around all day. Take me back to the hotel."

His voice sounds strange.

15

Marianne Leblanc. It has taken a real effort to get used to it. Sophie has always hated the name Marianne, though she is not sure why. Probably some girl at school who bullied her. But Sophie had no choice. This is what she has been given: Marianne Leblanc, whose date of birth is eighteen months from her own. It hardly matters, though. It is almost impossible to guess Sophie's age. She can pass for thirty or for thirty-eight. The certificate is stamped October 23. "As you know, notarised copies of birth certificates are valid for only three months," the supplier told her. "But that should give you enough time to sort yourself out."

She can picture him that night as he sets down the birth certificate and slowly counts the money. He does not even have that satisfied smirk of a businessman who has just made a good deal. He is methodical. He is a cold man. Sophie probably did not say a word. She cannot remember now. The next thing she can picture is arriving home, the gaping wardrobe, the open suitcase. She sees herself haphazardly cramming everything into the case, pushing back her fringe, feeling a wave of dizziness and clutching the kitchen door to steady herself. She takes a shower – the water is freezing. As she dresses again, dazed and exhausted, she makes a last tour of the apartment, checks that she has not forgotten anything important, but by now she cannot see anything. Already she is on her way down the stairs. It is a slow, clear night.

16

By now Sophie has got a nose for finding unlicensed studios, unauthorised sublets, cash-in-hand jobs, in short, all the little tricks she needs to settle into a new town. When she arrived here, she combed through the small ads, systematically looking for the worst jobs on offer, those for which no reference would be required. Two days later, she was working with a team of office cleaners – mostly black and Arab women – under the firm hand of a motherly sadist from Alsace. Salaries are paid in cash every fortnight. The managers of Quik-Kleen consider the quota for declared employees to be reached when half of its cleaners receive a pay slip. Sophie is part of the other half. For form's sake she protests, while praying to God they will not listen.

At 10.00 every night, Sophie goes outside and waits on the pavement. A shuttle bus comes to pick her up. The teams are dropped off, first at an insurance firm and later at an I.T. company. The "day" finishes at 6.00 a.m. sharp. "Lunch" is eaten in the bus en route between the two jobs.

*

She has only two and a half months to carry out her plan and it is vital that she succeeds. At the beginning of the month, she had her first meetings. She signed up with a dating agency. Later, she may subscribe to others, but even a single agency is expensive. She stole 1,400 euros from the manager's office, just enough to fund her initial searches.

Her identity as Marianne Leblanc was guaranteed only as a "medium-term solution", which means she does not have long. She has settled, therefore, on a golden rule: take the first man who comes along. Although she is utterly desperate, trembling constantly from head to foot, sleeping barely three hours a night and shedding weight with every passing day, on her first date Sophie realised that the word "first" was meaningless. She had drawn up a short checklist: the man must have no children, an uncomplicated private life – as for everything else, she is prepared to make do. At the agency, she pretended that she was not particularly fussy in her criteria. She offered banal phrases: "a simple guy", "a quiet life".

17

René Bahorel, forty-four, a simple, quiet guy.

They had agreed to meet in a brasserie. She recognised him at once, a chubby-cheeked farmer with terrible B.O. He looked exactly as he had sounded on the telephone. A hearty character.

"I'm from Lembach," he says knowingly.

It takes her twenty minutes to realise that this means he is a wine-grower who lives somewhere in the back of beyond. Sophie lit a cigarette. He tapped the pack on the table with his finger.

"Let me tell you straight off, if you're with me, you'll have to quit."

He smiled broadly, visibly proud of expressing his authority in what he considers a tactful manner. Like all men who live alone, he is garrulous. Sophie does not need to do anything, she merely stares at him and listens. Her mind is elsewhere. She feels a desperate urge to get away. She imagines the future, visualises the first physical submission to this man and feels the need for another cigarette. He talks about himself, about his smallholding. There has never been a wedding ring on his finger, or if there was, it was long ago. Perhaps it is the stifling heat of the brasserie, the clamour from the tables where diners are ordering their main courses, but Sophie feels a wave of nausea rising in her stomach.

". . . I mean, obviously, we get E.U. subsidies, but it's still a nightmare. What about you?"

The question comes out of the blue.

"What about me?"

"What do you think? Are you interested in farming?"

"Not particularly, to be honest . . ."

Sophie said this because, regardless of the questions, it was the right answer. René says, "Oh." But the guy is a Weeble, he might wobble, but he won't fall down. You have to wonder how farmers end up being run over by their own tractors. His vocabulary might be limited, but certain words recur with a worrying insistence. Sophie tries to decode what she is hearing.

"So, your mother lives with you?"

René says, "Oh, yes", as though reassuring her. Eighty-four years old. And still "fit as a fiddle". It is terrifying. Sophie imagines herself lying beneath the weight of this man while the old woman prowls the corridors, the shuffle of slippers, the smell of cooking. For a second, she pictures Vincent's mother in front of her, her back to the stairs, Sophie places her hands on her shoulders and pushes so hard that the old woman seems to soar, her feet do not even touch the first steps, it is as though she had just had a shotgun blast in the chest.

"Have you met a lot of women, René?" Sophie says, leaning towards him.

"You're the first," he says, as though this is some kind of achievement.

"Well, take your time deciding . . ."

Sophie put the birth certificate into a transparent plastic folder. She is afraid of mislaying it as she has mislaid so many important things, terrified of losing it. Every night, before she goes to work, she picks up the folder and says aloud:

"I open the wardrobe."

She closes her eyes, visualises the gesture, her hand, the wardrobe and repeats: "I have opened the wardrobe."

"I pull out the right-hand drawer; I have pulled out the right-hand drawer . . ."

She repeats each gesture several times, trying, by sheer force of will, to fuse the words to the actions. As soon as she comes home, before she even undresses, she rushes to the wardrobe to check that the folder is still there. Then she sticks it to the fridge door with a magnet until she has to go out again.

Perhaps she could kill him one day, this husband she is trying to find? No. When she is finally safe, she will go back and see someone like Doctor Brevet. She will keep two notebooks, three if she has to, she will start writing everything down, and this time, nothing will distract her. It is like a child's resolution: if she pulls through, she will never again let madness engulf her.

18

Five dates later, Sophie is no further forward. Theoretically, the agency is supposed to introduce her to potential partners who meet her criteria, but the woman at Odyssée, like an estate agent who shows you properties that have nothing to do with what you are looking for, is sending her everyone she has. First, there was a dull-witted soldier proud to have risen to the lowly rank of *sergent-chef*, next a depressive draughtsman who, she discovered after three hours of tedious conversation, had an ex-wife and two children and a poorly negotiated alimony settlement that ate up three-quarters of his unemployment benefit.

She had stumbled out of a tea room, crushed by boredom, having spent a couple of interminable hours listening to a former priest whose finger bore the mark of a wedding ring he had clearly taken off an hour earlier, probably in an attempt to spice up his bleak sex life. And then there was the tall, self-confident guy who proposed a marriage of convenience for 6,000 euros.

Time seems to be passing ever faster. However much Sophie tells herself that she is not looking for a husband (she is recruiting a candidate), the fact remains that they will have to marry, to sleep together, to live together. In a few weeks, in a few days, she will no longer have the luxury of choosing, she will have to make do with whatever she can find.

Time passes and with it her opportunity to be free, and this is something to which she cannot reconcile herself.

19

Sophie is on the bus. Go faster. She stares vacantly ahead. What can she do to make it go faster? She checks her watch: she just has time to get home, catch two or three hours' sleep. She is shattered. She slips her hands into her pockets. It is curious how they tremble at times and not at others. She stares out of the window. Madagascar. She turns and, for a fleeting instant, looks at the poster that caught her eye. A travel agency. She cannot be certain. But she stands up, presses the button, ready to get off at the next stop. It feels as though she has travelled kilometres before the bus finally comes to a halt. She trudges back up the boulevard, moving like a wind-up toy, as always. As it turns out, it is not far. The image on the poster is of a young black woman with an innocent, beguiling smile. She is wearing a kind of turban, the sort of thing with a name you would find in a crossword puzzle. Behind her is a picture-postcard beach. Sophie crosses the street and turns to look at the poster from a distance. The better to think.

"Affirmative," the soldier had said. "Not really my thing, I have to say. Never been much of a traveller, but, yeah, we've got lots of opportunities like that. I've got a mate, a *sergent-chef* like me, he's being posted to Madagascar. In his case it kind of makes sense, his wife lives there. In general, though, there aren't many lads who are keen to leave France! Not as many as you might think . . ."

Not as many as you might think.

She thinks about this all the way home. Before she reaches her door she stops at a telephone booth, delves into her bag.

"Look," the soldier had said shyly. "This might sound bad, I mean, the thing is, I don't really know how to go about this . . . I can't really ask you for your number, so I'm going to give you mine. It's my private number. I mean, you never know . . ."

By the end of their date, the soldier had lost much of the superciliousness he had had when he arrived. He no longer looked like a conquering hero.

"I know I'm not really your type . . . You need someone who's, well, more intellectual."

He had smiled awkwardly.

"Hello?"

"Hi," Sophie said. "It's Marianne Leblanc, I'm not disturbing you am I?"

In fact, the soldier is not as short as he at first seemed. He is half a head taller than Sophie, but everything about him is marked with a crippling shyness that makes him seem smaller. When Sophie walks into the café, he gets clumsily to his feet. She sees him now in a new light, but new or old, there is only one thing to be said about him: he is ugly. "Well, plain," she tries to reassure herself only for a little voice to whisper: "No. Ugly."

"What would you like to drink?"

"I don't know – a coffee? What about you?"

"Same. A coffee."

They spend a while like this, smiling uncomfortably at each other.

"I'm really glad you called. Do you always tremble like that?"

"I'm just nervous."

"I suppose that's normal. I am too, well, I don't want to talk about me . . . It's really hard to know what to say, isn't it?"

"Perhaps we've got nothing to say to each other."

She regrets this immediately.

"I'm so sorry."

"That's a negative! I . . ."

"Please, I'm begging you, don't say 'negative' and 'affirmative' all the time, it's really irritating."

She has been brutal.

"It's just, I feel like I'm talking to a computer," she says by way of apology.

"You're right. Force of habit. It comes with the job. I suppose in your job you must pick up strange habits, no?"

"I work as a cleaner, so my habits are much the same as anyone else's. Well, anyone who does their own cleaning, that is."

"It's weird, I didn't mention it last time, but I'd never guess you were a cleaner. You seem really educated."

"Well, yes . . . I did study, but that kind of thing doesn't appeal to me anymore. Let's talk about it some other time, if you don't mind?"

"No, no, I don't mind. Nothing much bothers me, I'm pretty easy-going."

And this declaration, uttered with disarming sincerity, makes

Sophie think that there is nothing more annoying in life than people who are easy-going.

"Right," Sophie says, "let's start again from square one, shall we?"

"I'm not sure we ever got past square one!"

He is not as dumb as he seems.

Why not? Sophie hears a small voice in her head. But first, she needs to know; right now, the fact that he could be posted abroad is his one attractive quality. This is what she needs to confirm.

Sophie decided they should meet in the late afternoon. They have been here for an hour. The soldier weighs his every syllable so as not to say anything that might scupper the flimsy raft on which he is afloat.

"Why don't we get something to eat?" Sophie says.

"If you like."

From the moment they met, this has been the pattern: the man is weak, he is needy, he wants whatever she wants. She feels a little ashamed of what she is planning to do to him, but she knows what she will have to give him in exchange. As she sees it, he is hardly losing out. He is looking for a wife. Any woman would fit the bill. A wife. Even Sophie would do.

As they leave the café, she is the one who decides to turn right. He does not question her decision, he carries on chattering as he walks beside her, harmless. He is content to have Sophie lead him by the nose. It feels a little pathetic.

"Where do you fancy going?" she says.

"I don't know . . . How about Le Relais?"

Sophie is convinced that he has had that line prepared since the night before.

"What kind of place is it?"

111

"A restaurant. A brasserie . . . I mean, I've only ever been there once, but it's not bad. Well, I'm not sure you'd like it."

Sophie manages to smile.

"Let's find out, shall we?"

And in the end, it is indeed not bad. Sophie was afraid it might be a restaurant full of squaddies, but did not dare ask.

"It's really nice," she says.

"To tell you the truth, I picked it out beforehand. I even walked past this morning to do a quick recce. I couldn't really remember where it was."

"You haven't actually been here before, have you?"

"That's a neg. I get the feeling it's not going to be easy to lie to you." The soldier smiles.

As she watches him choose from the menu (waiting to see whether he lingers over the prices), she wonders how a man like him will come through this unscathed. But he has to fend for himself. And since he will want to know the pleasures of the flesh, he has to accept that sooner or later she will exact a pound of his. It will be a true marriage, the two will be one flesh.

"Do you tend to lie to women?" Sophie picks up the thread of the conversation.

"No more than most men, I reckon. Less, actually, I think. Let's say I'm probably somewhere in the middle."

"So, on our first date, what did you lie about?"

Sophie lights a cigarette, then remembers he does not smoke. She does not care. As long as he leaves her be.

"I don't know. We didn't talk for long, did we?"

"When it comes to lying, some men don't take much time."

He stares at her.

"I can't compete."

"Sorry?"

"In conversation, I can't compete with you. I'm not much of a talker, you know that. Of course you know that. It's probably the reason you picked me. Well, I say 'picked' . . ."

"I don't understand."

"Well, I know what I mean."

"The conversation might be easier if we both knew."

The waiter appears. Mentally, Sophie makes a bet.

"What are you having?" he says.

"Rib-eye steak and a side salad. What about you?"

"Let's see . . ." He scans the menu one last time. "I'll have the same, steak and salad."

"How would you like it cooked?" the waiter says.

"Rare. Both rare," Sophie says, stubbing out her cigarette.

Jesus, what a stupid thing to say.

"You were saying?"

"Me? Nothing, why?"

"That's why I picked you . . .? What the hell is that supposed to mean?"

"Oh, don't mind me. I'm a born bumbler. I can't help it. My mother always used to say if I was walking through a field and there was a single cow pat ('scuse my language), I'd be the one to step in it."

"I don't follow you."

"Not much to follow, I'm not particularly complicated."

"It seems that way. Sorry, I meant . . ."

"Don't keep apologising or we'll be here all night."

The waiter brings the two identical steaks. In silence they begin to eat. Sophie feels she should say something nice about the steak, finds she cannot think of another word. The vast desert separating them has just grown wider, like a pool spreading, spreading . . .

"It's not bad, in fact."

"Yeah, it's good. Really good."

But there is nothing to be done, Sophie does not have the energy to revive the conversation, it is too much effort. She has to eat her steak and hang in there. For the first time, she studies him closely. A metre seventy-five, maybe a metre eighty. A decent body, probably, broad shoulders – soldiers tend to be pretty fit – large hands, impeccable nails. And the face: like a spaniel puppy. His hair probably stuck up before he had it cropped, his nose is a little flat, his eyes a little vacant. But he is well built. Strange that the first time they met, she thought he was small. Probably just the way he carries himself, as though he has not quite grown up. There is an innocence to him. For an instant Sophie envies him. For the first time she genuinely envies his simplicity. She realises that, until now, she has seen him as an object, that she has been sneering without even knowing him. She reacted like a man.

"We made a bit of a hash, didn't we?" she says.

"A hash?"

"Of the conversation . . . It sort of petered out."

"Well, it's not easy," he says. "When you find something to talk about, it's easy, you just keep going, but sometimes it leads nowhere. We started off well, it's a pity the waiter didn't come at that point."

Sophie cannot help but smile.

What she is feeling now is not boredom, it is not contempt. What is it? A hollowness. An emptiness. Perhaps it comes from him.

"So, what was it you said you do, exactly?"

"I'm in the Signals Corps."

"Well, that helps."

"Sorry?"

"What does that mean, the Signals Corps? Tell me."

The soldier launches into an explanation. Now that he is in his element, he is quite talkative. She is not listening. Discreetly she glances at the clock. But could it really have been any different? What did she expect? Another Vincent? She sees herself in their house just after they moved in. The day she started painting the living room. Vincent came up behind her and simply laid his hand on the back of her neck and Sophie felt his strength flow into her.

"You're not really interested in the Signals Corps, are you?"

"No, no, I am."

"So you find the whole thing fascinating?"

"Well, I wouldn't go as far as that."

"I know what you're thinking."

"You do?"

"Yes. You're thinking 'Nice enough guy, with his stories about the Signals Corps, but boring as fuck.' Excuse my language. You're checking the time, your mind is elsewhere. I should probably tell you right now, I feel the same. You make me uncomfortable, you're trying to be nice because, well, what choice do you have? So here we are, talking away. But we haven't got much to talk about. I can't help but wonder . . ."

"I'm really sorry, you're right, my mind was elsewhere. It's just that it's very technical, what you do."

"It's not just because it's technical. It's mostly that you don't fancy me. I wonder . . ."

"What?"

"I can't help wondering why you called me back. What is it that you really want? What's your story?"

"Oh, It's a lo-o-ong story – it could take a year or two, maybe three. Most people never get the chance. My ex-boyfriend doesn't know how damn lucky he was."

They both laugh. At the end of the meal, she no longer knows where she stands. They walk along the river bank. A biting cold. A hundred metres on, she slips her arm through his. A moment of complicity has brought them closer together. In the end, he manoeuvred skilfully: he gave up trying to impress. He said simple things: "The way I see it, you might as well just be yourself. Because sooner or later, people will find out who you really are. You might as well let them know from the start."

"You were talking about postings to overseas territories."

"Not just French *départements*! You can get yourself posted to foreign countries too. Though I have to admit, that's pretty rare."

Sophie is working out a timeline. Meet, marry, move abroad, work, divorce. Perhaps it is an illusion, this thought that she will be safer thousands of kilometres from here. But intuitively she knows she will be better able to hide. While she is thinking, the soldier lists friends who have been posted abroad, those who put in for transfers, those who are still hopeful. God, but the man is so tedious, so trite.

20

I am afraid. The dead are surfacing. In the darkness. I can count them one by one. In the darkness, I see them sitting at a table, side by side. In the darkness. At the head of the table is Léo with a bootlace around his throat. He looks at me reproachfully. He says: "Are you mad, Sophie? Why did you strangle me? Is it really true that you're mad?"; his eyes are probing, piercing. I recognise that puzzled expression, his head tilted to one side as though he is thinking. "It's true, but it's nothing new, she was always mad," Vincent's mother says. She is trying to be reassuring. I recognise that grim expression, the shrill voice, the eyes like a hyena's. "She was crazy long before she started killing people and destroying everything around her, I said as much to Vincent, I said, 'That girl is crazy . . .'" She says this solemnly, she closes her eyes for so long when she speaks you wonder if she will ever open them, she spends most of her time with her eyelids closed, gazing deep within herself. "You hate me, Sophie, you always hated me, but now that you've killed me . . ." Vincent says nothing more. He shakes his fleshless head as though pleading for mercy. Now they are all staring at me. They say nothing.

I wake with a jolt. When this happens, I can't get back to sleep. I

go to the window and I stand there for hours, smoking and sobbing.
I even killed my own baby.

21

They have been seeing each other for about two weeks. It took Sophie only a few hours to work out what makes the soldier tick. Now, she is simply honing her skills to match his interests, but she remains vigilant.

He allows her to drag him to see "24 Heures de la vie d'une femme" and pretends to enjoy it.

"In the novel it was different, there were only two generations of women," Sophie explains, lighting a cigarette.

"I haven't read it, but I'm sure it's pretty good."

"Yes," Sophie says, "the book is pretty good."

She has had to reconstruct a whole biography based on her new birth certificate: who her parents were, where she studied, it is a story she shrouds in mystery for fear of saying too much. The soldier is tactful. As a precaution, she encourages him to talk most of the time. In the evening, when she gets home, she makes notes, she has a jotter that contains everything she knows about him. There is nothing convoluted about his past. Nothing interesting, either. Born October 13, 1973 in Aubervilliers, just outside Paris. Unremarkable primary and secondary schools, technical college, qualification in electromechanical engineering, enlisted in the army, assigned to the Signals Corps, certificate in telecommunications, *sergent-chef*, possible promotion to *adjudant*.

"So, squid, huh?"

"They're sometimes called calamari . . ."

He smiles.

"D'you know, I think I'll go for the steak."

It is Sophie's turn to smile.

"You make me laugh."

"Usually when women say that, it's not a good sign."

The advantage of soldiers is their directness, that what you see is what you get. He turns out to be very much as Sophie supposed on their first few dates. She has discovered that he is unexpectedly sensitive, the man is not an idiot, he is simple and down to earth. He wants to marry, to have children, he is kind, and even caring. And Sophie has no time to lose. She had little trouble seducing him: he was already seduced, and Sophie was as good a catch as any other woman. In fact she was rather better because she is quite pretty. Since they started dating, she has gone back to buying make-up, she pays a little more attention to what she wears but is careful not to overdress. From time to time, it is clear that the soldier fantasises about certain things. It has been years since any man looked at her with such passionate longing – it feels strange.

"Where exactly are we heading?"

"I thought we said we were going to see 'Alien.'"

"No, I mean us. Where do we stand?"

Sophie knows exactly where they stand. She has barely two months to carry out her plan. Less the time required to publish the banns. She cannot change her mind now. There's no time. With any other guy, she would have to start again from scratch. There is no time. She looks at him. She has become accustomed to his face. Or perhaps she just needs him. The result is the same.

"Do you know where you stand?"

"Me? Yes, I think so. But you already know that. What I don't understand is why you changed your mind, why you called me back."

"I didn't change my mind, I just took time to think."

"No. You changed your mind. On our first date, you'd already made a decision, and it was 'No'. I don't understand what made you change your mind. Or why."

Sophie lights another cigarette. They are in a brasserie. The evening has not been as dull as she had expected. She has only to look at him to know that this man has fallen in love with her. Has she been canny enough to be convincing?

"You're right. The first time we met, I wasn't blown away . . . I . . ."

"You met other guys. And they were worse, so you thought to yourself . . ."

Sophie looks him in the eye.

"Well, didn't you?"

"Marianne, I get the feeling that you're a terrible liar. No, actually, what I mean is you're a very good liar, and you've lied to me a lot."

"About what?"

"How would I know? Maybe about everything."

Sometimes, she sees such anxiety in his face that she feels a pang of guilt.

"I suppose you have your reasons," he says. "I've got my own ideas on the subject, but maybe I'm better off not prying."

"Why?"

"When you decide to tell me, you'll tell me."

"So what *are* your ideas on the subject?"

"There are things in your past that you can't bring yourself to talk about. But I don't mind."

He looks at her, hesitates. He pays the bill. Finally, he takes the plunge.

"I think maybe – I don't know . . . maybe you were in prison or something like that."

He looks at her again, a sidelong glance. Sophie thinks rapidly.

"Let's say something like that. Nothing terribly serious, but I don't like to talk about it."

He nods sympathetically.

"But what is it exactly that you want?"

"I want to be an ordinary woman, with a husband and kids. That's all."

"I have to say, you don't exactly seem the type."

Sophie feels a cold chill down her back. She tries to smile. They have left the restaurant, the night is ink black, the cold wind whips their faces. She has slipped her arm through his as she always does now. She turns to face him.

"I was thinking of asking you to come home with me. But maybe you're not the type."

He swallows hard.

He does his best. He is very attentive. When Sophie sobs, he says,

"We don't have to . . ." She says, "Help me." He wipes away her tears. She says, "It's not about you, you do know that." He says, "I know." Sophie thinks that this man might be able to understand everything. He is calm, unhurried, careful, all things that she never expected of him. It has been a long time since she had a man inside her. For a while, she closes her eyes as though she is drunk and desperately wants the world to stop spinning so fast. She guides him. She encourages him. She breathes in his familiar smell which until now she has caught only at a distance. It is the anonymous smell of male lust. She manages to choke back her tears. He is careful not to put his weight on her, he seems to be deferring the moment of climax, she smiles up at him. She says, "Come . . ." He is like a callow boy. She hugs him to her. He is under no illusion that this is love.

They lie there in silence, she looks at the time. Each of them knows what they do not have to say to the other. They are both casualties of life, and for the first time she wonders what happened to him that hurt so.

"What about your story, the real story?" she says, coiling his chest hair between her fingers.

"I'm a pretty ordinary guy."

And Sophie wonders whether this is his answer.

When you work night shifts, everything is out of sync. As he is drifting off to sleep, Sophie gets up and goes downstairs to catch the shuttle bus.

*

They are still together: Véronique and the manager from the fast-food restaurant. She killed them both in the same way. She cannot remember how. They are lying side by side on the steel autopsy table in the morgue. Like man and wife. Covered by a white sheet. Sophie walks past the table and, although they are both dead, their eyes are open and they watch eagerly as she passes. Only their eyes move. As she moves around the end of the table, passing the backs of their heads, blood slowly begins to ooze, they smile.

"'fraid so!"

Sophie whips round.

"It's like your hallmark. A few swift blows to the back of the skull."

The manager of the agency is wearing a pale-yellow shirt and a green tie. His tight trousers make his paunch look bigger, his flies are undone. He steps forward like a pathologist, he is pedantic, self-assured, precise, surgical. And smiling. A sardonic smile.

"Sometimes just the one."

He is standing at one end of the slab, looking down at the skulls of the deceased. Blood drips to the floor, fat drops splashing on the concrete, spattering the turn-ups of his trousers.

"Take our friend here [he bends down and reads the tag] . . . Véronique. That's right, Véronique. Five stab wounds to the stomach. To the stomach, Sophie, honestly! Well, never mind, let's move on. This man here [he reads the tag] . . . David. In his case, you had a weapon to hand. A baseball bat David kept purely for decorative purposes, and here he is, his skull caved in with the logo of the Cincinnati Reds. Some deaths are absurd, don't you think?"

He moves away from the table and walks towards Sophie. She backs against the wall. Still he keeps coming, smiling:

"And then there is me. I was a little luckier: there was no knife, no baseball bat around, I had it easy, I can't complain. I'm sure if you could have, you would have smashed my head against the wall and I would be dead, like the others, from a fractured skull. I, too, would be bleeding from the back of the head."

Sophie watches as a bloodstain suddenly spreads down the back of his yellow shirt. He smiles.

"Just like that, Sophie."

He is standing right in front of her, she can smell his acrid breath.

"You are a very dangerous woman, Sophie. And yet men fall in love with you, don't they? You have killed many. Do you plan to kill all the people you love, Sophie? All those who get close to you?"

22

These smells, these gestures, these moments . . . In Sophie's mind they are an omen of what is to come. She will need an escape plan. When the time comes. But all of that is in the future; right now she needs to fake it. To fake it convincingly. No outward show of passion, this is a relationship based on mutual benefit, but one that promises more. They have spent four nights together. Tonight is the fifth. The second in a row. Because she needs to speed things up. She has managed to swap shifts for a few days with one of the girls on the other cleaning team. He comes to pick her up. She slips her arm through his, tells him about her day. By the second time, it is already a habit. As for everything else, he is attentive to the smallest detail. Sometimes it seems as though every gesture is a matter of life and death to him. She tries to reassure him, tries to make their new-found tenderness seem less contrived, less artificial. She cooks for him on the two-ring hotplate in his tiny apartment. Gradually, he relaxes. In bed, he does nothing unless she makes the first move. She does so every time. And every time it terrifies her. She pretends. Sometimes, for an instant only, she imagines she could be happy. The very thought makes her cry. It is something he never sees because it comes at the end, when he has fallen asleep, when she is staring at the dreary bedroom in the murky darkness. At least he does not snore.

Sophie spends long hours like this, watching the images of her life unspool. As always, the tears come of themselves, foreign to her, unrelated to her. Little by little, she slides towards the sleep she finds so terrifying. Sometimes, she reaches for his hand and grips it tightly.

23

It is a dry cold. They are leaning on the wrought-iron railings, the fireworks have just begun. Children scamper along the tree-lined avenue, parents stare into the heavens, mouths agape. The sound of war. The explosions are sometimes preceded by an ominous whistling. The sky glows orange. She presses herself against him. For the first time she needs him, truly needs to nestle in his arms. He slips an arm around her shoulders. It could be anyone. It is him. It could be worse. She strokes his cheek, turns his face towards her. She kisses him. The sky glimmers blue and green. He says something she does not catch because a rocket explodes at that moment. From the look on his face, it was something nice. She nods.

Parents try to shepherd their children, hackneyed jokes spark from one group to the next. They start to head home. The couples go arm in arm. They try in vain to find a pace to suit them both; his strides are longer than hers, he marks time, she smiles, gives him a shove, he laughs, she smiles. They stop. It is loveless, and yet something about it feels good, something that feels like an overwhelming weariness. For the first time, he kisses her with an air of authority. In a few short seconds, the New Year will have begun, some cars are already blaring their horns in their eagerness to be first. Suddenly, everything explodes, there are screams, sirens, laughter, lights. A wave of collective happiness sweeps briefly over everyone, the event is carefully stage-managed, but the joy is real.

Sophie says, "So are we getting married?" She has asked the question.

"I'm up for it . . ." he says, as though apologising. She hugs his arm.

There.

It is done.

In a few weeks, Sophie will be married.

Farewell, Sophie the Psycho.

A new life.

She can, for a short while, breathe freely.

He looks around at the world and smiles.

FRANTZ

I've just seen her for the first time. Her name is Sophie. She was coming out of her apartment block. I barely caught a glimpse. She's obviously a woman in a hurry. She got into a car and sped off so fast I had difficulty keeping up on my motorbike. Luckily she had trouble finding somewhere to park in the Marais, and that made things a bit easier. I followed her at a distance. At first I thought she was going shopping, in which case I would have had to stop tailing her, too risky. But in fact she was meeting someone. She went into a tea room on rue des Rosiers and headed straight for another woman about the same age, looking at her watch to make it obvious she was rushed off her feet. I knew for a fact that she had left home late. Caught red-handed in a lie.

I hung around outside for about ten minutes, then went in and sat in the back room where I found the perfect seat from which I could discreetly keep an eye on her. Sophie was wearing a print dress, flat heels and a pale-grey jacket. I could see her in profile. She is a good-looking woman, the sort most men probably find attractive. Her friend, on the other hand, looked to me like a slut. Too much make-up, too vain, too *female*. At least Sophie knows how to be natural. They stuffed themselves with cupcakes like a couple of schoolgirls. Watching them, I could tell they were joking about breaking their diet. Women are forever going on diets and forever breaking them. Women are so shallow. Sophie is very slim. Much slimmer than her friend.

I soon regretted coming into the tea room. It was a foolish risk, she might have spotted me and, for some reason or other, remembered my face. Why take unnecessary risks? I resolved to be more careful in future. Though I have to say, I like this girl. She's bubbly.

I feel in a very strange state of mind. All my senses are heightened. This was why I was able to turn a futile incident into a fruitful opportunity. I left about twenty minutes after they did, and as I was taking my jacket from the coat rack, I noticed a man had hung his coat there. I quickly slipped my hand into the inside pocket and left with a rather handsome wallet. Its owner was one Lionel Chalvin, born in 1969, so only five years my senior. He lives in Créteil. He still has one of the old-style identity cards. Since I have no intention of using it if asked for my papers, I tinkered with it, pasted a photograph of myself on it – I did a pretty good job, too. There are days when I am glad that I'm good with my hands. If you don't study it too closely, it looks legit.

June 15

It took me about ten days to come to my decision. I've just suffered a terrible blow, years of hopes and waiting dashed in the space of a few short minutes. I never thought I'd get back on my feet so quickly, but, oddly, I think I am over it. I'm a little surprised, to be honest. I followed Sophie Duguet wherever she went, I deliberated, I watched her. I finally came to a decision last night while staring up at the windows of her apartment. I saw her appear for a moment, she drew the curtains with a broad, sweeping gesture. As though sowing the stars. Something in me clicked. I realised that I was going to take the plunge. I needed a Plan B in any case, I couldn't just give up on everything I had ever dreamed about, everything I had longed for. I decided that, all in all, Sophie would fit the bill.

I opened my notebook. There are a lot of things I need to prepare and taking notes will help me think. Because this plan is much more complicated than the previous one.

Sophie's husband is a tall guy who seems intelligent and very self-assured. I like that. Well dressed, elegant in fact, though in a casual way. I showed up early this morning so I would be here when he left and I could follow him. They're doing well for themselves. They own two cars and a luxury apartment. They could be a perfect couple with a bright future ahead of them.

June 20

Vincent Duguet works for Lanzer Gesellschaft, a petrochemical company about which I have managed to track down a lot of information: I don't understand all the details, but basically it's a German limited-liability company with branches all over the world and one of the market leaders in solvents and elastomers. The headquarters of Lanzer Gesellschaft are in Munich, the French head office is in La Défense (where Vincent works), and they have three research centres across the country, in Talence, Grenoble and Senlis. In the company's organisational chart, Vincent appears close to the top, as Assistant Director of Research and Development. He has a Ph.D. from the Université de Jussieu. The photograph in their promotional leaflet looks just like him. It is obviously recent. I cut it out and pinned it to my corkboard.

Sophie works for Percy's, the auction house (antiquarian books, fine art, etc.). I don't know what exactly she does just yet.

I started with the easier part, gathering information on Vincent. As for Sophie, things seem a bit more complicated. Percy's is reluctant to give out anything. With companies like that, you only ever get to see the shop window. Percy's itself is quite well known, but if you try to track down any information, you come up only with vague details. This is not enough for me. There is no point hanging around Saint-Philippe-du-Roule where their showrooms are, because of the risk of being spotted.

July 11

I need more detailed information about Sophie and I have noticed that, of late, she has been using her car more frequently – it being July, the streets of Paris are pretty quiet. It didn't take me long to put two and two together. I had new number plates made for my motorbike and, yesterday, I followed her car at a distance. Every time we stopped at a traffic light, I mentally rehearsed the scene. And when Sophie's car stopped at the front of the line at a red light, I was ready. Everything went to plan. I felt calm. I rode up on her right-hand side, careful to leave myself room to manoeuvre. As soon as the lights turned amber, I had only to reach out to open the passenger door, grab her handbag, accelerate away and take the first turn to the right. In no time I had covered several hundred metres, zigzagged through three or four side streets, and five minutes later I was casually sailing along the *Périphérique*. If everything were this simple, it wouldn't be any fun.

A woman's handbag is such a wonder! What a marvel of grace, intimacy and childishness! In Sophie's bag I found a pile of things that defy all classification. I worked through them in order. I began with those that told me nothing about her: a travel card (I clipped out the photograph), a nail file, a shopping list (probably for tonight's dinner), a black biro, a pack of tissues, a packet of chewing gum. The remainder proved more enlightening.

Firstly, about Sophie's tastes: a "Multi-Active Hand Cream" from Cebelia; lipstick by Agnès b. ("Perfect", pink spice), a notebook with a few scribbles, mostly illegible, including a list of books she plans to read (Grossman: *Vie et destin*; Musset: *Confessions d'un enfant du siècle*; Tolstoy: *Resurrection*; Citati: *Portraits de femmes*; Ikonnikov: *Dernières nouvelles du bourbier* . . .) She clearly has a thing for Russian authors. At the time she was reading Coetzee's *Le Maître de Petersbourg*. She had got to page 63.

I read and re-read her notes. I like her handwriting, though barely legible, it is decisive, spirited: it gives a sense of her determination, her intelligence.

About her private life: an open box of tampons (Nett "mini") and a pack of Nurofen (maybe for period pain). Just in case, I put an X on the wall calendar at home.

About her habits: from her company card, I can see she rarely eats at Percy's in-house canteen, that she loves movies (she has a loyalty card for Cinéma Le Balzac), that she does not carry much cash (barely thirty euros in her purse), that she has signed up for a series of conferences at La Villette on the cognitive sciences.

Most importantly: the keys to her apartment, her car, her mailbox, her mobile phone – I immediately made a copy of her contacts – an address book that must be ancient, since the handwriting and the colour of the pen varies, a recently issued identity card (she was born on November 5, 1974, in Paris), a birthday card addressed to Valérie Jourdain, 36 rue Courfeyrac, Lyon, that reads:

My little poppet,

I can't believe that a little girl so much younger than me is all grown up now.

You promised to come and visit me in Paris: your present is waiting.

Vincent sends his regards. I am sending much more: my love, and lots of hugs and kisses.

Happy birthday, poppet. Be crazy.

Lastly, there is a diary that offers a great deal of precious information on the past weeks and those to come.

I photocopied everything and pinned it to the corkboard, I had copies made of all the keys (some of which I don't recognise), and then I went and handed in everything – apart from the wallet – at the police station in the next arrondissement. A relieved Sophie got her bag back the following morning.

A nice little trick. And a nice result.

Best of all is finally to feel that I'm doing something. I spent so much time (so many years) thinking and going round in circles, filling my head with images, poring over the family album, my father's military record, the wedding photos with my mother looking so beautiful . . .

July 15

Last Sunday, Sophie and Vincent went to a family lunch. I followed them from a respectable distance and, from what I knew of Sophie's address book, I soon worked out that they were going to Vincent's parents' house in Montgeron. I went there via a different route and discovered, on that beautiful summer Sunday (why did they not go on holiday?), that they were having lunch in the garden. The long afternoon stretched out ahead of me. So I went back to Paris and investigated their apartment.

At first, I was in two minds about this visit. I was happy at the considerable potential offered by the situation – unrivalled access to the most private parts of their life – yet at the same time I felt sad, for no reason I could put my finger on. It took me a little while to understand. The fact is, I do not like Vincent. I realise, in fact, that I disliked him on sight. I'm not going to be sentimental, but there is something about that man that I immediately found unpleasant.

The apartment has two bedrooms, one of which has been converted into a study with a relatively up-to-date computer set-up. For the most part, it's equipment I'm familiar with, but I will probably download the technical manuals anyway. They have a nice kitchen, large enough to have breakfast in, a beautiful bathroom with twin washbasins and separate cabinets. I will have to check later, but an apartment like this must be very expensive. Admittedly, they both earn a comfortable living (I found their payslips in the desk).

There was plenty of light, so I was able to take a lot of photographs from various angles, enough to reconstruct the whole apartment. Photos of open drawers and wardrobes, of various documents (Vincent's passports, photographs of Sophie's family, snaps of her and Vincent together which seem all to date from several years ago). I checked their sheets. They seem to have a pretty average sex life.

I disturbed nothing, I took nothing. My little visit will go unnoticed. I plan to come back soon in order to scan for their login details for e-mail, banking, messaging, company intranet. It should take two or three hours – my I.T. certificate will come in useful for once – so I need to be very wary. After my next visit, I will only come back when I have very good reasons to do so.

July 17

I did not need to rush: they have just gone away on holiday. Since I have access to Sophie's e-mail I know that they're in Greece and won't be back before August 15 or 16. That gives me all the time I need. Their apartment is at my disposal the whole time they are away.

I need a contact who is close to them, a neighbour perhaps, or a colleague, someone who can give me information about their life.

August 1

Calmly, I prepare for battle. Napoleon apparently used to say: "I would rather have a general who was lucky than one who was good." However great your patience and your determination, sooner or later you are bound to rely on luck. Right now, I'm a happy general. Even if I feel sad when I think about Maman. I think about her too much. About her love, which is what I miss most. I miss her terribly. Luckily, I have Sophie.

August 10

I've enquired with a number of estate agents, but so far without success. I had to visit several apartments I knew would be of no interest to me, but I need to be careful not to attract attention. It has to be said, it was difficult to explain my criteria. After the third agency, I decided to give up the idea. But I hesitated. Then an idea came to me as I was walking along Sophie's street. I believe in signs. I went into the building opposite theirs. I knocked politely at the lodge of the concierge, a fat woman with a jowly face. I had nothing prepared, and this is probably why things went so well. I asked her if there were any apartments for rent. No, there was nothing. Well, not nothing exactly. Nothing "that would be worth your trouble". My ears pricked up immediately. She took me up to see an apartment on the top floor. The owner lives in the country somewhere, and he rents out the apartment to students. I say "apartment", but actually it's a tiny studio with a kitchenette; the toilets are along the landing. This year, the student who rented the room has just given notice and the owner has not had time to put it back on the market.

It is on the sixth floor. The lift only goes to the fifth. As I walked up the stairs, I tried to get my bearings and, as we went along the corridor, I sensed that we were very close to Sophie's apartment. It was opposite, directly opposite. When we went inside, I was careful not to rush to the window, in spite of my excitement. Once I had looked around the room (a quick glance was enough, there was nothing to see), and while the concierge was explaining the rules imposed on her "tenants" (a depressing, exhaustive list of dos and don'ts), I wandered over to the window. It looked directly onto Sophie's apartment. This was not just luck, it was a miracle. I pretended to hesitate, to think about it. The furnishings are old junk, the bed probably sags worse than an old whore's tits, but that doesn't matter. As I pretended to check the plumbing and study the ceiling, which has obviously not been painted for generations, I asked her how much the rent would be. And then I told her, yes, it suited me, and asked what the next steps were.

The concierge stared at me pointedly, as though wondering why a man who is clearly no longer a student would want to live in such a place. I smiled. That is something I know how to do, and the concierge, who looks as though she has not been with a man in decades, was utterly charmed. I told her I lived out of town, that I would have to come to Paris often for my work, that a hotel was not a viable solution and that, for a couple of nights a week, somewhere like this would be perfect. I broadened my smile. She said she would call the owner and we headed back downstairs. Her lodge, like the building, looks like a throwback to the last century. Everything in it seems to date from the same period. The overpowering smell of wax polish and vegetable soup made my stomach lurch. I am very sensitive to smells.

The owner asked to speak to me. He reeled off the same litany of rules "of propriety" to be respected. He's a cantankerous old codger. I played the meek tenant. When I handed the receiver back to the concierge, I could tell he was asking for her opinion, her gut instinct. I pretended to search for something in my pockets while I studied the framed photographs the old dear had on her sideboard, and the nineteenth-century print of a street urchin pissing. I didn't think such things still existed. I passed the final exam with flying colours. The concierge was whispering "Yes, yes, I think so . . ." and by 5 p.m., Lionel Chalvin had officially rented the room, paid the exorbitant deposit – three months' rent in advance – in cash, and had been given permission to visit the apartment again before leaving in order to take some measurements. The old biddy even lent me the tape measure she used for sewing.

This time, she let me go up on my own. I went straight to the window. It was even better than I had hoped. The storeys in the two buildings are not quite aligned, so I found myself looking down on Sophie's apartment. I had not noticed that, in fact, I had a view of two of her windows, the living room and the bedroom. Both are hung with net curtains. I took out my pen and in my notepad jotted down a list of things to buy.

As I left, I gave the concierge a generous tip.

August 13

I am very happy with the telescope. The salesman in the Galerie de l'Astronomie seemed to know his stuff. The shop has an excellent reputation among amateur astronomers, and perhaps also among voyeurs with a little savvy and a lot of money. This occurred to me because he suggested an infrared unit that attaches to the lens, making it possible to see at night and, if need be, take digital photographs. It is absolutely perfect. My studio is now impeccably equipped.

The concierge was plainly disappointed that I did not offer to give her a copy of the key, as I assume the other tenants do, but I did not want her snooping around my command centre. Not that I have any illusions, she probably has a key. So I set up a rather cunning lock-and-chain system that prevents the door from opening fully, and I made sure there was nothing incriminating in that part of the room visible through the gap. It is rather clever, even if I say so myself. She would be hard pushed to come up with any reason to mention it to me.

I attached a whiteboard and a corkboard to the wall, and I have a small table. I brought over everything I already had. I bought a new laptop and a small colour printer. The only problem is that I can't come here as often as I'd like, or not for a while anyway, otherwise I might arouse suspicion and sabotage the story I gave for renting in the first place. In a little while, I can tell her there has been a change at work that means I have to come more regularly.

August 16

I haven't had a panic attack since I first met Sophie. From time to time, when I'm drifting off to sleep, I feel a twinge of anxiety. Before now, this was a sure sign that I would have night terrors and wake up in a cold sweat. It is a good sign. I think Sophie can help to make me well. Strangely, the calmer I feel, the more I am aware of the presence of Maman. Last night, I laid her dress out on the bed to look at it. It is a bit crumpled now, the fabric does not have the same velvety softness, and despite having it dry-cleaned several times, if you step back you can clearly see a dark mottling. There was a lot of blood. For a long time, the stains bothered me. I wanted the dress to have the same unsullied whiteness it had on her wedding day. But now I don't mind that, although almost invisible, the stains are there. Because they spur me on. They are evidence of my existence, they symbolise my willpower.

I lay down on it and fell asleep.

August 17

Sophie and Vincent got home last night. I allowed myself to be caught off guard. I would have liked to be there to welcome them. When I woke up this morning, their windows were wide open.

It doesn't matter, everything was set for their return.

Tomorrow morning, Vincent is leaving early, he is going away on business and Sophie is dropping him at the airport. I won't bother getting up to see them off. It was enough to take in the news when I read Sophie's e-mails.

August 23

The weather has been sweltering, sometimes all I can bear to put on is a T-shirt and shorts. I don't like to open the window when I am keeping watch, so the heat quickly becomes unbearable. I brought over a fan, but I find the noise it makes irritating. There is nothing to do but sit and sweat at my observation post.

My surveillance programme has been richly rewarded. They obviously don't worry about being seen. Firstly, because they live on the top floor, and secondly, because the building opposite – my building – has only four windows facing their apartment. Two of these are boarded up. My window is permanently closed, which no doubt gives the impression that the room is uninhabited. The room to my left is occupied by a weird guy, a musician or something like that, who lives in the dark and goes out at all hours, although he abides by the building rules like everyone else. Twice or three times a week, I hear him creeping home furtively.

No matter what time they come home, I am ready at my lookout post.

I am particularly attentive to their routine. Routine is what people depend on, it is the protocol by which we live. The thing people are least likely to question. This is what I need to work on. For the time being, I make do with little tasks. For example, I've been timing certain habits and activities, so I know that between showering and personal grooming, Sophie spends at least twenty minutes in the bathroom. To me that seems an awful lot, but she is a woman. And even then, she comes out in a bathrobe, goes back later to do her face, and sometimes one last time to freshen her make-up.

Having carefully timed everything, and knowing that Vincent was away, I made the most of it. As soon as Sophie went into the shower, I crept into their apartment, took her watch from the bedside table and left. It's a pretty watch. From the inscription engraved on the back, her father gave it to her in 1993 when she graduated from university.

August 25

I have just met Sophie's father. The family resemblance is striking. He arrived yesterday. From the size of the suitcase, he is not planning to stay for long. He is a tall, thin man in his sixties, very elegant. Sophie adores him. They go out to dinner together like lovers. Looking at them, I can't help but think about the time when Sophie's mother, Mme Auverney, was still alive. I suppose they talk about her sometimes. But they do not think about her as much as I do. If she were still alive, we would not be in this situation. Such a shame . . .

August 27

Patrick Auverney, born August 2, 1941 – Graduated as an architect, 1969 (Paris) – Married Catherine Lefebvre, November 8, 1969 – Founded the Agence R'ville in 1971 in partnership with Samuel Génégaud and Jean-François Bernard, head offices: 17 rue Rambuteau, later 64 rue de la Tour-Maubourg (Paris) – 1975, the couple move to 47 avenue d'Italie in Paris – Divorce granted September 24, 1979 – Buys a house in Neuville-Sainte-Marie, 1980, and moves in – Second marriage to Françoise Barret-Pruvost, May 13, 1983 – Françoise dies, October 16, 1987 (road traffic accident) – Sells his shares in his company that same year – Lives alone – Continues to work as a part-time consultant

architect and town planner, particularly for local community
associations.

August 28
M. Auverney stayed for three days. Sophie drove him to the station. Since she had to get to work, she did not hang around. I hung around, I watched the man. I even took a few quick snaps.

August 29
It is difficult to find a place to park. Even in August, when Paris is deserted, I often see Sophie driving round and round the neighbourhood before she finds a spot, sometimes quite far away.

As a rule, Sophie and her husband take the *métro*. She only uses her car when her work takes her out into the suburbs, or she has something bulky she needs to transport. There are only two streets in the neighbourhood that don't have parking meters. Everyone knows them and swoops as soon as a space becomes free. Occasionally, Sophie is forced to leave her car in the nearby public car park.

Tonight, when she arrived home at about 7 p.m., there were no free spaces so she left the car in a disabled parking bay (not very nice, Sophie, not very public-spirited!), just long enough to carry three heavy parcels upstairs. She raced down again at the speed of light. I immediately noticed that she wasn't carrying her handbag, she had left it upstairs. I didn't hesitate for a second; by the time Sophie climbed into her car and set off to find another parking space, I was on my way up to her apartment. I felt feverish, but in my head I had rehearsed what I was doing dozens of times.

Sophie had left her bag on the small sideboard by the front door. In it, I found her wallet and I swapped her new identity card for the one I stole in July. It will take a while before she notices. When does anyone ever look at their own I.D. card?

I've started to sow doubts.

September 1

I looked at their holiday photographs. Vincent left the flash card in the digital camera. God, but their pictures are banal. Sophie at the Acropolis, Vincent on a boat sailing past the Cyclades. Deathly dull. But still, there were other treasures. After all, they're thirty, they have an active sex life, so they take dirty pictures of each other. Oh, nothing terribly risqué. The first one shows Sophie thoughtfully stroking her breasts (they are outdoors in the blazing sun). There are a few blurred shots of them going at it doggie-style, but in the end I found my thrill (if I can put it like that): four or five shots of Sophie giving Vincent a blow job. She is clearly identifiable. I made a copy of the digital files and a few colour prints.

September 5

It is the sort of mistake a woman cannot afford to make often. Tonight, Sophie realises that she has somehow miscalculated in taking the pill. It's something she does as a matter of routine, but tonight, when she takes out the blister strip, she discovers it is empty. It is not as though she got the days mixed up, there is one pill missing.

September 10

It is all a matter of skill, of ingenuity. You have to be subtle, to play the piece with finesse. For example, I've spent brief but frequent periods watching Sophie from a distance as she does her shopping at the Monoprix on the corner. People don't really realise how much they act out of habit, even in the smallest things. So Sophie usually buys much the same things, follows much the same route, makes much the same gestures. For example, after she has been through the checkout, she always sets her plastic bags down on the ledge next to the shopping trolleys while she queues at the bakery. Last night, I replaced her pack of butter with a different kind and switched her brand of coffee. Little touches: discreet, gradual. It's a simple process, the key is to ramp things up by degrees.

September 15

Yesterday, Sophie booked a couple of tickets online for the Théâtre Vaugirard on October 22. She is going to a production of "The Cherry Orchard" (still the same obsession with Russian writers) starring some film actor whose name I can never remember. She booked early, because the production is bound to sell out fast. This morning, I sent an e-mail from her account asking to postpone the reservation to the following week. I was lucky, there were only a few seats left. I planned the date carefully, because I know from Sophie's diary that she and Vincent are going to a company event at Lanzar that night. She underlined it twice, so it must be important. I was careful to delete my e-mail requesting the change of reservation, and the confirmation from the theatre.

September 19

I don't know whether Sophie had a meeting this morning, but if she did she would have been late. Someone stole her car! She came downstairs – for once she had found a space with no parking meters – and it was gone. So she has to go to the police station, make a statement, these things take time.

September 20

You can say what you like about the police, but sometimes it is reassuring to have them there. Sophie could have done without the hassle. She said as much in an e-mail to Valérie, her best friend. It did not even take a day for the cops to find her car . . . in the next street. She had reported it stolen when in fact she had simply forgotten where she parked it. The police were sympathetic, but even so, it creates a lot of paperwork, maybe if she were not so scatterbrained . . .

If I felt I could, I would advise Sophie to check her headlights, they seem to be on the blink.

September 21

Since coming back from their holidays, the lovebirds have taken to going away for the weekend, and sometimes they even take a day off during the week. I don't know where they go, but it is a bit late in the year for long walks in the country. So yesterday, I decided to follow them.

I had set my alarm to go off early. It was a struggle to get up, because lately I have not been sleeping much, I have disturbing dreams and wake up exhausted. I made sure the motorbike had a full tank of petrol. As soon as I saw Sophie close the curtains, I went downstairs and waited on the corner of the street. They emerged from their building at 8.00 sharp. I had to use all my wiles to make sure they didn't spot me. I even had to take a few risks. And all for nothing. Just before the *autoroute*, Vincent switched lanes, edging between two cars so he could get through before the lights changed. Instinctively I tried to slip in behind him, which was reckless. I had just enough time to brake to avoid ploughing into the back of his car. I swerved, lost control, the bike toppled and we skidded about ten metres. I didn't really know whether or not I had been injured, or whether it was only physical pain that I felt . . . I heard the traffic coming to a standstill, it was as if I were in a movie and someone had turned off the sound. I should have been confused, dazed by the shock, but in fact I felt hyper-alert. I saw Vincent and Sophie getting out of their car and running towards me, and then other drivers – a whole crowd of rubberneckers – descended on me even before I had time to pick myself up. I felt a wild energy coursing through me. While the first people to arrive were bending over me, I managed to disentangle myself from the motorcycle and scrabble to my feet. I found myself face to face with Vincent. I was still wearing my helmet, the Plexiglas visor was down, I could see him standing right in front of me: "It's probably best not to move," was what he said. Next to him, Sophie looked worried, her lips parted. I had never been this close to her. Everyone suddenly started to chime in, offering advice, the police were on their way, I should take off the helmet, sit down on the verge, the motorbike had slipped, it was going too fast, no, the car had swerved suddenly, then Vincent put his hand on my shoulder. I turned and looked at the motorbike. The idea came to me when I noticed the engine was still running. The petrol tank did not seem to be leaking. I took a step towards it and, for the second time, someone turned off the sound. Everyone fell silent, wondering why I was gently pushing away this man in the grubby T-shirt and bending over my motorcycle. Then they realised that I was trying to right it. The babble of advice started up again. Some people seemed to be prepared to stop me forcibly, but I already had the bike upright. I was cold as ice, it felt as though my blood had stopped flowing. In seconds, I was ready to go. I could not help myself turning back for a last look at Sophie and Vincent, who were staring at me, speechless. My determination must have been frightening. I roared off to screams from the onlookers.

They have seen my motorbike, my riding gear, I'll have to change all that. More money. In her e-mail to Valérie, Sophie insinuates that the rider probably drove off because it was a stolen bike. I only hope that I can keep a low profile. The incident shocked them, it's likely that for a while at least they will be more aware of people on motorbikes, they will look at them differently.

September 22

I woke up in the middle of the night, bathed in sweat, my chest tight, my whole body shaking. Hardly surprising, given the scare I had yesterday. In my dream, Vincent slammed into me. I soared across the handlebars, my motorcycle leathers changed colour, they turned a pristine white. You don't need to be a psychologist to understand the symbolism: tomorrow is the anniversary of Maman's death.

September 23

For days now, I've been feeling sad and listless. I should never have taken the risk of riding the motorcycle in such a weak and nervous state. Since Maman's death, I have had all kinds of dreams, but sometimes what I see are actual scenes my mind has recorded at a particular moment. I am constantly astonished by the almost photographic detail of these memories. Somewhere, deep inside my brain, is a crazed projectionist. He shows me scenes such as Maman at my bedside, telling me stories. These commonplace images are heartbreaking enough, but hearing her voice . . . That particular timbre makes me quiver from head to foot. Maman never went out without first coming to spend a little time with me. I remember a babysitter, an exchange student from New Zealand. Why she should turn up in my dreams more than the others, I don't know . . . You'd have to ask the projectionist. Maman spoke English with an impeccable accent. She spent hours and hours reading me stories in English. I was never very good at languages, but she was patient with me. Recently, I dreamed about our holidays together. The two of us in the house in Normandy (Papa only came at weekends). Laughing on the train. A whole year of memories re-emerging. Though the projectionist tends to show the same reels over and over: Maman, dressed all in white, sailing through the window. In that dream, her face is exactly as it was when I saw her for the last time. It was a beautiful afternoon, she had been standing, gazing out of the window. She always said she loved trees. I was sitting in her bedroom, I wanted to talk to her, but the words wouldn't come. She seemed so tired. As though all her energy was focused on staring at the trees. From time to time, she would turn to me and smile affectionately. How could I know that the vision of her at that instant would be the last? And yet, my memory of it is of a silent but deeply happy moment. We were one person, she and I. I knew that. As I left the room, she planted on my forehead one of those feverish kisses I have never known since. She said: "I love you, my little Frantz." She always said that when I left.

In the projectionist's footage, I leave the room, I go downstairs and a few seconds later, she leaps into the void, as though nothing and no-one could stop her. As though I did not exist.

This is why I hate them so much.

September 25

I've just had confirmation. Sophie e-mailed her friend Valérie to tell her she and Vincent are looking to buy a house somewhere north of Paris. She is being very mysterious on the subject. I have to say I find that childish.

Today is Vincent's birthday. I went up to their apartment in the early afternoon. I had no trouble finding her present, a prettily wrapped package the size of a book, with a tag stamped Maison Lancel, no less. She had put it at the back of her knicker drawer. I took it away with me. I can imagine her panic tonight when she wants to give him his present. She'll search the apartment from top to bottom. In a couple of days, I'll put it back. I've decided to put it in the bathroom cabinet, behind the cosmetics and the boxes of tissues.

September 30

My neighbours seem to live their lives with their windows wide open. This is how, two days ago, when Sophie and her husband got home at the end of the day, I was able to watch them making love. Unfortunately I couldn't see everything, but it was pretty hot. My little turtledoves don't seem to have any taboos: blow jobs, various contortions and positions, the picture of beautiful, intoxicating youth. I took photos. The digital camera I bought is perfect. I touch up the images on the laptop, print out the best shots and pin them to the corkboard. In fact, there were far too many, and half the room is now plastered with photographs of the lovebirds. They help me to concentrate.

Last night, after Sophie and her husband turned out the light, I lay on my bed and studied these imperfect photographs. I felt vaguely aroused. I decided it was best to turn over and go to sleep. Sophie is charming, and from what I've seen she's a good fuck, but let's not get carried away. I know it's important that I keep my distance from her emotionally, and I have trouble enough dealing with my loathing for her husband.

October 1

I've done several technical dry runs using free e-mail accounts I signed up for with various providers. Now I've got my ducks in a row, as they say, we can start Operation E-mail Fuck-up. It will take Sophie a little while to figure it out, but from now on some of her e-mails will be dated the day before or the day after she thinks she wrote them. The brain can play strange tricks sometimes . . .

October 6

I finally sold my old motorbike, bought a new one and got some different leathers. I didn't take a whole month, obviously, but I had a bit of a crisis of confidence. The sort of thing that happens to riders when they fall off their horse and are wary of getting back in the saddle. I had to overcome my fears. But as a result, although I'm not as confident as I was before, this time everything went according to plan. They took the *autoroute* and headed north, towards Lille. Since they always come back the same day, I assumed they were not going far, and I was right. Actually, it's pretty straightforward: Sophie and her husband are looking to buy a house in the country. They had a meeting with an estate agent in Senlis. They only went into the office for a few moments and reappeared with a guy in full body armour: the suit, the shoes, the haircut, the folder under the arm, that overfamiliar "I'm-an-expert-but-I'm-your-friend" manner that is standard-issue in this business. I followed them, and that's when things got complicated, because of the narrow country lanes. After the second house they visited, I decided to head back. They show up at a house, stare at it from a distance, they think hard and wave their hands about like architects, go inside and take a tour, come out again, wander around the grounds, ask a few more questions and set off for the next property.

They are looking for a big house. They have money. Most of the ones they've seen are in the country, or on the outskirts of dreary little villages, all of which have extensive gardens.

I don't think I'll do anything for the moment about their desire to spend weekends in the country, which has no place in the plan I have been formulating.

October 12
I can see from the test e-mails she has been sending herself that Sophie is beginning to doubt her memory. I took the opportunity

156

to mix up the second test, changing the date stamp. I only change the dates every now and then, it's much more devious because there is no apparent logic. Sophie does not know it yet, but gradually, I will be her logic.

October 22

Tonight I sat by the window waiting for the lovebirds to come back from the theatre. They got home very early. Sophie seemed anxious and angry with herself, Vincent had a face three feet long, as though irritated that he has married such an airhead. The scene played out in the theatre foyer must have been quite dramatic. Two or three little incidents like that and you begin to doubt everything.

I wonder if Sophie has found her old identity card, and how she felt when she found Vincent's birthday present in the bathroom cabinet.

October 30

Things aren't going too well for Sophie. The tone of her e-mail to Valérie speaks volumes about her self-esteem. Plainly, the things that have been happening are all minor, but that's precisely the problem: with a major event you can draw a line under it, try to work out what went wrong, whereas here, everything is so fluid, so inconsequential. What is worrying is the sheer number. Forgetting . . . no, that's not right, *losing* one of her contraceptive pills? Or taking two without realising? Making mistakes when buying tickets, forgetting where the car is parked, mislaying your husband's birthday present. Taken individually, such things are trivial. But finding the present in a ludicrous place like the bathroom and not remembering that you put it there. Being convinced you sent an e-mail on Monday when in fact it was sent on Tuesday, having proof in black and white that you changed your theatre reservations but no memory of doing so . . .

Sophie explains it all to Valérie. Things have been escalating slowly. So far, she has not said anything to Vincent. But if this carries on, she will have to.

She is having trouble sleeping. In their bathroom I found a "herbal remedy" to help her sleep, the sort of thing a girl would buy. She bought a syrup rather than tablets, one tablespoon at night before going to bed. I didn't think it would happen so quickly.

November 8

I went to the head offices of Percy's yesterday. Sophie had the day off. She and Vincent had set out in the car early in the morning.

Pretending to be interested in a forthcoming auction, I flirted with the receptionist.

My strategy is simple: statistically, there are more women in the world than men. More specifically, the ideal prey is a single woman with no children, aged between thirty-five and forty.

The receptionist is overweight, chubby-cheeked and wears too much perfume, there is no ring on her finger and she is instantly won over by my smile (and by a few stupid and gratuitous remarks about some of the contemporary artwork in the auction catalogue). I know I will have to play it safe, but I think I may have found just the person I'm looking for. As long as she knows Sophie reasonably well. If not, she might unknowingly point me in the direction of a better candidate.

November 12

The internet is a vast market run by killers and degenerates. You can find anything there: guns, drugs, women, kids, anything that takes your fancy. It's simply a matter of having the patience and the means. I have both. So eventually I found what I was looking for. It cost a small fortune, that was no problem, but having to wait almost two months for delivery was driving me insane. It doesn't matter now, the package has finally arrived from the States, a hundred little pink capsules. I tested the product, and it is perfect: completely odourless and tasteless. It was originally devised as a revolutionary anti-obesity drug. In the early 2000s, the pharmaceutical company sold the tablets in their thousands, chiefly to women. It had everything going for it: in terms of weight loss, it was unrivalled. But the drug also turned out to have an excitatory effect on monoamine oxidase, an enzyme that destroys certain neurotransmitters in the brain: what had been developed as a weight-loss drug was also a "depressant". The side effects quickly became evident from the level of suicides. In the greatest democracy in the world, the pharmaceutical company had no problem hushing up the scandal. A class-action lawsuit was circumvented using the most powerful judicial inhibitor: the chequebook. The formula is simple: the greater the resistance, the more zeroes you add. Nothing can resist that. The drug was taken off the market, but it was impossible for the company to recall the thousands of boxes of capsules already sold, which instantly began to be trafficked to the world at large via the internet. You could not make it up: this thing is a veritable anti-personnel mine, and yet people are desperate to get their hands on it. There are thousands of women out there who would rather be dead than fat.

While I was about it, I also bought some Rohypnol. They call it the "date-rape drug". It leaves the subject confused, disorientated and passive, and causes anterograde amnesia. I don't think I will need it anytime soon, but I need to be prepared. Lastly, for my first-aid kit, I found a powerful sleeping tablet with a hypnotic-anaesthetic effect. According to the patient information leaflet, it works in seconds.

November 13

At last I have come to a decision. For the past two weeks I have been hesitating, weighing the advantages and the risks, researching the various technical complexities. Fortunately, technology has advanced considerably in recent years, this was what finally decided me. I settled on three microphones, two in the living room and the third, obviously, in the bedroom. They are very inconspicuous, barely three millimetres in circumference, they are voice-activated and record onto high-capacity D.A.T. tapes. The only challenge is recovering the recordings. I hid the recorder in the cubby-hole that houses the water meter. I will have to watch out for the meter reader. Usually, the building supervisor posts a notice next to the mailboxes a few days beforehand.

November 16

The results are excellent: the recordings are crystal clear. It is like being in the room. And in a sense, I am. It is a pleasure to hear their voices.

As though Fate wanted to reward me for my initiative, on the very first night I was able to listen to them making love. It's quite strange. I know so much about her private life.

November 20

Sophie can't work out what is going on with her e-mails. She has just created a new account. As usual, to avoid forgetting her password, she saves a link on her desktop. I have only to click on it to access her account. Thanks to her trusting nature, I have access to everything. If ever she should decide to change the process, it would not take me long to crack her password. In her e-mails to Valérie, she talks about being "tired". She says that she doesn't want to bother Vincent with such insignificant details, but she is suffering frequent memory lapses, and sometimes she does "crazy stuff". Valérie suggests she see a professional. I have to say, I agree.

Especially since she hardly sleeps. She has opted for a different remedy, this one comes in blue caplets. This makes it much more practical for me; the caplets are easy to open and re-close and the drug itself is never in direct contact with the tongue, which is just as well since my sleeping tablets have a slightly bitter taste. I have learned to titrate the dose according to her sleeping and waking hours (thanks to the microphone, I know that the drug makes her snore a little). Through her, I am becoming something of a drug expert, a molecular artist. Sophie confides her problems to Valérie, complains that her sleep is like a coma and that when she wakes, she has trouble getting through the day. The pharmacist wants to refer her to a doctor, but Sophie refuses. She likes her little blue caplets. I'm quite fond of them myself.

November 23

Sophie set a trap for me! She is doing some detective work. I've known for a while now that she has been trying to find out if she is being followed. Of course she has no idea she is also being recorded. But that doesn't change the fact that her recent tactic worries me. If she is already starting to be suspicious, that must mean I have made some mistakes. And I don't know where. Or when.

As I was leaving their apartment that morning, by sheer fluke I noticed a scrap of brown paper, the same colour as the door. Sophie must have slipped it between the door and the doorframe as she was leaving so that it fell when I opened the door. I could not hang around on the landing, so I went back inside to think, but I could not resolve what to do. If I took the scrap of paper away, it would simply confirm her suspicions. If I slipped it back in a different place, that would also prove that she was right. How many traps had she set that I had blithely walked into? I had absolutely no idea what to do. I settled on the radical solution: upstage her little trap with one of my own. I went and bought a short crowbar and went back up to her apartment. I forced the crowbar in at several points, I even opened the door to give the impression that I had used great force. I had to work quickly because the noise – though I muffled it as best I could – was easily audible, and even in the middle of the day the building is never completely deserted. I took just enough time to examine the result: it looked convincingly like an attempted break-in, and the door being forced with a crowbar would explain why the scrap of paper was on the floor.

I'm still a little worried, I have to say. In future, I will have to be extra vigilant.

November 25

At Monoprix I buy the same groceries she does. Exactly the same. But just before I reach the checkout I add a bottle of expensive whisky. I am careful to choose Vincent's favourite tipple, the one they have in their drinks cabinet. While Sophie is queuing at the bakery, I swap my bags for hers and as I am leaving I have a word with the security guard about the woman in the grey coat.

On the other side of the street, I go to the A.T.M. to withdraw money because it is the perfect observation point, and I see Sophie's shock as she is stopped by the security guard. She laughs, but not for long. She has to go with him so he can check her purchases.

Sophie did not emerge from the supermarket for more than an hour. Two uniformed police officers turned up. I don't know what happened. When she came out of Monoprix, she looked crushed. This time, she really will have to go and see a shrink. She has no choice.

December 5

Since September, there have been several auctions at Percy's, but I can't work out what determines whether or not Sophie goes. It seems completely unpredictable, because I don't have the information that informs her decision. There was an auction last night at 9.00. I waited until 9.15 and, since Sophie seemed determined to spend the evening in front of the television, I decided to go myself.

There was a large crowd. The receptionist was greeting customers with a smile, distributing handsome glossy catalogues. She recognised me immediately and gave me a particularly winning smile which I returned, without insisting unduly. The sale was a long-drawn-out affair. I waited for at least an hour before popping out to the lobby where the receptionist was counting the catalogues that remained and handing them to the few stragglers.

We talked for a bit. I played my cards well. Her name is Andrée – a name I despise. She looks fatter standing up than she does behind the desk. Her perfume is just as cloying, if anything it was even more nauseating at close range. I told her a few jokes and made her laugh. I pretended I had to get back for the rest of the auction, but at the last moment, having already taken a couple of steps, I turned and asked if she would allow me to buy her a drink when the auction was over. She simpered pathetically, I could tell she was thrilled. For form's sake, she pretended she would have a lot to do after the sale, but she did little to put me off. As it turned out, I only had to wait fifteen minutes. I hailed a taxi and took her to the *grands boulevards*. I remembered a bar opposite l'Olympia that had muted lighting and served cocktails and English beers, and where you can also eat. It was a painfully dull evening, but one that I am sure will prove fruitful in the future.

I feel sorry for the girl.

Last night I watched my lovebirds romping in bed, though Sophie's heart didn't seem to be in it. She probably has other things on her mind. I slept like a stone.

December 8

Sophie is wondering whether her computer might be the problem. She suspects that someone might have remote access, but doesn't know how to find out. She created yet another e-mail account and this time she did not store the password on her computer. It took me six hours to hack in. The mailbox was empty. I changed the password. Now she is the one who cannot access it.

Vincent is visibly worried about her. Deep down, he's a sensitive soul. He simply asked Sophie how things were going, but that was euphemistic. On the telephone to his mother, he raised the possibility that Sophie might be "depressive". From what I could gather, his mother was sympathetic, which just goes to show what a hypocrite she is. She and Sophie cordially loathe each other.

December 9

Through a friend of her late mother she has vaguely kept in touch with, Sophie quickly managed to get an appointment to see a specialist. I don't know what's going on in that head of hers, but choosing a "behavioural therapist" seems dumb to me. Why didn't she go for a decent psychiatrist? The sort of guy who's bound to drive you insane. It's as if she learned nothing from her mother. Instead, she visits a Doctor Brevet, a quack who, from what she has written to Valérie, offered her advice on how to "confirm the validity, the objective reality, of her fears". So she has to keep lists of things, lists of dates, she has to note everything down. It promises to be exhausting.

That said, she is still keeping the whole thing secret from her husband, which is a good sign. For me. And what's good for me is good for Sophie.

December 10

I'm really worried about something I heard them say last night: Vincent was talking about trying for a baby. Listening to them, it's not the first time they've had this conversation. Sophie is reluctant. But I can tell from her voice that she wants to be persuaded. I don't think she particularly wants a kid, I think she just wants something normal to happen for a change. In fact, it's hard to say whether Vincent is being honest about the whole thing. I've been wondering whether he thinks Sophie's depressive behaviour has something to do with her longing for a child. Pure psychobabble. I could tell him a thing or two about his wife.

December 11

A few days ago, I found out that Sophie has to go to Neuilly-sur-Seine this morning for some public relations event. There is my Sophie looking for a parking spot, driving round and round and finally finding a place. An hour later, the car is gone. This time, she didn't go rushing to the police station, she went round in circles – on foot this time – and eventually found the car parked several streets away. This is not like her own neighbourhood, she does not recognise the landmarks. A nice little story to start off her new notebook.

December 12

I am not about to set down in the diary the unspeakable horrors I have to put up with from that fat bitch Andrée. She is just about becoming useful to me, but there are times when I can hardly bear to be in her presence.

This is what I've found out so far.

As a press officer, Sophie is responsible for certain P.R. campaigns, those related to particularly high-profile auctions, for example. The rest of the time, she works on "corporate communications", ensuring the company's "brand image" is "well positioned".

Sophie has been working at Percy's for two years. There are two of them in the department, Sophie and a man called Pencherat, who is Head of P.R. "pro tem", according to Andrée. He's a dipso. Andrée pulls comic faces when she describes him. Talks about the stink of wine on his breath. It's a bit rich, coming from someone who uses perfume as a weapon, but never mind . . .

Sophie has a degree in economics. She got the job at Percy's through a friend who has since left the company.

She and Vincent were married in 1999 at the town hall in the sixteenth arrondissement. May 13, to be precise. Andrée went to the reception. I was treated to a detailed description of the food I could well have done without, especially since she told me nothing about the other guests. All I can remember is that "the husband's family are well off". Not exactly helpful. And that Sophie hates her mother-in-law, and calls her a "poisonous bitch".

Sophie is popular at Percy's. Her superiors trust her. Although lately, rumour has it, her reliability has been called into question: she misses meetings, she lost a company chequebook, she damaged two company cars in recent weeks and she accidentally wiped a client file that was, so they said, critical. I can see what they mean.

Andrée describes her as friendly, approachable, very cheerful, and generally dependable. She is, it seems, something of an expert. Though recently she has not been very well (no shit . . .). She isn't sleeping, she claims to have bouts of depression. She says she is seeing someone. To put it bluntly, she seems a little lost. And alone.

December 13

Everyone is rushing around trying to get ready for Christmas, and Sophie is no exception. This evening, she did some late-night shopping at F.N.A.C. The place was heaving! People pushing and shoving at the checkouts. You put down your plastic bag, bicker with the customer behind you, stumble and . . . when you get home and look in the bag, you discover that instead of *Swordfishtrombones,* there is a different Tom Waits C.D., *Blue Valentine*, and that you have a copy of Salman Rushdie's *Midnight's Children* but you can't remember who you bought it for. And you can't find the till receipt to take it back. So you write it down in your little notebook.

Sophie and Andrée mostly confine themselves to small talk, they are not what you would really call friends. Is the information I've managed to gather about Sophie and Vincent really worth the excruciating time spent with this dumb bitch? Because it is pretty thin. Vincent is apparently working on a "major deal" at work, which is taking up most of his energy. Sophie is bored at Percy's. Since her mother's death, she increasingly misses her father, who lives in Seine-et-Marne. She wants to have children, but not yet. Vincent doesn't like her friend Valérie. I think I'll have to give up on the fat bitch and find myself a more useful source of information.

December 14

Sophie writes everything down, or almost everything. She sometimes wonders whether she is even remembering to note things down. Then she realises that she has written the same thing twice. Her arrest for shoplifting at Monoprix a month ago has left her badly shaken. The security guards took her into a windowless room and took turns trying to get her to sign a confession. From what she wrote to Valérie, they are utter bastards, but they're good at their job. At harassing people. She did not really understand what they wanted. Then the police arrived. They were in a hurry. They did not pull their punches. She had the choice of being taken down to the station and referred to the magistrate's court, or to admit to shoplifting and sign a statement: she signed. She couldn't bring herself to tell Vincent, she simply couldn't. The problem is, it has just happened again. This time it will be more difficult to hide. A bottle of perfume and a manicure kit were found in her bag. But Sophie was lucky. She was taken to the commissariat – it was action stations out there in the street – but released two hours later. She had to make up an excuse for her husband, who was waiting for her.

The following day, she lost her car again, and a number of other things.

Noting everything down is probably the best solution, but, as she writes, "I'm starting to get obsessive, even paranoid. I'm forever monitoring myself as though I am the enemy."

December 15

My relationship with Andrée has reached a critical point, the one where I am supposed to suggest that we sleep together. Since that is out of the question, I feel a little awkward. I've already been out with her five times, we've done all sorts of tedious things, but I have stuck to my plan: never ask her about Sophie, avoid the subject of her work – the only thing that interests me – as far as possible. Luckily, Andrée is a chatterbox, she can be very indiscreet. She has told me lots of funny stories about Percy's and I pretended to be interested. I laughed. I couldn't stop her taking my hand. She brushed against me in a way I found infuriating.

Last night, we went to the cinema and then to a bar she knows near Montparnasse. She said hello to several of the regulars and I felt embarrassed to be in public with her. She babbled a lot and smiled as she introduced me to people. I realised she had brought me here to show me off, chuffed to be on the arm of someone who is obviously a "good catch", since she's no oil painting. I played along diffidently. I did the best I could. Andrée was in her element. We took a table together and she was more attentive than she has ever been. She held my hand all evening. After what I reckoned was a reasonable amount of time, I said I was a little tired. She told me she had had a "fabulous" evening. We took a taxi, and that was the point at which I realised things were going to turn sour. As soon as we were in the back seat, she brazenly pressed herself against me. She had had a bit too much to drink. Enough to put me in an awkward position. By the time we got to her place, I had been forced to accept her invitation to "come up for a nightcap". I felt deeply uncomfortable. She kept smiling at me as though dealing with a painfully shy teenager and, needless to say, as soon as we got through the door, she stuck her tongue down my throat. I cannot describe how disgusted I felt. I thought about Sophie and that helped a little. Faced with her insistence (I should have been prepared, but I simply could not imagine myself in this situation), I told her that I "wasn't ready". Those were my very words, it was the first thing that popped into my head, and the only truthful thing I ever said to her. She gave me a strange look and I managed to smile self-consciously. And I said: "It's difficult for me . . . I'll tell you about it sometime." She assumed

I was hinting at some sexual confession and felt reassured. She's the kind of woman who likes to play the nursemaid with men. She squeezed my hand fiercely as if to say "Don't worry, it'll be alright". I made the most of the awkward atmosphere to get the hell out of there, deliberately making it seem as though I were running away.

I walked along the river and tried to choke back my anger.

December 21

The day before yesterday, Sophie came home with an important project for the management committee. It took two days, working late into the night, to finish. Sitting at my observation post into the early hours, I followed her progress; I watched as she wrote, deleted, corrected, did more research then rewrote and re-edited. Two long nights. At least nine hours by my calculation. Sophie is a hard worker, I'll give her that. And then this morning – *wham!* – she can't find the C.D. on which she burned the file, even though she remembers putting it in her bag last night. She rushed over to her computer, and when she started it up – by now she was already late – she found that the original file had also disappeared. She spent an hour doing everything she could think of, searching, scanning, she was almost in tears. In the end, she had to go to the management committee meeting without the work she had been entrusted to do. I suspect the meeting didn't go too well.

It could not have happened on a worse day: today is Vincent's mother's birthday. From the look on his face – he loves his mother, that boy – I worked out that Sophie was refusing to go. Vincent was pacing up and down the living room, and screaming. I can't wait to listen to the recording. Eventually she gave in and

171

agreed to go with him. But of course when they were leaving she couldn't find the present (it's been here in my room since last night, I will put it back in a few days): Vincent hit the roof again. By the time they left the apartment, they were running very late. Moody. When they'd gone I went upstairs to change the dose of her depressant.

December 23

I'm extremely worried about Sophie. This time she really lost it. Spectacularly.

On Thursday night, when they came back from the birthday party, I could tell things had gone badly (Sophie has always hated her mother-in-law, and there's no reason why things should be any different at the moment). They had a blazing row. I think Sophie may even have insisted on leaving before the party was over. His mother's birthday! Given that Sophie had already lost his mother's present, she can ill afford to make such a scene.

I don't know exactly what was said: most of the argument must have taken place in the car on the way home. By the time they got back to the apartment, they were hurling insults. I have no way of working out exactly what happened, but I feel sure the old bag was condescending and cantankerous. I'm with Sophie – the woman is a nightmare. She is constantly making insinuations, she's manipulative and hypocritical. At least that is what Sophie screamed at Vincent before he furiously slammed every single door in the apartment and insisted on sleeping on the sofa. Personally, I found the whole episode a little histrionic, but there's no accounting for taste. Sophie was absolutely livid. This is the point at which she should have had her breakdown. The sleeping pills plunged her into a coma but, inexplicably, this morning she was up and about. Staggering, but on her feet. She and Vincent did not exchange a word. They ate breakfast separately and before Sophie was overwhelmed by sleep again, she had a cup of tea and checked her e-mails. Vincent slammed the door as he left. Sophie contacted Valérie on MSN Messenger and told her about the dream she had had in which she pushed her mother-in-law down the stairs of her suburban house; the old woman tumbled down the steps, slamming against the wall and the banister, and ending up sprawled at the bottom, her spine snapped. Stone dead. The image was so real it jolted Sophie awake. "It was weird, it felt so unbelievably real." Sophie did not go in to work immediately. She did not have the energy to do anything. Being a good friend, Valérie chatted to her online for an hour after which Sophie decided to go shopping so that Vincent would not come home to find there was nothing for dinner. This is what she told Valérie: a quick trip to the supermarket, a cup of strong tea, then a shower and she would still be able to go to the office, if only to show her face. I intervened between stages one and two, slipping in to take care of the tea.

Sophie did not get to the office at all. She spent the whole day drifting in and out of sleep and cannot remember a single thing she did. In the late afternoon, Vincent got a call from his father: Mme Duguet had had an accident, she had fallen down a flight of stairs. Sophie was almost hysterical when she heard the news.

December 26
The funeral was this morning. I watched the lovebirds drive off with their suitcases last night. They looked devastated. They must

have gone to see Vincent's father, to keep him company. Sophie is a changed woman. She is shattered, her face is pale and gaunt, she moves like an automaton and looks as though at any moment she might collapse.

In her defence, it must be hard to celebrate Christmas with the body of the old bag laid out upstairs. I crept up and put the present to Vincent's late mother among Sophie's things. It should make for a touching surprise when they get back from the funeral.

January 6, 2001

Sophie is deeply depressed. Since the death of her mother-in-law, she feels panicked about the future. When I heard that there was an investigation, I was worried. Thankfully, it was only routine. The case was quickly classified as an accidental death. But we know better, Sophie and I. Now I need to increase my surveillance. It is vital that nothing should escape my notice, otherwise Sophie herself might escape. My every sense is heightened, I am razor-sharp. Sometimes I feel myself quiver.

Given recent events, Sophie can no longer think of confiding in Vincent. She is condemned to her solitude.

January 15

This morning, they set off for the country. It has been a long time since they went back to the Oise. I left Paris half an hour after them, overtook them on the *autoroute* and calmly waited for them at the slip road by the Senlis exit. Following them did not prove too difficult this time. They dropped into the estate agent, but re-emerged without the agent. They seemed to be heading to a house I remembered them visiting in some godforsaken hole near Crépy-en-Valois. By the time I arrived, they weren't there. For a moment, I thought I had lost them, but I saw their car parked in front of a gate a few kilometres away.

The house is vast and quite extraordinary. Very different from most of the places you get around here: a stone mansion with wooden balconies; the architecture is intricate, with hundreds of nooks and crannies. There is a disused barn they will probably convert into a garage, and a shed where the model husband will probably spend his weekends tinkering. The grounds are bordered by high stone walls, except at the northern boundary where part of the wall has collapsed. This is how I managed to get in, having left the motorbike on the edge of a patch of woodland behind the property. With a little cunning, I managed to find them. I watched them through my binoculars. Twenty minutes later, they were walking through the grounds, their arms around each other's waists. They were whispering sweet nothings to each other. It was pathetic. As if anyone could overhear them in the desolate gardens of an empty mansion on the outskirts of a village that time seems to have forgotten. But maybe that's what people call love. In spite of Vincent's slightly mournful expression, they seemed good together, they looked happy. Especially Sophie. From time to time she pulled Vincent's arm more tightly around her as though to remind him of her presence, her support. All the same, it was a little sad, the two of them traipsing through the grounds in the dead of winter.

When they went back into the house, I didn't know what to do. I'm not familiar with the area yet, and I was beginning to worry that someone might walk past. You are never really alone in a place like this. It looks dead, but try to find a bit of peace and quiet and before you know it you run into some farmer on his tractor, a hunter looking you up and down, a kid on a bicycle setting off to build a den in the woods. After a little while, since I hadn't seen them come out again, I left the motorbike behind a low wall and crept closer to the house. All of a sudden I had a premonition. I raced round to the back of the house. By the time I got there, I was out of breath and had to wait until my heart had stopped hammering so I could listen for noises. Not a sound. I inched along the wall, taking care to watch where I placed my feet, until I came to a pair of shutters with the bottom slats missing. Stepping onto a stone curb, I hoisted myself up a little until I could peer inside. The kitchen. It was horribly old-fashioned, and would need a lot of expensive work. But my lovebirds had other things on their mind. Sophie was leaning against the carved stone sink, her dress hiked up to her hips; Vincent, with his trousers around his ankles, was conscientiously fucking her. Clearly his mother's death has not left the lad completely at a loss. From my vantage point, I could only see his back and his buttocks which clenched as he pumped into her. It looked ridiculous. What was beautiful, on the other hand, was Sophie's face. Her arms clasped around her husband's neck as though carrying a basket, she was standing on tiptoe, her eyes closed, the pleasure so intense it transfigured her. A pretty face, so pale and taut, utterly absorbed as though in sleep. I managed to take a couple of decent photographs. Vincent speeded up his perfunctory in–out motions, his pale buttocks clenched faster, harder. I could tell from Sophie's face that she was about to come. Her lips parted, her eyes flew wide and a passionate wail rose in her. It was magnificent. Exactly what I hope to see the day I kill her. Her head jerked back and she suddenly slumped onto Vincent's shoulder, sinking her teeth into his jacket as she quivered.

Enjoy the ride, my angel, make the most of it.

At that moment, it occurred to me that I hadn't seen her pills lying around the bathroom for a while. They seem to have decided to try for a baby. Not that it worries me. On the contrary, it gives me ideas.

I let them head back to Paris at their own pace. I waited around until noon, when the estate agent closed for the day. The house in the window is marked SOLD. Fine. It will mean spending weekends in the country. Why not?

January 17

Ideas are curious things. They evidently come from a certain receptiveness of mind. So, the day before yesterday, as I was wandering aimlessly around their apartment, I began leafing through some books Sophie has stacked next to the desk in the study. Almost at the bottom of the pile, there were two titles from the Press Research Library: a monograph about the journalist Albert Londres, and a *French-English Glossary of Media and Marketing Terms*. Both borrowed on the same day. I returned them. There is an "express counter" where people in a hurry can simply deposit their books. It saves time. I found it very practical.

January 18

Something else to put in her notebook: Sophie somehow missed two final demands for the phone bill. Now they've been cut off. Vincent isn't happy. Sophie is crying. Things are bad at the moment, they argue a lot. For all that, Sophie is doing her best to pay careful attention to her actions, to Vincent, to everything

– she may even be trying not to dream. She contacts her therapist to see whether she can bring her next appointment forward. Her sleep patterns are chaotic, they fluctuate wildly, some nights she feels as if she has slipped into a coma, other nights she cannot get a wink of sleep. She spends long hours standing at the open window, smoking. I'm worried she'll catch a cold.

January 19

The bitch! I don't know what she thinks she's playing at, I don't even know if she's doing it deliberately, but I'm furious with her, and furious with myself. Of course, I have to wonder whether Sophie has worked things out, whether this was a trap. In anticipation of her appointment with her therapist, I snuck into the apartment to take from her desk drawer the black Moleskine notebook in which she jots everything down. I know it well, I read it often. So I didn't check it immediately. It is completely blank. It looks exactly the same, but every page is blank. This means she has two notebooks and I wonder whether this was a decoy intended to trick me. She must have noticed tonight that the notepad was missing.

After careful consideration, I conclude that she has not become aware of my presence. Perhaps I'm just trying to reassure myself, but if she had made the connection there would surely be other signs, when in fact everything seems to be working perfectly.

I don't know what to think. I have to say, this business with the notebook has got me worried.

There is a God, after all. It seems I'm out of the woods. To be honest, I was really panicked: I didn't dare go back to the apartment; I had the vague feeling that it was dangerous, that I was being watched, that I was about to get caught. And I was right.

When I got to her place, I put the blank notebook back in the desk drawer but I had to search the entire apartment for the other one. I knew she wouldn't have taken it: her constant fear of losing things was my salvation. It was bound to take time and I don't like to stay long, I know it's not wise, I have to minimise the risks. I was searching for more than an hour, sweating in my latex gloves, freezing every time I heard a board creak. I was beginning to feel jittery, I couldn't fight it. Then, finally, there it was, behind the toilet cistern. This is not good, it means she's beginning to suspect something. Though not necessarily me . . . It occurred to me that she might be suspicious of Vincent, which would be a good thing. I had just fished it out when I heard a key turn in the lock. I was still in the bathroom. The door was ajar. I just managed to stop myself reaching out to pull it closed: it's right at the other end of the hallway from the front door. If it had been Sophie, it would have all been over – women always head straight for the bathroom when they get home. But it was Vincent, I could tell by the footsteps it was a man. My heart was pounding so loudly I couldn't hear a thing, couldn't even think. Panic surged through me. Vincent walked straight past, slamming the door shut. The noise was terrifying. I almost passed out, I had to steady myself on the washbasin. I felt as if I was going to throw up. Vincent went into the study, turned on the stereo, and at that point it was my panic that saved me. In a sort of trance, I pushed the door open and tiptoed quickly down the hallway, opened the front door and without even closing it I hurtled down the stairs. I was convinced the plan had been compromised, that I would have to give up. I felt utterly distraught.

A vision of Maman appeared before me and I began to sob. It was as though she had died a second time. Instinctively, I clutched Sophie's notebook in my pocket. I walked away, tears streaming down my face.

January 21

Listening to the recording today was like reliving the whole thing. It was a nightmare! I heard the stereo being cranked up (something by Bach, I think), I imagined I could make out the patter of my feet in the hallway, but it was very faint. Then I distinctly heard Vincent walking to the front door, and there was a long silence before I heard it close. I think he must have been wondering if someone had just come in, maybe he stepped out onto the landing, went down a couple of steps, peered over the banister or something like that. The door was closed carefully. He probably thought he had not shut it properly when he came in. That night, he didn't even mention the incident to Sophie – if he had, it would have been a disaster. I got such a fright.

January 23

A hysterical e-mail to Valérie. She was due to see her therapist tomorrow morning, but try as she might she cannot find her notebook. She is sure she hid it in the bathroom, but now it is gone. She broke down in tears. Despite her exhaustion, she feels anxious, constantly on edge. Depressed.

January 24

Appointment with her therapist. When she told him about losing the notebook, he was very supportive. This kind of thing often happens when you're trying too hard, he told her. Overall, he found her very level-headed, not panicked at all. She burst into tears when she related the dream about her mother-in-law. She felt she had to tell him how the accident had happened in precisely the same circumstances. How she could not remember anything she had done that day. He listened calmly, he does not believe in prophetic dreams. He offered a theory that she did not quite understand, did not quite hear, since her mind was working too slowly. It was something he terms "minor tragedies". But at the end of the session, he asked whether she might like to go somewhere "for a rest". This was what really scared her. I think she thought he was planning to have her sectioned. That is something that terrifies her.

Valérie always responds to her e-mails immediately. She wants to show how supportive she's being. Valérie suspects – and I know for a fact – that Sophie is not telling her everything. Maybe it's a kind of magical thinking. What she doesn't talk about does not exist.

January 30

I was starting to give up hope about her watch. It's been almost five months since she lost the beautiful watch her father gave her for her graduation. God knows, she turned the apartment upside down looking for it. No luck. Eventually she had to write it off. She was so upset.

But now, all of a sudden, it has turned up. And you'll never guess where? In her mother's jewellery box. Right at the bottom. Now it's not something she opens every day, obviously, since she doesn't really wear that kind of thing. But all the same, she must have looked inside it half a dozen times since late August. In her mind, she tries to work out precisely how often she has opened the box since they got back from their holidays – she even wrote down a list for Valérie, which was pointless, as though that would prove anything. But not once did she notice the watch. Granted, she was not at her best, but it's not a particularly large box and there's not really that much in it. And besides, why would she have put it there in the first place? It's insane.

Sophie doesn't seem particularly happy to have found the watch, which is a little rich.

February 8

Everyone loses money from time to time, but having too much is pretty rare. And in this case, it is baffling.

My little lovebirds have big plans. Sophie is very discreet on the subject in her e-mails to Valérie. She says "It's not definite yet", that she will tell her soon, that she'll be "the first to know". The fact is that she has decided to part with a painting she bought five or six years ago. She put the word out to her colleagues and clients at the auction house, and sold it yesterday. She was asking for 3,000 euros. Apparently that's a fair price. A man came to look at the painting. Then a woman. Eventually, Sophie settled for 2,700 on condition it was paid in cash. She seemed happy. She put the money in an envelope in the writing desk, but she does not like to keep so much money in the apartment. So Vincent took it to the bank this morning to deposit it into their account. And this is where it becomes baffling. Vincent seems quite shaken by the episode. They have been going round in circles talking about it ever since. There were 3,000 euros in the envelope. Sophie is absolutely certain it was 2,700. Vincent is just as certain: 3,000. My little lovebirds suddenly seem to be certain about everything.

Vincent, it has to be said, has been giving Sophie strange looks. He even said that lately she has been "acting weird". Sophie did not realise he had noticed anything wrong. She cried. They talked. Vincent suggested she go and see someone. That it was the right time.

February 15

The day before yesterday, Sophie took everything back. Her library card cannot be wrong, it says she took out two books, she remembers borrowing them because she flicked through them. She didn't read them, just leafed through them. She had borrowed them out of curiosity, prompted by an article she had read a few weeks earlier. She can picture them clearly. But she cannot find them anywhere. The monograph on Albert Londres and the Glossary. These days, everything panics Sophie. The slightest little thing and she falls apart. She called the library to ask if she could extend the loan. They told her she had already brought the books back. The librarian even gave her the date: January 8. She checked her diary, she had a meeting with a client in the suburbs that day. She must have dropped them off on the way. But she has no memory of taking the books back. She asked Vincent if he knew anything, but she didn't insist: these days he's like a bear with a sore head, she tells Valérie in the e-mail. The books are still there, still available, they have not been lent out since. She could not stop herself, she went to the library and asked when they had last been returned. They confirmed the date.

I saw her as she came out. She looks very distressed.

February 18

A week ago, Sophie organised a press conference to publicise a major auction of rare antiquarian books. She brought a digital camera and, during the cocktail party afterwards, took photographs of journalists, of board members and of the finger buffet for the company newsletter. This also meant the press did not have to send their own photographers. She spent a whole day and much of the weekend on her computer at home, cropping and retouching the photographs she needs to submit to the board and send to the various journalists. She stored the images in a folder labelled "Press 11/02", which she plans to send as an e-mail attachment. There must be a lot at stake because she thinks long and hard, checks the images, does a little more retouching, checks them again. I can tell she is nervous. Professional pride, I suppose. Eventually, she is satisfied. Before sending the e-mail, she carefully compresses the images into a single ZIP file. I have never abused the fact that I have remote access to her machine. I'm always worried that she will notice. But this time I couldn't resist. While she was zipping the file, I added two additional photographs to the folder. Same format, same EXIF data, guaranteed from the same camera. But these are not of journalists or of prestigious clients. They are of the press officer on a sunny beach in Greece, giving her husband a blow job. Admittedly, the husband is not as recognisable as the press officer.

February 19

Understandably, there is uproar at Percy's. News of the mix-up with the press kit is spreading like wildfire. Sophie is dumbfounded. First thing Monday morning, a member of the board called her at home. Several journalists called as soon as they got to their desks. Sophie is in complete meltdown. She has not mentioned what has happened to anyone, certainly not to Vincent. She must feel completely mortified. I only learned of it myself from an e-mail sent by one of her journalist "friends". A devastated Sophie had no idea what he was talking about and asked him to forward the offending photographs. Though I say so myself, I've got an eye for good composition: her mouth full, Sophie is gazing up at Vincent with a deliberately lascivious smile. When nice middle-class girls play the whore in private, they're better than the real thing, let me tell you. The second image is even more compromising, if that's possible. It was taken at the climax, and proves that she's a natural and that his equipment is in good working order.

It's a disaster. Sophie did not go in to work and spent the whole day sprawled on the sofa. Vincent is distraught, but she refuses to tell him anything. All she could bring herself to tell Valérie was that "something terrible" had happened. Shame is a terrible thing, it can be crippling.

February 20

Sophie cried all day. She stood for a long time at the window, smoking countless cigarettes. I got a lot of good pictures of her. She has not set foot in the office, where I'm sure the rumour mill is going round like crazy. I bet that the images have leaked, that the people around the coffee machine are passing them back and forth. This is probably what Sophie is imagining too. I don't think she would be able to go back. That would explain why she seemed indifferent when she found out that she had been suspended. One week. Apparently, they managed to limit the extent of the damage, but personally I think the harm has been done. And in career terms, this is the sort of thing that can come back to haunt you.

Sophie certainly looks like a ghost.

February 23

From the very start, the evening felt like a trap: I was supposed to pick her up at her apartment and take her out to dinner. I'd reserved a table for two at Chez Julien, but my determined paramour had other plans. As soon as I stepped through her front door, I saw the table set for two. The mindless bimbo, whose noxious perfume is enough to confirm that nothing is too tasteless, had even put a candelabra on the table, one of those revolting objects that masquerades as contemporary art. I gave a little yelp of surprise, but now that I was inside and could smell something cooking in the oven, it was difficult, indeed impossible, to refuse her invitation. I protested for the sake of form, vowing never to see this woman again. My decision was made. This thought comforted me, and since the round table made it impossible for Andrée to paw me as she usually does whenever she has the opportunity, I felt safe.

She lives in a cramped apartment on the fourth floor of an ageing, charmless building. The living-dining room has only one window, which admittedly runs floor to ceiling but gives little light since it overlooks the courtyard. It's the sort of place where you have to keep the lights on at all times if you don't want to sink into a depression.

Like the evening itself, the conversation lagged. As far as Andrée is concerned, I am Lionel Chalvin, I work in the property business. Both of my parents have passed on, meaning that it takes only a mournful look whenever the subject is raised to avoid having to talk about my childhood. I live alone, and of course the stupid bitch believes that I'm impotent. Or that I have trouble getting it up, at least. This is another subject I have largely managed to avoid, or to limit to practicalities. I play it by ear.

We talked about holidays; last month Andrée spent a few days at her parents' place in Pau, so I was treated to little anecdotes about her father's eccentricities, her mother's phobias, the dog's antics. I smiled. Honestly, it was as much as I could do.

I was treated to what is called "fine dining". Well, what she calls "fine dining". Only the wine could have been called "fine", but that had been recommended by her local merchant. She knows nothing about wine. She had made a "signature cocktail" which was almost indistinguishable from her perfume.

As I feared, when dinner was over, Andrée served coffee on the low table next to the sofa. When she had settled herself next to me, and after a long pause that she no doubt intended to be meaningful and compassionate, the fat sow informed me that she could "empathise" with my "problems in that department". She said it with the religious fervour of a nun. I bet she thinks it's a godsend. She's obviously desperate to get laid, since I'm guessing she doesn't often get the chance, so finding a lover who has "problems in that department" makes her feel useful. I pretended to be embarrassed. There was an awkward silence. Whenever this happens, she tries to distract me by talking about her work, like anyone who has nothing much to say. Always the same stories. But at some point, she mentioned the press department. I was instantly on the alert. Within a few minutes I had managed to steer the conversation towards Sophie, subtly at first, talking about how the big auctions must create so much work for everyone. Having rambled on about half the people in the company, she finally got onto the subject of Sophie. She was dying to tell me about the photographs. She laughed like a drain. With friends like her . . .

"I'll miss her when she leaves," she said. So she was definitely leaving.

I pricked up my ears. And this was when I got the whole story. Sophie was not only leaving Percy's, she was leaving Paris. It was not *a country house* they had been looking for over the past month, it was *a home in the country*. Sophie's husband has just been appointed director of a new research facility in Senlis, and they are planning to move there.

"But what is she going to do?" I said.

"What do you mean?" She seemed surprised that I should be interested.

"Well, you've always said she's a career woman, so I was wondering . . . what could she find to do out in the country?"

Andrée flashed me a conspiratorial smile and told me that Sophie is "expecting a baby". Although this is hardly news, I was shaken. It seems a rash thing to do, given the state she is in.

"So have they found somewhere?"

According to Andrée, they've found "a beautiful house in the Oise", with easy access to the *autoroute*.

A baby. And moving to the country, too . . . I had hoped my little trick with the press kit would force her to stop work temporarily, but now she is pregnant and leaving Paris. I needed to give serious thought to these new factors. I got up and stammered something. I had to leave, it was getting late.

"But you haven't even touched your coffee."

I didn't give a damn about her coffee. I went and fetched my jacket and headed for the door.

I don't know quite how it happened. Andrée followed me to the door. She had a very different plan for the evening. She said it was a shame, that it was not yet late, especially for a Friday night. I mumbled something about having to work in the morning. I knew I had no further use for Andrée, but to avoid burning my bridges completely I said something that I intended to be reassuring. It was at this point that she pounced. She pulled me to her, kissed my neck. She must have felt my resistance. I don't remember what she whispered, something about "taking care" of me, she would be patient, I didn't need to worry, after all, such things happen to most men at some point . . . I could have tolerated all that had she not slipped her hand around my waist. Dangerously low. I could not control myself any longer. Coming on top of the evening I'd just had, the devastating news, it was all too much. I shoved her hard. She was startled by my reaction, but still tried to press her advantage. She smiled at me, a grotesque, double-chinned leer – ugly women are so crude when it comes to sexual desire – I couldn't stop myself. I slapped her. Hard. She brought her hand up to her cheek. Her eyes registered absolute astonishment. Immediately I realised the enormity of the situation, and how useless she had been. After everything I had forced myself to do for her. So I slapped the other cheek, and I went on hitting her until she began to sob. I was no longer afraid. I looked around the room, at the table and the remnants of the meal, at the sofa and the coffee we had not touched. I felt an overpowering disgust. I took her by the shoulders and hugged her towards me as though to comfort her. She offered no resistance, assuming that this painful interlude was at an end. I walked over to the window and opened it wide, as if to get a breath of fresh air, and I waited. I knew that she would follow. It only took two minutes. I heard her snuffling pathetically behind me. Then I heard her footsteps and an acrid cloud of perfume enfolded me one last time. I held my breath, I turned and once again I took her by the shoulders, and when she was pressed against me, whimpering like a puppy, I wheeled around gently as though to kiss her, and with a vicious shove, I pushed her. I just had time to see the terror on her face as she toppled out of the window. She did not even scream. Two, maybe three seconds later, I heard a gruesome sound from the courtyard below. I began to sob. I was shaking from head to foot, trying to stop the image of Maman from rising up before me. But I must have had some last vestige of self-control, because an instant later I had grabbed my jacket and was running wildly down the stairs.

February 24

It goes without saying that Andrée's fall was a terrible ordeal for me. Not because the dumb bitch died, but because of the *way* she died. In retrospect, I am surprised that I felt nothing when Vincent's mother died. But in that case, I was dealing with stairs. That night it was not Andrée flying through the window, but Maman. But it was not as upsetting as it has been in the dreams that have haunted me for years now. It is as though I have begun to make my peace with things. That is something I owe to Sophie. It's probably what shrinks call "transference".

February 26

This morning, Sophie attended the funeral of her beloved colleague. She wore black. When I saw her leave in her mourning clothes, I thought she looked rather pretty for a dead woman walking. Two funerals in such a short space of time must be unsettling. In fact, I have to admit I feel rather unsettled by Andrée's death myself, and especially by how it happened. It feels blasphemous. Like an affront to my mother. Painful images from my childhood came flooding back, and I had to fight them every inch of the way. Perhaps all the women who love me are destined to throw themselves out of windows.

I reassessed the situation. Things are far from brilliant, it goes without saying, but it has not been a complete disaster. I will have to be more careful. As long as I don't make any more mistakes, I should be alright. No-one at Percy's knows me, I never went back there after the night I met Andrée.

Of course my fingerprints will be all over her apartment, but I don't have a police record so, barring accidents, it's unlikely that they will be able to link her to me. Even so, I need to be very cautious. Another fuck-up like that could put my whole plan in jeopardy.

February 28

As for Sophie's decision, it's not the end of the world. She's moving out of Paris, so I will simply have to deal with that. What is frustrating is seeing my elaborate technical set-up become obsolete. But what is done is done. There's no way I will be able to find an observation post as perfect as this out in the country, but I'm sure I'll find something.

The baby is due in the summer. I have begun to factor this in to my strategy for the coming months.

March 5

All systems go: this morning the removals van pulled up outside. It was not even 7.00 a.m., but the lights in the apartment had been on since 5.00 and I could see Sophie and her husband rushing around. At about 8.30, Vincent went to work, leaving his wife to cope with everything. The guy is a complete shit.

I can't see any point in keeping this room on now: it would be a painful reminder of the wonderful moments living so close to Sophie, of a time when at any moment I could look onto her windows, see her moving around, take photographs . . . I have hundreds now. Sophie in the street, in the *métro*, at the wheel of her car. Sophie, naked, at her bedroom window. Sophie kneeling in front of her husband, Sophie painting her toenails in the living room . . .

The day will come when I will truly miss Sophie, I know that. But that day is still a way off.

March 7

Minor technical glitch: I managed to recover only two of the three microphones. The third obviously disappeared during the move; those things are so small.

March 18

It's freezing cold out in the country. And God, but it's bleak. I can't understand what Sophie is doing here. I suppose she's traipsing after her husband. A good little wife. I'll give it three months before she's bored to death. She'll have her big belly to keep her company, but she'll have so many other things to worry about . . . I recognise that it was a good promotion for Vincent, but I think he's being very selfish.

Sophie moving out to live in the Oise will mean me having to travel long distances, and in the dead of winter. So I checked into a little hotel in Compiègne. I told them I'm a writer. Finding a lookout post, on the other hand, took a lot longer. But I managed in the end. I slip through the crumbling section of wall at the rear of the house. The motorbike I park in a rickety shack with only half the roof still in place. It's quite some distance from the house and the bike is not visible from the road. Not that many people pass this way.

Apart from the cold, everything is going well for me. I can't say the same for Sophie. Hardly had she moved in than the problems started. Even for someone who is very active, the days tend to drag in such a vast house. For the first few days, the builders offered some distraction, but then there was a cold snap and they had to stop working. Who knows when they will be back. The upshot is that the ground in front of the house churned up by the trucks has frozen over and Sophie sprains her ankle whenever she tries to go out. To make matters worse, the weather is still miserable. When they didn't need it, the stack of firewood seemed close by, but now . . . Worst of all, she is completely isolated. From time to time she takes her cup of tea out onto the front steps. It's hard to keep cheerful when you're alone all day and your husband comes home at all hours.

Proof, if it were needed, came this morning when the door opened and a cat slunk out. Not a bad idea, really. It sat on the threshold staring out at the gardens. It is a handsome black-and-white cat. After a few minutes it went to do its business, never straying far from the house. This must have been one of its first forays into the wild. Sophie was watching from the kitchen window. I skirted round to the back of the house and we came nose to nose, the cat and I. I stopped dead. It's not at all feral. It's a rather sweet animal. I crouched down and called it. It hesitated a moment and then padded over, arching its back so I could stroke it. I took it in my arms and it began to purr. I felt a tautness, a fevered anxiety. The cat was still purring as I carried it towards the shed where Vincent keeps his tools.

March 25

I have not been to visit for several days, not since the night Sophie found her cat nailed to the door of her husband's shed. It was a terrible shock, understandably. I arrived at about 9.00 p.m. just as Sophie was leaving. I saw her putting an overnight bag into the boot of her car. I waited half an hour, just to be sure, then jemmied one of the shutters at the back of the house and crawled inside to take a look. Sophie has been busy. She has already painted most of the downstairs rooms – the kitchen, the living room and another room, although I don't know what they'll use that for. A pretty pastel yellow edged with a darker yellow. The exposed beams in the living room are painted pistachio green (as far as I can judge), but it all looks very pretty. It must be a painstaking task. Countless hours of work. The builders have left the concrete bathroom walls unplastered, but everything is working, there is hot water. The kitchen is also being completely refurbished. The workmen have left the new cabinets in the middle of the floor; I suppose they have to deal with the plumbing before they can be mounted. I made some tea and had a little think. I wandered through the rooms, took two or three trinkets as souvenirs, the sort of thing no-one would ever miss, but they're a surprise when you stumble upon them. Then, having made my decision, I fetched the tins of paint and the rollers. It took me a lot less time than Sophie to redecorate from floor to ceiling, though my style is a little more "spontaneous". The kitchen cabinets have been reduced to sticks and kindling, I cleaned up the dribbles of paint with the table linen and used this to add a dash of colour to the furniture, I hacked through the pipes in the bathroom and the kitchen and turned on the taps before I left.

I don't need to come back for a while.

March 26

Shortly after they moved in, Sophie met Laure Dufresne, who teaches at the village school. They are about the same age, and they hit it off immediately. I went and had a nose around Laure's place when she was in class. I wouldn't want to be caught. Nothing to report. A nice quiet life. A nice quiet girl. She and Sophie see a lot of each other. Laure pops by for coffee when she finishes work. Sophie went round to help move new furniture into the classroom. Through my binoculars, I saw them laughing and joking together. I have a feeling this new friend is just what Sophie needs.

I have started to make plans. The question is how to make use of all this new information. I think I've come up with something.

March 27

Though Laure has done her best to be supportive, Sophie is devastated. After her cat was killed, the house was vandalised while she was away; she has been knocked for six. She is convinced it must be the work of some spiteful neighbour. Laure insists that the people around here are lovely, that they have made her feel very welcome. Sophie is doubtful. And the facts as she outlines them are in her favour. To make matters worse, it will take time to get a loss adjuster to come round, to re-hire builders, order new furniture. It could take weeks (or months, who knows?). Then everything will have to be painted again. If that were not enough, Vincent has just started his new job and gets home late every night, and tells her that this is normal, that it's always like that at the beginning. She feels as though they have got off to a bad start with the house. She does not want to focus on the negative (quite right, Sophie: try to stay rational). Vincent has had an alarm installed to reassure her, but still she feels uneasy. Their honeymoon period in the Oise did not last long. The pregnancy is coming along. Three and a half months. Though I have to say, Sophie looks very peaky.

April 2

This is the last straw: there are rats in the house. There were none when they moved in, and now they are all over the place. And they say when you see one rat there are nine more in the walls. You start out with a couple, but they breed so fast. The place is teeming, you see them scurrying into dark corners, it can be very frightening. At night you hear them scrabbling in the dark. You set traps, put down bait to lure and kill them. There seems to be no end. I'm the one who has to do all the work, ferrying panicked rats in the panniers of the motorbike. That is the most tiresome part.

April 4

It is to Laure that Sophie turns for comfort. I went back to the teacher's house to check on a few things. I even began to wonder whether she might not be a lesbian, but I don't think so. Though this is precisely what has been said in the anonymous letters circulating around the village. The council were the first to receive one, followed by social services and the school inspections board: they paint an ugly picture of Laure, claiming that she's a thief (one letter claims she has been embezzling school funds), a tyrant (allegations of the cruel treatment of pupils), a deviant (claims that she is involved in an intimate relationship with Sophie Duguet). The atmosphere in the village becomes hostile. Unsurprisingly, feelings are all the more intense because this is a godforsaken village where nothing ever happens. In her e-mails, Sophie describes Laure as "an extremely brave young woman". Finding herself in a position where she can be of help to someone else, Sophie feels useful.

April 15

So here she is at last, the famous Valérie! The two women are rather alike, I think. They met in secondary school. Valérie works for an international haulage company based in Lyon. The internet throws up no results for "Valérie Jourdain", but by widening the search to "Jourdain" alone I manage to trace the family lineage from the grandfather, the source of the family wealth, to the grandson, Henri – Valérie's elder brother. By the late nineteenth century, the family had already amassed a considerable fortune in the textile industry when, by a rare stroke of genius, the grandfather, Alphonse Jourdain, filed a patent for a synthetic cotton thread which was to ensure a generous income for his family for two generations. This was all that was needed for his son, Valérie's father, to consolidate their wealth with a series of judicious investments (principally real estate), so that the family would be secure for at least eight generations more. From what I've been able to glean of Valérie's personal finances, the sale of her Lyon apartment alone would allow her to live comfortably for a hundred years without working a day in her life.

I watch them stroll together in the grounds of the house. A distraught Sophie shows her how all the plants are dying, even some of the trees. No-one knows what the problem is. They would rather not find out.

Valérie proves to be cheerful and enthusiastic. She helps with painting the walls, but after a while she sits on the stepladder smoking cigarettes and chatting until she realises that Sophie has been working on her own for more than an hour. The problem is that she is terrified of rats, that the alarm randomly going off as many as four times a night sends her into a blind panic. (Although it requires a lot of work on my part, the results are deeply rewarding.) Valérie complains that they're stuck in the middle of nowhere. I wouldn't disagree.

Sophie introduced Valérie to Laure. They seem to get along famously. But what with Sophie's chronic depression and Laure's persistent anxiety about the wave of poison pen letters circulating in the village, it's not much of a holiday for Valérie.

April 30

If things carry on like this, even Valérie is going to get annoyed with Sophie. Vincent is a sphinx, it is impossible to know what he is thinking; Valérie, on the other hand, is impulsive and spontaneous. She has no ulterior motives.

For some days now, Sophie has been pleading with her to stay a little longer. Just a few more days. Valérie tried to explain that she simply can't. Sophie insisted, called her "darling" and "poppet", but though Valérie might be able to take more time off, she hates the place. I don't think anything in the world could persuade her to stay. But then, just as she is about to leave, her train ticket goes missing. She cannot help but think that perhaps Sophie is doing everything in her power to keep her here. Sophie swears that she had nothing to do with it, Valérie shrugs it off, Vincent makes it out to be just a trivial incident. Valérie books a new ticket over the internet. She is more reserved than usual. They kiss goodbye at the station, Valérie patting a sobbing Sophie on the back. I think Valérie is ecstatic to be getting out of here.

May 10

When I saw that Laure's car had broken down, I immediately realised what would happen next and planned accordingly. It worked exceptionally well. The following day, Laure asked to borrow Sophie's car so she could do her weekly shop. Sophie is always happy to help. Everything was prepared. I had arranged things meticulously, though I also had a stroke of luck. When she opened the boot of the car, Laure might not have noticed anything. But as she was loading the bags from her shopping trolley, she saw the stack of magazines poking out of a plastic bag. Given that recently her whole life has been dominated by the poison pen letters, she was of course intrigued. When she saw that there were words and letters cut from the pages of the magazines, she made the connection. I was expecting her to explode. But she didn't. Laure is a very calm, very organised person; in fact this is what Sophie likes about her. Laure went home to pick up copies of the anonymous letters she has been collecting over recent weeks and took them and the magazines directly to the police station in the nearest town, where she pressed charges. Sophie was beginning to worry by the time Laure finally came back from her shopping trip. Laure barely said a word. Through the binoculars, I could see them standing facing each other. Sophie's eyes widened. Hardly had Laure left when the police arrived with a search warrant. It didn't take them long to find the other magazines I had secreted here and there. The libel action should keep tongues wagging in the village for the next few weeks. Sophie is at her wits' end. This is all she needs. She will have to tell Vincent. Sometimes I think that Sophie wishes she were dead. And she is pregnant.

May 13

Sophie is distraught. These past few days she has literally had to drag herself around. She did a little work on the house, but her heart was not in it. She seems reluctant to set foot outside.

I don't know what is going on with the builders, but there has been no sign of them. I suspect the insurance company are not being cooperative. Perhaps they should have had the alarm installed earlier, I don't know, insurers can be sticklers for regulations. In short, no work is being done. Sophie looks haggard and dispirited. She spends hours standing outside smoking. Hardly the best in her condition.

May 23

Huge black clouds have been rolling across the sky all afternoon. At about 7.00 p.m., the rains started. By the time Vincent Duguet passed me at 9.15, the storm was raging wildly.

Vincent is a cautious, attentive man. He is driving at a reasonable speed, and is punctilious in his use of indicators. As he turns onto the trunk road, he accelerates. For several kilometres, it is a straight stretch of road and then it swerves sharply to the left, I would even say savagely. Despite the warning signs, many drivers have probably been caught out, especially since at that point the road is lined with trees that conceal the hairpin bend: it can quickly sneak up on an unsuspecting driver. Not Vincent, obviously; he has been driving the same route for weeks and is not given to bursts of speed. Even so, being familiar with a road can make you complacent; you stop thinking about the dangers. Vincent approached the bend with the confidence of someone who knows the area well. The rain was lashing hard now. I was just behind. I overtook at precisely the right moment and cut in front of him so brutally that the rear wheel of the motorcycle grazed his front bumper. At exactly that moment, I went into a carefully controlled skid, then braked hard to right the bike. The element of surprise: the rain, the motorbike appearing out of nowhere, scraping against the car and spinning out in front – Vincent Duguet literally went round the twist. He braked too hard, swerved and tried to turn into the bend. Just then, I pulled a wheelie right in front of him. He could visualise himself ploughing into me, wrenched the steering wheel wildly and . . . that was that. The car spun around, the tyres mounted the hard shoulder, it was already the beginning of the end. It veered right, then left, the engine roared and the shriek of metal as it hit the tree was terrible: the car wrapped itself around the trunk, balanced on the rear wheels, the bonnet half a metre off the ground.

I got off the motorcycle and ran towards the car. Despite the torrential rain, I was afraid there would be a fire, I needed to work fast. I approached the driver's door. Vincent's chest was buried in the dashboard, the airbag must have exploded – I didn't realise that was possible. I don't know why I did what I did next, I probably needed to make sure he was dead. I pushed back the visor on my helmet, then grabbed him by the hair and twisted his face towards me. Blood was streaming everywhere, but his eyes were wide open and he was staring at me intently. I stood, completely paralysed. The driving rain poured into the car, Vincent's face was gushing blood and yet he went on staring at me so fixedly that I was petrified. For a long moment we looked at each other. I let go of his head and it lurched heavily to one side and I swear, his eyes were still open. They now had a different fixity. As though he were finally dead. I ran to my bike and raced off back the way we had come. A few seconds later, I passed a car whose dipped headlights I had noticed earlier in my rear-view mirror.

I could not sleep for seeing Vincent's eyes gazing into mine. Is he dead now? If not, would he be able to remember me? Would he realise that I am the motorcyclist he knocked down a few months ago?

May 25

I keep up to date by way of Sophie's e-mails to her father. He tries to insist that she come to stay with him, but she always refuses. She says she needs to be alone. When it comes to solitude, she has all she could wish for. Vincent was rushed to Garches hospital. I am desperate for news of his condition. I have no idea how things are going to pan out now. But I feel reassured: Vincent is in a bad way. A very bad way.

May 30

I had to take extreme measures, otherwise I risked losing her. Now I know where Sophie is at any moment of the day. It is safer that way.

I look at her: you wouldn't think she was pregnant. Some women are like that, they only start to show at the very end.

June 5

It was bound to happen. It may be the predictable outcome of months of disaster and distress, and the way things have recently accelerated: Laure's libel action, Vincent's accident. Last night, Sophie went out in the middle of the night, something she never does. She went to Senlis. I wondered what it might have to do with Vincent. Nothing, as it turns out. Sophie has miscarried. Probably because she has been overwrought.

June 7

I was not at all well last night. I was woken by an overpowering feeling of dread. I recognised the symptoms at once. Anything related to motherhood does this to me. Not always, but often. When I dream about my own birth, when I imagine Maman's beaming face, the pain of missing her is excruciating.

June 8
Vincent has just been transferred to the Clinique Sainte-Hilaire for physiotherapy. The news is worse than I had feared. They expect him to be discharged in about a month.

July 22

It has been some time since I last saw Sophie. She took a little trip to visit her father. She stayed only four days, then came back to be at Vincent's bedside.

Truthfully, the prognosis is not good . . . I am anxious to see what happens next.

September 13
My God, I'm still in shock . . .

Of course I had been expecting it, but even so. From an e-mail to her father, I learned that Vincent is being discharged today. First thing this morning, I found a spot in the grounds of the clinic from where I could see the whole complex. I had been there for twenty minutes when I saw them emerge through the door to the main building. Sophie at the top of the wheelchair ramp, pushing her husband. I could barely make them out.

I scrambled to my feet and took one of the adjacent paths so I could move closer. What a surprise! The man in the wheelchair is a shadow of his former self. His spine was badly damaged, but that is not all that's wrong. It would be quicker to list the things that are still functioning. He cannot weigh more than 45 kilos. He is a shrunken relic; he wears a surgical collar to stop his head lolling and, from what I can make out, his eyes are glazed and his complexion sallow. When you think that the guy is not even thirty, it's terrifying.

Sophie pushes the wheelchair with admirable altruism. She is calm, she stares straight ahead. Her gestures are a little mechanical, but that's understandable, she has a lot on her mind. What I love about her is that, even in such tragic circumstances, she doesn't lapse into mawkishness, she doesn't adopt the martyred air of a nun or a nursemaid. She simply pushes the wheelchair. Though she must be wondering what she is going to do with this human wreck. As indeed am I.

October 18

It is heart-rending. The Oise is not a cheery region to say the least, but we seem to have reached rock bottom. This vast mansion and this forlorn young woman who, at the first ray of sunshine, drags her husband's wheelchair out onto the front porch, her husband who takes up all her time, saps all her energy. It's terribly moving. She wraps him in blankets, pulls a chair up next to his and chatters to him while she chain-smokes. It's impossible to tell whether he understands what she is saying. He nods constantly, whether she is talking or not. Through the binoculars I can see him drooling, it is painful to watch. He tries to express himself, but he cannot speak – by which I mean he can no longer articulate words. He lets out little cries and grunts, they both do their utmost to communicate. Sophie is so patient with him. I couldn't do it.

Otherwise, I am very discreet. It's important not to overdo it. I come by during the night, between 1.00 and 4.00 a.m., I slam one of the shutters and half an hour later I smash an outdoor lightbulb. Once I see a light go on in Sophie's room, then on the stairs, I can go home in peace. The important thing is to maintain the atmosphere.

October 26

Winter has arrived a little early.

I have discovered that Laure has dropped the charges against Sophie. She even came round to visit. Things may never be the same between them, but Laure is a good person at heart, she is not one to hold a grudge. Sophie is so pale she is almost translucent.

I visit about twice a week (I adjust her medication, read any opened letters and carefully put them back), the rest of the time, I keep up to date by way of her e-mails. I have to say I don't like the turn events are taking. We could languish in this listless depression for months, for years. Something needs to be done. Sophie is trying to get herself organised, she has requested a home help, but they are hard to come by around these parts, and obviously I'm against the idea. I intercepted her letters. I have opted for a more fitful approach, I am counting on the fact that, given her age, regardless of the love she feels, Sophie will get bored, she will start to wonder what she is doing here, how much longer she can stand it. I can tell she has been looking for solutions: she has considered buying another house, she is thinking of moving back to Paris. Personally, I'm not fussed. What I don't want is to have the human vegetable hanging around much longer.

November 16

Sophie never gets a moment's peace. When he first came home, Vincent would sit in his wheelchair like a good little boy, and she could get on with other things, checking on him every now and then. But as time went on, things became more difficult. Recently, they have been very difficult indeed. If she leaves him out on the front steps, within minutes his wheelchair has rolled forward and is liable to topple over. She had someone come and install a ramp and protective rails anywhere he is likely to venture. She does not know how he does it, but sometimes he makes it all the way to the kitchen. Now and then, he manages to get hold of some implement that could be dangerous, or he starts screaming. She quickly rushes to his side, but can never work out what it is that has set him off. Vincent and I are old friends now. Every time I show up, his eyes grow wide, he starts to grunt. He is visibly afraid, he feels terribly vulnerable.

Sophie writes to Valérie, telling her about his misadventures. Valérie keeps promising to visit, but – surprise, surprise! – she never quite gets around to it. Sophie is having trouble coping with her anxiety, she is taking all sorts of medication, she has no idea what to do for the best. She seeks advice from her father, from Valérie, she spends hours on the internet looking for a house, an apartment, she feels completely helpless. Her father, Valérie, everyone she has talked to suggests that she put Vincent into residential care, but she will not hear of it.

December 19

The second home help has just quit. She did not even give a reason. Sophie worries what to do, the agency has written to say it will be difficult to find anyone else.

I did not know whether her husband still had urges, whether he could still function and, even if he could, how she might go about it. Actually, it's quite simple. Obviously, Vincent is not the strong, masterful hunk he was a year ago on their (now infamous) Greek holiday. These days, Sophie "services" him. She does her best, but it is evident that her heart is not in it. At least she doesn't cry while she's doing it. Only afterwards.

December 23

As Christmases go, it is pretty cheerless, especially as this is also the anniversary of Vincent's mother's death.

December 25

Christmas Day! The fire started in the living room. Vincent seemed particularly calm, he was dozing. Within minutes, the Christmas tree had caught fire – it makes an impressive blaze. Sophie just had time to drag Vincent's wheelchair away (he was screaming by this time) and douse the flames while she called the fire brigade. They were more shaken than hurt. But they were very shaken. Even the volunteer firemen, to whom she served coffee in the dank, charred remnants of the living room, gently advised her to place Vincent into care.

January 9, 2002

She had only to make up her mind. I allow the letters containing the official paperwork to arrive unhindered. Sophie has found a residential home in the suburbs of Paris. Vincent is well looked after, he had first-class private health insurance. She drove him there, she kneels next to the wheelchair, takes his hands in hers, whispers softly, explains the advantages of the situation. He grunts something incomprehensible. As soon as she finds herself alone, she bursts into tears.

February 2

I have eased up a little on Sophie to give her time to get organised. I just mislay a few objects, juggle with her calendar, but she is so used to such things that she no longer finds them disturbing. She muddles through. And, in doing so, she begins to recover her strength. In the beginning she went to visit Vincent every day, but such good intentions never last. And then she finds herself crippled by guilt. It's most obvious in her e-mails to her father: she cannot even bring herself to mention it.

Now that Vincent is safely installed in the suburbs, she has put the house on the market. And she's flogging everything at knock-down prices. She has had a curious collection of people come by, vans show up at all hours with antique dealers, bric-a-brac merchants, the Emmaus Homeless Charity. Sophie waits for them and stiffly greets them at the top of the front steps; she is never around when they leave. In the meantime, they load up boxes and furniture, a whole pile of junk. It's strange, when I saw those same things in her house the other night, I found them charming, but now, watching them being cleared out and packed up, they suddenly seem ugly, damaged. Such is life.

February 9

Two nights ago, at about nine o'clock, Sophie jumped into a taxi.

Vincent's room is on the second floor. He somehow managed to push the safety bar on the door that leads to the vast stone staircase and launched his wheelchair down the steps. The nurses are at a loss to know how he did it, but obviously he still had considerable strength. He took advantage of the general kerfuffle after dinner, when groups are getting together to play games and the pensioners are gathered in front of the television.

He died instantly. Curious that he died the same way as his mother. Talk about fate . . .

February 12

Sophie decided to have Vincent cremated. The ceremony was poorly attended: her father, Vincent's father, a handful of former colleagues, a few relatives she rarely sees. It is at times like this you realise how completely she has cut herself off. At least Valérie showed up.

February 17

I expected her to be relieved by Vincent's death. For weeks, she must have been imagining herself having to visit him for years and years. But in fact her reaction was completely different: she is tormented by guilt. If she had not "put him in a home", if she had had the strength to care for him to the end, he would still be alive.

Despite Valérie's e-mail saying that the life he was living was no life at all, Sophie is devastated. But I believe that, sooner or later, reason will prevail.

February 19

Sophie has gone to stay with her father for a few days. I didn't feel I needed to tag along. Besides, she took her medication with her.

February 25

I have to admit that it's a decent neighbourhood. It's not one I would have chosen, but it's fine. Sophie moved into a third-floor apartment. I will have to find a way to visit some day. It's unlikely I'll be able to find an observation post as convenient as I had back when Sophie was a radiant young woman. But I'm working on it.

She brought almost nothing with her. There cannot have been much left after her clearance sale in the Oise. The removals van she has rented is tiny compared to the one they used when they moved out of Paris. I'm not one for symbols generally, but even I can see it as a sign, and a good one, too. A few months ago, Sophie moved house with a husband, with tons of furniture, books and paintings, and with a baby in her belly. She has come back alone, with nothing but a small van. She is no longer the young woman who radiated life and energy. Far from it. Sometimes I look at the photographs from back then, her holiday snaps.

March 7

Sophie has decided to look for work. Not in her own field, she no longer has any contacts in P.R., and besides, she no longer has the ambition or the drive. Then there is the problem of why she left her last position. I watch from a distance. I'm not bothered one way or the other. She visits offices, arranges interviews. She obviously doesn't care what she does. She barely mentions it in her e-mails. It is strictly utilitarian.

March 13

Well, I didn't see that coming: a nanny. The advertisement was for a "child-minder". The manager of the agency took a liking to Sophie. And it took no time at all to find her a position: that same evening, she was hired by "M. and Mme Gervais". I will have to do a little digging about them. I saw Sophie with a little boy of about five or six. It is the first time I've seen her smile in months. I haven't yet figured out her work schedule.

March 24

The cleaning woman arrives at about noon. Sophie usually lets her in. But since she lets herself in when Sophie isn't there, I assume she has her own keys. She is a plump woman of a certain age who goes everywhere with a brown plastic bag. She does not clean for the Gervais on weekends. I watched her for days on end, I have learned her routine, her habits. I'm an expert. Before starting her shift, she stops at Le Triangle, the café on the corner, for one last cigarette. She is evidently not allowed to smoke in the apartment. Her big thing is the horses. I sat at the table next to her as she was filling in her betting slip, and then, when she went to give it in, I slid my hand into the brown plastic shopping bag. It hardly took me a moment to locate the keys. On Saturday morning I went out to Villeparisis (it's ridiculous how far the woman has to come to work), and while she was doing her shopping, I slipped the keys back into her bag. I'm sure it was a load off her mind.

Now, I have my access to the Gervais' apartment.

April 2

Nothing much has changed. It was less than two weeks before Sophie lost her identity card, for her alarm clock to go on the blink (she showed up late in her very first week). I am piling on the pressure and waiting for the right opportunity. So far, I have been pretty patient, but now I'd like to move on to Plan B.

May 3

Although she loves her new job, for the past two months Sophie has found herself facing the same psychological problems she did a year ago. Exactly the same. But one thing is new: the furious outbursts. Even I have trouble understanding her sometimes. Her unconscious mind seems to be rebelling, driving her into wild rages. It was different before. Sophie was resigned to her madness. Since then, something inside her has snapped and I don't know what. I see her getting angry, she has no self-control; she is rude to people, it's as though she finds everyone infuriating, as though she no longer likes anyone. But it's hardly anyone else's fault that she is like this! I find her aggressive. It did not take long for her to get a terrible reputation in the neighbourhood. She has no patience. For a nanny, that is a serious drawback. And though I admit she has a lot to deal with right now, she takes out her personal problems on other people. There are times when I think she is capable of murder. If I were the parent of a six-year-old kid, I wouldn't leave him in the care of someone like Sophie.

May 28

I was dead right. I saw Sophie with the boy in place Danremont. Everything was calm. Sophie was sitting on a bench, daydreaming. I don't know what can have happened, but a few minutes later she was striding down the street in a towering rage. Trailing a long way behind her, the boy was evidently sulking. When Sophie turned and ran at him, I knew things would not end well. She slapped him. A vicious smack, the sort that is meant to hurt, to punish. The kid was dumbfounded. As was Sophie. As though she had woken from a nightmare. They stood for a moment staring at each other, not speaking. The traffic light turned green and I drove away. Sophie was looking around wildly, fearful that someone might have seen, that someone might say something. I get the feeling she hates this child.

Last night, she slept at the Gervais' apartment. This is rare. As a rule, she prefers to go home, no matter how late it is. I know the layout of the apartment. When Sophie stays over, there are two possibilities, because there are two guest bedrooms. I watched the lights flicker on and off in the various windows. Sophie read the boy a bedtime story, then I saw her at the window smoking a last cigarette, the light went on in the bathroom briefly, then the apartment was dark. The bedroom. To get to the boy's bedroom you have to go through the room in which Sophie sleeps. I'm sure that when the nanny sleeps over, the parents don't dare check on their son for fear of waking her.

Mme Gervais arrived home at 1.20 a.m. The light came on in the bathroom again, and their bedroom lights went out at about 2.00. I waited until 4.00 before I went up. I made a detour to the cloakroom to find her hiking boots, to remove the laces, then retraced my steps. I stood listening to Sophie sleeping for a long time before slowly, silently, creeping through her room. The little boy was sound asleep, his breathing made a soft, high-pitched whistle. I don't think he suffered much. I wrapped the laces around his throat, pressed the pillow down on his face with my shoulder, and it was all over quickly. But it was horrifying. He writhed and thrashed furiously. I felt that I was going to throw up, tears came to my eyes. And suddenly, with absolute terrible certainty, I knew that in those few seconds I became someone very different. I managed to finish the job, but I could never do it again. Something in me died with that boy. Something of the child in me that I had not realised was still alive.

In the morning, I was concerned when I did not see Sophie emerging from the building. It's not like her. There was no way of knowing what was happening in the apartment. I telephoned, twice. And a few minutes later, a few interminable minutes later, I saw her suddenly appear, clearly in a blind panic. She took the *métro*. She raced back to her apartment to pick up some clothes, and then called into the bank just as it was closing for lunch.

Sophie was on the run.

The following morning, the headline in *Le Matin* read: "SIX-YEAR-OLD STRANGLED IN HIS SLEEP. POLICE SEARCH FOR NANNY".

January 2004

In February of last year, *Le Matin* ran the headline: "WHERE IS SOPHIE DUGUET?"

It had just been discovered that, after murdering little Léo Gervais, Sophie had bumped off a woman named Véronique Fabre and stolen her identity in order to escape. No-one could know that the following June, she would murder the manager of a fast-food restaurant who was employing her cash in hand.

Sophie Duguet proved more resourceful and determined than anyone imagined. Myself included, and I know her better than anyone. "Survival instinct" is not an empty phrase. For Sophie to get away, she needed a little help from me, though always at a distance, but I suspect she might have managed it without my help. Whatever the case, the fact remains that Sophie is still a free woman. She has moved several times, changing her hairstyle, her clothes, her routine, her job, her friends.

Despite the difficulties posed by her being on the run, living incognito, never staying in the same place for long, I have managed to keep up the pressure on her because my methods are effective. Over the months, she and I were like two blind actors in a tragedy: we were destined to meet, and that moment was fast approaching.

They say that it was by constantly changing tactics that Napoleon won his wars. This is also how Sophie succeeded. She has changed course a hundred times. Recently she has changed her plans again. And she is about to change her name once more. This is a recent development. With the help of a prostitute, she has managed to purchase genuine/forged papers. The papers themselves are forgeries, but the identity is genuine, almost verifiable, irreproachable, the name of someone to whom nothing much has ever happened. As soon as she had her new identity she moved again to another city. I have to say that, at the time, I could not really work out what good it would do her to spend an exorbitant amount of money on a forged birth certificate, given that they are only ever valid for three months after issue. But when I saw her signing up with a dating agency everything fell into place.

It is an ingenious solution. Credit where credit is due: Sophie may still be suffering harrowing nightmares, shaking like a leaf all day long, obsessively keeping a check on her every action, but I have to admit she has an extraordinarily ability to come up with imaginative ideas. And this one means I need to think on my feet, and fast.

I'd be lying if I said it was difficult. I know her so well. I knew how she would react, what would interest her. Because I was the only person who knew precisely what she was looking for and, I believe, the only person in a position to play the role. To be really plausible, I had to make sure I did not come across as the perfect candidate; it was a matter of striking just the right balance. Initially, Sophie knocked me back. Then time worked its magic. She hesitated, she came back. At that point, I had to appear awkward enough to seem convincing, yet cunning enough not to put her off. As a *sergent-chef* in the Signals Corps, I can pass for an acceptable moron. As of a few weeks ago, Sophie had three short months to seal the deal, so she decided to speed things up. We spent a couple of nights together. Here, again, I think I played my role with admirable delicacy.

As a result, the day before yesterday, Sophie asked me to marry her.

I said yes.

FRANTZ
AND SOPHIE

The apartment is not very large, but it is practical. It is perfectly fine for a couple. This is what Frantz said when they moved in, and Sophie agreed. Three rooms, two with French windows overlooking the building's small communal garden. They are on the top floor. The place is quiet. Shortly after they moved in, Frantz took her to see the military base twelve kilometres away, though they did not go inside. He just waved to the orderly on duty, who nodded vaguely in response. Since his hours are flexible, he leaves home late and gets back early.

The wedding took place at Château-Luc town hall. Frantz took responsibility for finding two witnesses. Sophie was rather expecting him to ask two of his colleagues from the base, but he said no, he would rather it remained private. (He must be pretty creative: he managed to get one week's leave.) Two men of about fifty who seemed to know each other were waiting for them on the steps of the town hall. They shook Sophie by the hand a little self-consciously, but when it came to Frantz they simply gave a curt nod. The deputy mayor ushered them into the wedding hall and when she saw there were only four of them, asked "Is that all?", then bit her lip. She seemed keen to get the ceremony over with.

"She turned up the wick a bit, but at least she got the job done," Frantz said.

A military expression.

Frantz could have got married in uniform, but he preferred to wear civvies which means that Sophie has never seen him in uniform, not even in a photograph; she bought herself a print dress that accentuated her hips. A few days earlier, blushing to the roots of his hair, Frantz had shown her his mother's wedding dress. Though somewhat threadbare now, Sophie had been spellbound: a lavish creation of chiffon as insubstantial as snow, which had since been in the wars. There are patches of darker fabric that looked like ancient stains. She realised that Frantz had an ulterior motive in showing her the dress, but when she saw the condition it was in, she dismissed the idea. Sophie expressed her surprise that he had kept the relic. "Yes," he said, startled, "I'm not sure why myself . . . I should probably throw it out, it's just an old thing." Then he carefully packed it away into the hall cupboard, something that made Sophie smile.

When they emerged from the town hall, Frantz handed his camera to one of the witnesses and explained how to focus. "Then all you have to do is press this button." Reluctantly, she stood next to him on the steps of the town hall. Then Frantz wandered off a little way with the witnesses. Sophie turned her back, she did not want to see the money changing hands. "It's still a marriage," she thought a little foolishly.

Now that he is her husband, Frantz seems quite different from the impression Sophie had of him when he was her fiancé. He is more subtle, less boorish in his manner. As often with simple souls, Frantz will sometimes say things that seem particularly astute. Though he is more reticent now that he does not feel he has to keep up the conversation, he still gazes at Sophie as though she were one of the wonders of the world, a dream come true. He calls her "Marianne" with such tenderness that Sophie has become accustomed to the name. He is the epitome of a caring, attentive husband. Sophie is surprised to find herself noticing his good qualities. The first, and the most unexpected, is that he is a powerful man. Sophie has never fantasised about muscular men, but on their first night together, she was thrilled by his strong arms, his taut stomach, his well-developed pectorals. She was naïvely charmed when one night he smiled and effortlessly lifted her up and set her on the roof of a car. She felt a sudden longing to be protected. Something deep within her, something weary and worn out, slowly began to relax. Events in her life have robbed her of the hope that she might be truly happy; in its place she feels a contentment that is almost enough. Many marriages endure for decades with just that. She had felt a little contemptuous when she chose him because he was simple, ordinary. Now she is relieved to feel a certain respect for him. Without thinking, she curls up with him in bed, lets him take her in his arms, allows him to kiss her, to make love to her.

So the first weeks passed, still in black and white, though the ratio was different. On the black side, though the faces of the dead did not fade, they appeared less frequently now, as though distancing themselves. On the white side, she was sleeping better, and if she did not exactly feel completely alive, she could feel a certain stirring: she took a childlike pleasure in doing the housework, cooking the meals – like a little girl playing at having a tea party – and looking for a job – though half-heartedly since

Frantz assured her that his salary was enough to keep them both.

At first, Frantz would leave for the base at 8.45 a.m. and come home between 4.00 and 5.00 p.m. In the evenings, they would go to the cinema or have dinner at the Brasserie du Templier, a short walk from where they lived. Their path was the reverse of that of other couples: they had started by getting married, now they were getting to know each other. Even so, they did not talk much. Sophie would have been unable to explain what made their evenings together pass so smoothly. But then again . . . One subject did come up regularly. As with every couple in the early days, Frantz was very interested in Sophie's life, her past, her parents, her childhood, her studies. Had she had many lovers? How old was she when she lost her virginity? All the things that men claim are not important but never stop harping on about. So Sophie created plausible parents, talked about their divorce (this part was based largely in reality), invented a new mother who had little in common with her real mother, and of course she made no mention of her marriage to Vincent. As for her lovers and losing her virginity, she drew upon stock clichés, which seemed to satisfy Frantz. As far as he is concerned, Marianne's life seems to stop abruptly five or six years ago and begin again on the day they were married. Between the two, there is still a yawning gap. She knows that sooner or later she will have to come up with a credible story to cover this period. But she has time. Frantz may be an inquisitive lover, but he is no sleuth.

Overcome by her new sense of calm, Sophie has begun to read again. Frantz regularly brings home paperbacks from the newsagent's. Being out of touch with what has been published in recent years, she has had to trust to chance – to trust to Frantz – and he has proved very lucky in his choices: he has brought home some potboilers, of course, but also Citati's *Portraits de femmes* and, as though he sensed her passion for Russian writers, Vasily Grossman's *Vie et destin* and Ikonnikov's *Dernières nouvelles du bourbier*. They watch films together on television, and he brings home videos. Here, too, his choices are sometimes fortuitous: this is how she finally got to see the famous "Cherry Orchard" with Michel Piccoli. As the weeks passed, Sophie felt overcome by an almost voluptuous lassitude, something approaching the marvellous marital numbness sometimes felt by wives who do not go out to work.

The numbness was misleading. Far from being a symptom of new-found tranquillity, as she imagined, it was a precursor to a new bout of depression.

One night, she began thrashing about in the bed, turning this way and that. And Vincent's face suddenly appeared.

In her dream, Vincent was a huge, distorted face, as though photographed with a fish-eye lens or reflected in a concave mirror. It was not really the face of *her* Vincent, the man she had loved. It was of Vincent after the accident, the eyes perpetually tearful, the head lolling to one side, the mouth half open but robbed of words. But no, Vincent does not communicate with grunts. He speaks. As Sophie tosses and turns in her sleep, trying to get away, he stares at her and speaks in a soft, deep voice. It is not really his voice, just as it is not really his face, but it is him, because he says things that only he could know. His face barely moves, his pupils dilate to become huge, hypnotic saucers, *I am here, Sophie my darling, I am speaking to you from beyond the grave, where you consigned me. I have come to tell you how much I loved you, to show you how much I love you still.* Sophie struggles, but Vincent's eyes pin her to the bed, her thrashing arms are ineffective. *Why did you send me to my death, my darling? Not once, but twice, remember?* In the dream, it is night-time. *The first time, it was simple fate.* Vincent is driving carefully along the road in the driving rain. Through the windscreen, she watches as he becomes tired, sees his head drooping, his eyelids fluttering, watches him screw up his eyes to ward off sleep as the rain lashes harder, flooding the road ahead, and the blustery wind plasters sycamore leaves against the windshield. *I was just tired, Sophie my dream, I was not dead then. Why did you want me dead?* Sophie tries to answer, but her tongue is heavy, numb, it seems to fill her mouth completely. *You've got nothing to say, have you?* Sophie would like to say something, to tell him: My darling, I miss you so much, I miss life now that you are dead, I am dead now you are gone. But no words come. *Do you remember how I was? I know that you remember. Since my death, I do not move nor speak, I simply drool, you remember how I drooled, my head is heavy, my soul, my soul is heavy, and how heavy my heart is to see you stare at me tonight. I picture you exactly as you were on the day of my second death. You are wearing the blue dress I never liked. You are standing by a fir tree, Sophie my gift, your arms folded, and so silent* (move, Sophie, wake up, do not be a prisoner of memory, it can only bring you grief. Do not accept it), *you look at me and I merely drool, I cannot speak, but I gaze lovingly at my Sophie, while you look at me with such cruelty, such bitterness, such loathing, I know that now my love can no longer move you: you have begun to hate me, I am the dead weight hung about your life for centuries to come* (don't accept this, Sophie, turn over, do not allow the nightmare to engulf you, these lies will kill you, this is not you, wake up, whatever the cost, force yourself to wake up) *and you calmly turn, to grasp one of the branches of the Christmas tree, to stare at me, your eyes vacant as you strike a match, and you light one of the candles* (don't let him say such things, Sophie. Vincent is mistaken, you could never have done such a thing. He is in pain, his suffering is great because he is dead, but you are still alive, Sophie. Wake up!), *the tree flares, a vast, all-consuming blaze and at the far end of the room, I see you disappear behind the wall of flames licking at the curtains and, terrified but paralysed in my wheelchair, I tense every muscle, but in vain, I watch you leave, Sophie, my flame* (if you cannot move, Sophie, scream!), *Sophie my vision, I see you now at the head of the stairs, standing on that wide landing from which you hurled my wheelchair. You have just performed your act of mercy. How headstrong you look, how single-minded* (resist, Sophie, don't allow yourself to be consumed by Vincent's death). *Before me, the abyss of the stone staircase, broad as a cemetery path, deep as a well, and you, Sophie my death, you gently stroke my face, this is your last farewell, your hand upon my cheek, you tense your lips, you clench your jaw and behind my back you grasp the handles of the wheelchair* (resist Sophie, fight, scream louder!) *and with a shove, the chair takes wing and I with it, Sophie my killer, and I am in heaven because of you, and here I wait, Sophie, because I need you here beside me, soon you will be here beside me* (scream, scream!), *scream if you will, my love, I know that you are on your way. Today, you resist, but tomorrow you will come to me for solace. And we shall be together for centuries to come . . .*

Panting for breath, bathed in sweat, Sophie jolts upright in the bed. Her terrified howl still echoes around the room. Next to her, Frantz looks on in alarm. He grasps her hands.

"What is it? What happened?" he says.

Her scream dies in her throat, she feels herself choking, her fists are clenched, her nails are stabbing into her palms. Frantz takes her hands in his, relaxes her fingers one by one, whispering to her gently, but to her, in that moment, all voices sound alike, even Frantz's voice sounds like that of Vincent. The voice in her dream. The voice.

This is the day that her childlike pleasures come to an end. Sophie concentrates hard, as she did during her worst episodes, so as not to founder. During the day, she tries not to fall asleep. Fearful of what dreams may come. But sometimes, there is nothing to be done, sleep overtakes her, engulfs her. Night and day she is visited by the dead. Sometimes Véronique Fabre, smiling and blood-streaked, mortally wounded but still alive. Véronique talks to her, describes her death. It is not her voice but *the voice* that speaks, always the same, the voice that knows every aspect, every detail of her life. *I am waiting, Sophie,* says Véronique Fabre, *ever since you killed me, I have known that you will join me. Dear God, the pain you caused me, you cannot begin to imagine. I will tell you all when we are reunited. I know that you are coming. Soon, you will long to be with me, to be with us. Vincent, Léo, me. We are all eager to welcome you.*

During the day Sophie does not move, she lies prostrate. Frantz is alarmed, he wants to call a doctor, but Sophie adamantly refuses. She pulls herself together, tries to reassure him. But she can tell from his face that he does not understand, that to him, not calling a doctor in such circumstances is incomprehensible.

He comes home increasingly early. But he is too concerned. Before long, he tells her:

"I've applied for leave. I have a few days in hand."

Now he is with her all day. He watches television while she lies sprawled, only half-conscious. In the middle of the day. She can just make out Frantz's close-cropped head in silhouette against the television screen before sleep overcomes her. Always the same words, the same dead. In her dreams, little Léo speaks to her with the voice of the man he will never be. Léo speaks with the Voice. In agonising detail he tells her of the pain as the laces dug into his throat, how he struggled to breathe, how he thrashed and tried to scream. All the dead return, night after night. Frantz makes her hot drinks, herbal teas, tries to insist she call a doctor. But Sophie refuses to see anyone, she has managed to disappear, she does not want to trigger an investigation, she does not want to be insane, she does not want to be sectioned, she is determined to get through this alone. During these episodes her hands are frozen, her heart rate fluctuates alarmingly. She feels cold, but her clothes are soaked in sweat. Day and night, she sleeps. "They're just panic attacks." She tries to sound reassuring. "They come and go." Frantz smiles, but he does not seem convinced.

Once, she disappeared. Only for a few hours.

"Four hours!" Frantz says as though this were a sporting record. "I was worried. Where were you?"

He takes her hands in his, he is genuinely concerned.

"I came back," Sophie says, as though this is the response he is expecting.

Frantz tries to understand, Sophie's disappearance has made him nervous. He is a simple soul, but rational. What he cannot understand drives him crazy.

"What am I supposed to do if you go and disappear like that? I mean . . . how am I supposed to find you?"

She says that she does not remember. He insists.

"Four hours you were gone, how can you not remember?"

Sophie rolls her eyes, they are strangely glazed.

"In a café," she says, as though talking to herself.

"A café? You were in a café? Which café?" Frantz says.

229

She stares at him, utterly lost.

"I'm not sure."

Sophie started to cry. Frantz held her and she huddled in his arms. This was in April. What did she want? For it to be over, perhaps. And yet she came back. Does she remember what she did for those four hours? What could she possibly do in just four hours?

A month later, in early May, more exhausted than ever, Sophie escapes.

Frantz has gone out for a few minutes. "I'll be right back," he says, "don't worry." Sophie waits until the sound of his footsteps fade, then pulls on her jacket, hastily stuffs a few things into her pockets, grabs her purse and flees. She leaves the building by the side door next to the bins. It leads onto a different street. She starts to run. Her head is pounding like her heart; they bludgeon her from her belly to her temples. She keeps running. She feels flushed and hot, takes off her jacket and tosses it on the ground, never breaking her stride, she turns back every now and then. Is she afraid the dead will follow her? 6-7-5-3. She needs to remember this. 6-7-5-3. She pants for breath, her lungs ache, she keeps on running, reaches the bus and does not climb but rather leaps aboard. She forgot to bring any change. In vain she fumbles through her pockets. The driver looks at her as though she is mad – which she is. She digs out a two-euro coin. The driver asks a question she does not catch, but she replies: "Everything's fine", a stock answer designed to reassure others. Everything's fine. 6-7-5-3. Do not forget. There are only three or four people on the bus, they give her curious glances. She tries to straighten her clothes. She sits at the back, scanning the traffic through the rear window.

She feels a desperate urge to smoke, but smoking is forbidden and, besides, she left her cigarettes back at the apartment. The bus lurches towards the train station, stopping for endless minutes at traffic lights, setting off again, wheezing and rattling. Sophie gets her breath back, but as they approach the station, she feels fear overwhelm her again. She is afraid of the world, afraid of people, afraid of trains. Terrified of everything. She cannot get away so easily. She glances back continually. Do the faces behind her wear the mask of impending death? Her whole body is trembling and, after so many gruelling days and nights, the simple act of running for a bus and walking through a train station have left her shattered. "Melun," she says. 6-7-5-3. No, she does not have a rail card. Yes, she is prepared to travel via Paris. She proffers her debit card insistently, desperate for the cashier to take it now, desperate to have done with her message before she forgets it (6-7-5-3), desperate to get her ticket, to board the train, to watch the stations flash past, desperate to arrive at the other end . . . Yes, there will be a long wait while she has to change trains. Finally, the man taps on his keyboard, a printer rattles into life and her ticket is in front of her. "Just enter your code . . . " he says. 6-7-5-3. A small victory. Against whom? Sophie turns to leave, she has left her card in the machine. A woman gestures towards it with a smug smile. Sophie snatches it back. Everything smacks of *déjà vu*. Sophie has been reliving the same scenes, the same getaways, the same deaths since . . . when? It has to stop. She pats her pockets in search of cigarettes, finds the bank card she has just slipped in there and when she looks up Frantz is standing in front of her, panicked, saying "Where the hell are you going dressed like that?" He is holding the jacket she dropped on the street. He tilts his head left, then right. "Let's get you home. This time, we have to call a doctor. You have to recognise that . . ." For a moment she considers saying yes. But she stops herself. "No. No doctor . . . I'll come home." He smiles and takes her arm. Sophie feels a wave of nausea. Frantz grips her arm: "Let's go home," he says. "I'm parked just over there." Sophie watches the station recede, closes her eyes as though she needs to make a decision. Then she turns to Frantz, throws her arms around his neck, hugs him hard and says "Oh, Frantz . . ." She sobs as he half-carries her towards the exit, towards the car, towards home; she drops the crumpled train ticket on the ground, buries her face in his neck and sobs.

Frantz is always close at hand. As soon as she recovers her composure, she apologises for what she has put him through. Timidly, he asks for an explanation. She promises to tell him everything. She needs to rest first, she says. "Rest" is her constant refrain, the word that, for a few hours, closes every door, gives her time to breathe, time to gather her strength, to steel herself for the battles to come, for the dreams, the dead, the unwelcome visitors. Frantz does the shopping. "I don't want to have to go hunting for you all over town," he says, smiling as he locks the door behind him. Sophie smiles back gratefully. Frantz takes care of the housework, does the hoovering, cooks the meals, brings home roast chicken, Indian takeaways, Chinese food, rents videos and brings them to her hoping for a flicker of approval. Sophie finds him a good housekeeper, a great cook, she assures him that the films he brings are excellent, but by the time the opening credits roll, she is already asleep. Her heavy head falls and she finds herself among the dead, Frantz is holding her arms when she wakes lying on the floor, wordless, breathless, almost lifeless.

And so what was bound to happen finally happened. It is a Sunday, Sophie has not slept for days. She has been screaming so much she is hoarse. Frantz cossets her, he is always by her side, spoon-feeding her since she cannot bring herself to eat a mouthful. It is remarkable how this man has accepted the madness of the woman he has just married. He is almost a saint. He is devoted, ever ready to make sacrifices. "I just want you to accept that you need to call a doctor, that way you can start to get better," he says. She says that things will be "back to normal soon". He presses her. Tries to understand the logic of her refusal. He is worried he may be stepping into the uncharted territory of her life. What is going on in her head? She does her best to reassure him, knows that she needs to behave normally to allay his concerns. Sometimes she climbs on top of him, rocks back and forth until she feels him get hard, opens her legs, guides him inside, doing her best to pleasure him, she lets out little moans, squeezes her eyes shut, waits for him to surrender.

It is a Sunday. As calm as death. In the early morning, the building echoed with the voices of tenants coming back from the market, or washing their cars. Sophie spent the whole morning gazing through the French windows, smoking cigarettes, hands so cold she has stuffed them into the sleeves of her jumper. Tired. "I'm cold," she says. Last night, she woke up vomiting. Her stomach still aches. She feels dirty. The shower did not help, she wants to take a bath. Frantz runs the water – too hot, as he often does – adds the bath salts he likes but silently she loathes, they feel synthetic and the fragrance is cloying, but she does not want to offend him. It hardly matters. All she wants is for the water to be scalding, hot enough to warm her frozen bones. He helps her to undress. Sophie catches her reflection in the full-length mirror, the jutting shoulder blades, the angular hip bones, the gauntness, it is enough to make you cry, if it did not make you shudder. How much does she weigh? She finds herself saying aloud something that seems obvious: "I think I'm dying." She is shocked at the thought. She said it in the same tone in which, a few weeks ago, she said, "I'm fine." It is just as true. Sophie is slowly wasting away. As day follows night, as one nightmare follows another, Sophie is growing weaker, thinner. She is melting. Soon she will be translucent. She looks at her face again, the prominent cheekbones, the rings around her eyes. Frantz hugs her to him. He whispers sweet, foolish things. He pretends to laugh off this shocking thing she has just said. But he goes too far. He pats her on the back as one might a friend going away for a long time. He tells her that the water is hot. Sophie tests the surface. A shiver runs through her. Frantz runs the cold tap for a moment, she checks again and tells him it is fine. He goes out. He smiles encouragingly every time he leaves the room, but the door is always left ajar. As soon as she hears the television, Sophie gets into the bath, reaches for the shelf and takes down the nail scissors. She studies her wrists, the pale blue of the veins. She angles the blade of the scissors, adjusts the position, glances round and sees the back of Frantz's head, seeming to draw strength from this. She takes a deep breath and cuts deep and fast. Then she lets her muscles go slack and lies back in the bath.

*

The first thing she sees is Frantz sitting by her bed. Then her left arm, swaddled in bandages, lying limp against her body. Then the room. The pale glow streaming through the window could be dawn or dusk. Frantz gives her a compassionate smile. He cradles her fingertips, the only visible part of her hand. He strokes them gently, wordlessly. Sophie's head feels heavy. Next to them, a table on wheels and a tray.

"You need to eat something," he says.

These are his first words. It is not a question, not an admonition, not even a fear. No. Sophie does not want to eat. He shakes his head as though personally offended. Sophie closes her eyes. She remembers everything. Sunday, smoking cigarettes by the window, the chill in her bones, her face in the bathroom mirror like a death mask. Her decision. To slip away. To leave for ever. At the sound of a door opening, she opens her eyes. A nurse comes in. She smiles gently, steps around the bed and checks the I.V. drip that Sophie has not yet noticed. She places an expert thumb under Sophie's chin; a few seconds are enough for her to smile once more.

"Get some rest," she says as she leaves. "The doctor will come by soon."

Frantz stays behind, he looks out of the window and tries to compose himself. "I'm so sorry . . ." Sophie says, but he can think of nothing to say. He keeps staring out of the window, stroking her fingertips. There is an extraordinary stillness about him. She feels that he will be here for ever.

The doctor is a chubby little man with extraordinary energy. Fifty-something, supremely confident, reassuringly bald. A glance and a curt smile are enough for Frantz to feel obliged to leave the room. The doctor takes his place.

"I'm not going to ask you how you are. I can guess. You'll need to see someone, and that's all there is to it."

He says it in a single breath, the sort of straight-talking doctor who cuts to the chase.

"We have very good people here. You'll be able to talk."

Sophie looks at him. He must know that her mind is elsewhere, so he drives home the point.

"As for the rest, it was spectacular, but it didn't quite do the trick . . ."

He immediately corrects himself.

"Obviously, if your husband had not been there at the time, you'd be dead."

He has chosen the harshest, bluntest terms to test her reactions. The doctor slaps his knees and gets to his feet. Before he leaves, he nods towards the door and says:

"Do you want me to have a word with him?"

Sophie shakes her head, but her response is not sufficiently clear. She says:

"No. I'll talk to him."

"You gave me a fright."

Frantz smiles awkwardly. It is time for explanations. Sophie has none. What can she tell him? She forces herself to smile.

"I'll explain everything when I get home. But not here."

Frantz nods as though he understands.

"It's to do with a part of my life I've never talked about. I'll tell you everything."

"Is there really that much to tell?"

"There's a lot, yes. Afterwards, it's up to you."

He shakes his head in a way that is difficult to interpret. Sophie closes her eyes. She is not tired, she simply wants to be alone. She needs information.

"Did I sleep for long?"

"Almost thirty-six hours."

"Where are we, exactly?"

"The Anciennes Ursulines. The best clinic in the area."

"What time is it? Is it still visiting hours?"

"It's almost noon. Usually visiting doesn't start until 2.00 but they let me stay."

Ordinarily he would have added "given the circumstances", but today he is terse. She can tell he is working himself up to say something. She waits.

"All this . . ." He gestures vaguely to the bandages on her wrists. "Is it about us? Because things aren't working out, is that it?"

If she could, she would smile. But she cannot, she does not want to. She needs to stick to her limits. She curls her three free fingers around his.

"It has nothing to do with us, I promise you. You're so sweet."

He does not like the word, but accepts it. He is a sweet husband. What more could he hope for? Sophie wants to ask where her things are, but instead she closes her eyes. There is nothing that she needs now.

The clock in the hallways reads 7.44. Visiting time has been over for almost half an hour, but the clinic is not strict about the rules, and a chatter of visitors can be heard from several rooms. The smell of hospital food still lingers from the last meal of the day: clear soup and cabbage. How is it that clinics and hospitals all smell exactly the same? At the far end of the corridor, a large window lets in a faint, grey light. A few minutes earlier, Sophie managed to get lost. A nurse on the ground floor helped her to find her room. Now she knows the layout. She has seen the exit to the car park. She has only to make it past the nurses' station on her floor and she can get outside. In the wardrobe, she found some clothes that Frantz must have brought for her to wear when she is discharged. Nothing goes with anything. She waits, one eye pressed to the narrow gap of the door she has left slightly ajar. The nurse's name is Jennie. She is a slim, graceful woman with blonde highlights in her dark hair. She smells of camphor. She moves calmly, confidently. She has just walked away from the nurses' station, hands in the pockets of her white coat. She does this when she wants to go for a quick cigarette outside. She pushes the swing doors that lead to the lifts. Sophie counts to five, opens the door of her room and creeps down the hallway past Jennie's desk, but before she reaches the double doors, she turns right and takes the stairs. In a few minutes she will be in the car park. She clutches her handbag to her. She begins to recite: 6-7-5-3.

Jondrette the *gendarme*, his face sallow, his moustache grey. He is accompanied by another officer who does not say anything, but stares at his feet looking attentive and concerned. Frantz has offered them coffee. They said, sure, coffee, why not, but they remained standing. Jondrette is sympathetic, when he talks about Sophie he refers to her as "your lady wife", but he says nothing that Frantz does not already know. He stares back at the officers, playing his own role. His role is to look worried, which is not difficult because he *is* worried. He remembers sitting in front of the television; he enjoys general knowledge quiz shows because he can answer all the questions, although he always cheats a little. The applause, the patter of the game-show host, the asinine jokes, the canned laughter, the cheers that greet the results – television can be very noisy. Not that it mattered, Sophie did what she did in complete silence. Even if he had been doing something else at the time . . . Next category: Sport. Not really his specialised subject. But he gave it a go. He was never very good when it came to sport. Questions about the Olympic Games, the sort of trivia only a few obsessive nerds would know. He turned around. Sophie's head was tilted back, resting on the edge of the bath, foam rising to her chin. She was beautiful in profile. Even in her emaciated state, Sophie has always been pretty. Really pretty. He has often thought so. He turned back to the television, wondering whether he should check on her anyway: the last time she fell asleep in the bath and by the time he lifted her out she was frozen, he had to rub her with eau de cologne for several minutes before she got her colour back. It is no way to die. By some miracle, he came up with the answer, the name of a Bulgarian pole vaulter and . . . in a flash his internal alarm went off. He turned. Sophie's head had disappeared, he ran into the bathroom. The bubbles were crimson and Sophie's body had slid to the bottom of the bath. He screamed "Sophie!", plunged his hands into the water, gripped her shoulders and dragged her out. She did not cough, but she was breathing. Her whole body was deathly pale, blood still trickling from her wrists. Not much. It came out in little spurts to the pulse of her heart, the gashes in her arm swollen shut from being so long underwater. For a split second he panicked. He did not want her to die. "Not like this," he thought. He did not want Sophie to escape. This was the death *she* wanted. And this act of free will was like an affront to his carefully wrought plan, an insult to his intelligence. If Sophie were to die like this, he would never be able to avenge his mother's death. And so he dragged her from the bath, laid her on the floor, wound towels tightly around her wrists, talking to her all the while, then he stumbled to the telephone and called an ambulance. It arrived in less than three minutes, the station is nearby. While he waited for the paramedics, he worried about many things. How much might the bureaucrats and the pen-pushers find out? Would they discover Sophie's identity? Worse, would they tell her the truth about *sergent-chef* Frantz Berg who has never been in the army.

By the time he visited her in hospital, he was in full possession of his faculties, once again perfectly in character. He knew exactly what to do, what to say, how to respond, how to behave.

Now, he is furious again: Sophie has run away and it took six hours before the hospital even noticed! The nurse who called him did not know what to say. "Monsieur Berg, is your wife at home by any chance?" When Frantz said no, she beat a hasty retreat and handed the telephone to the doctor.

Since being informed of her disappearance, he has had time to think. The *gendarmes* can take their own set time over their coffee. No-one but Frantz could ever find Sophie. For three years he has been tracking the multiple killer that every police officer in France has been unable to find. He has rebuilt this woman with his own hands. Sophie has no secrets from him, and even he does not know where she might be right now, so the police . . . But Frantz needs to move quickly, he wants to tell the *gendarmes* to fuck off. Instead, his voice strained, he simply says:

"Do you think you'll find her soon?"

This is the sort of thing a husband would ask, surely? Jondrette raises an eyebrow. Not as dumb as he looks.

"We'll find her, monsieur, don't you worry."

Peering over the rim of the scalding coffee, taking small sips, the *gendarme* gives Frantz a probing look. He sets down his cup.

"She will have gone to stay with someone, she will call tonight or tomorrow. The best thing you can do is be patient, you under-stand?"

Then, without waiting for a response:

"Has she done it before? Run away like this?"

No, Frantz says, but she has been more or less suffering from depression.

"'More or less . . .'" Jondrette echoes. "And do you have any family, monsieur? I mean your lady wife, does she have any family? Have you called them?"

He has not had time to think things through and now everything is moving very fast. Marianne Berg, née Leblanc, what family does she have? When he questioned her over the past months, Sophie invented a family that the police would have great trouble tracking down. But that is dangerous ground. Frantz pours more coffee. To give himself time to think. He decides to change tactics. He puts on a scowl.

"So what you're saying is, you're not going to do anything? Is that it?" he says nervously.

Jondrette does not reply. He stares at his empty cup.

"If she doesn't come back in, say, three or four days, we'll launch an investigation. If it's any comfort, monsieur, in this sort of situation people generally come home after a few days of their own accord. They usually go to family or friends. Sometimes all it takes is a few phone calls."

Frantz says that he understands. If he hears anything, he will be sure to . . . Jondrette says that is for the best. Thanks him for the coffee. His lackey nods and stares at the doormat.

Frantz waited for three hours, this seemed to him a reasonable period.

He spent this time on his laptop, staring at a map of the area, watching the blinking pink dot that marked the location of Sophie's mobile. According to the map it was still in the apartment. He found it in the desk drawer. This is the first time in four years he has not been able to tell precisely where Sophie is, to within a second. He has to work fast. To find her. He thinks for a moment about her medication, but reassures himself: he has engineered a depressive state that is not likely to wear off too quickly. Even so, he needs to get her back. It is imperative. He needs to end this. To be done with it. He feels anger welling in him, but manages to control it with breathing exercises. He has been over and over the question in his mind. First stop, Lyon.

He checks his watch, then finally he picks up the telephone.

He is put through to Jondrette.

"My wife is staying with a relative," Frantz says rapidly, as though both happy and relieved. "Near Besançon."

He waits for the reaction. Double or quits. If the *gendarme* asks the name of this relative . . .

"Good." Jondrette sounds satisfied. "Is she alright?"

"Yes . . . well, from what I can tell. I think she's feeling a little lost."

"Good," Jondrette says again. "Is she coming back? Has she told you she wants to come back?"

"Yes, that's what she said. She wants to come home."

A brief silence.

"When, exactly?"

Frantz's brain is in overdrive.

"I think it might do her good to have a little break. I'll go and pick her up in a couple of days, I think that would be best all round."

"Good. When she gets back, she'll have to come to the *gendarmerie*. To sign a few forms. Tell her there's no hurry. It's more important that she gets some rest."

Then, just before Jondrette hangs up:

"One last little thing . . . You haven't been married long . . ."

"Six months . . . almost . . ."

Jondrette is silent. On the other end of the line, he probably has his probing look.

"And this . . . thing she's done, do you think . . . do you think it's related to your marriage in some way?"

Frantz responds instinctively.

"She suffered bouts of depression before we got married . . . But yes, obviously it could have something to do with it. I'll talk to her."

"That would be for the best, Monsieur Berg, believe me. Thank you for letting us know so promptly. Talk about it with your good lady wife when you go to collect her."

Rue Courfeyrac comes out more or less by place Bellecour. Frantz drives around the well-kept neighbourhood but he learns little that he did not know two years ago.

It was difficult for him to find a vantage point. Yesterday, he had to be careful to move frequently from café to café. This morning he rented a car from which it is easier to keep an eye on Valérie's building, and follow her if necessary. Back when she knew Sophie, she was working for a haulage company; now she seems to work for some boy as rich and feckless as she is, who has convinced himself he is a designer. The sort of company where you can work relentlessly for two years before realising that it is not bringing in a cent. Which, of course, would make little difference to Valérie or her friend. In the morning she leaves home, bright-eyed and bushy-tailed, and catches a taxi to work from place Bellecour.

As soon as he spotted her in the street, he knew that Sophie was not here. Valérie is a WYSIWYG girl – what you see is what you get. From her manner, from the ways she walks, Frantz can tell that she has no worries, no concerns, her bearing oozes self-assurance and an utter lack of care. He is virtually certain that Sophie has not come to find refuge here. Besides, Valérie Jourdain is much too selfish to take in Sophie Duguet – multiple murderer, wanted by the police – even if she is a childhood friend. Valérie has her limits. And they are narrow.

But what if she has? As soon as Valérie left, he went up to the floor where she lives. Reinforced door, three-point security lock. He stood for a long while, his ear pressed to the door. Every time one of the residents came into the building he pretended to be going up or down to a different floor, then returned to his listening post. Not a sound. He carried out the check four times over the course of the day. After 6.00 p.m., the sound from other apartments, from televisions, radios, conversations, however muted, made it impossible for him to detect the secret sounds that might indicate there was someone in Valérie's supposedly empty apartment.

At about 8.00 p.m., when the young woman came home, Frantz was waiting a few steps up from the landing. Valérie opened up without a word. As soon as she was inside, he pressed his ear to the door again and, for a few minutes, listened to the everyday sounds (kitchen, toilet, drawers), the music and finally to Valérie's voice in the hall, talking on the telephone. A clear voice. She is laughing, cheerful, but says, no, she does not feel like going out tonight, she has a deadline. She hangs up; more sounds from the kitchen, the radio.

Inevitably, he is a little uncertain, but he decides to trust his instincts. He leaves the building. Seine-et-Marne is less than four hours' drive.

Neuville-Sainte-Marie, thirty-two kilometres from Melun. Frantz drove around in circles for a while to make sure there were no police staking out the address. They probably did so in the early days, but they simply do not have the resources. And as long as public opinion is not stirred up by another murder . . .

He left the rental car in a supermarket car park on the outskirts of the village. Within forty minutes he has managed to walk to a small patch of woodland and from there to a disused quarry, where he forces open the entrance gate. From here he has an aerial view of the house. Not many people come here. A few couples, maybe, but they come by car. There is no risk of him being caught unawares: the headlights will alert him in time.

Sophie's father appears only three times. First, to do his washing (the laundry room is in an outbuilding not directly accessible from the house), then to pick up his post (the mailbox is fifty metres down the path). The third time, he got into his car and drove off. Frantz hesitated: follow him? Stay here? He stayed. In a small village it would be impossible to follow him unnoticed.

Patrick Auverney was gone for one hour and twenty-seven minutes, and Frantz spent this time studying every detail of the house through his binoculars. When he first saw Valérie in the street, he had felt certain that Sophie was not with her, but seeing her father now, he feels unsure. Perhaps it is the fact that time is passing, the hours ticking by at an alarming rate that makes him hope for a swift solution. But there is a more fundamental reason for his decision to wait: if Sophie is not here, he has no idea where she might have gone. Sophie is profoundly depressed, she has tried to kill herself. She is in a very fragile state. Ever since he heard that she fled the clinic he has been in a black rage. He wants to get her back. "I need to end this," he says to himself over and over. He blames himself for postponing the inevitable for so long. Surely he could have ended it long ago? Has he not already got everything he wanted? He needs to find her, to finish this.

Frantz wonders what is going on in Sophie's mind right now. What if she tries to kill herself again? No, in that case she would not have run away. There are lots of ways to end your life in a clinic, in fact it is probably the easiest place to die. She could have slashed her wrists again. Why run away? Sophie is completely disorientated. The first time she tried to escape, she sat for almost three hours in a café and came home without even remembering where she had been. He can think of only one answer: Sophie left without the faintest idea of where she might be going. She did not leave, she fled. She is trying to outrun her madness. She will eventually find sanctuary somewhere. And though Frantz has considered the problem from every angle, he cannot think where a wanted murderer like Sophie Duguet could turn for help if not her father. Sophie was forced to cut all ties in order to become Marianne Leblanc. Unless she has simply picked a destination at random (in which case she will have to come home soon), the only place she can come is here, to her father's house. It is simply a matter of being patient.

Frantz adjusts the binoculars and watches as M. Auverney parks his car in the garage.

She still has work to do, but it has been a very long day and she is eager to get back. Since, as a rule, she starts late in the morning, usually she does not leave before 8.30 p.m., sometimes 9.00. As she leaves, she calls out that she will come in early tomorrow, though she knows that this will not happen. On the drive back, she reminds herself over and over of the things she can and cannot do, the things she should and should not do. It is very difficult when you have never had much self-discipline. In the back of the taxi, she leafs through a magazine. In the street, she does not look around her. She keys in the door code and pushes it open. Since she never takes the lift, she does not do so today. She gets to her landing, takes out her keys, opens the door, goes inside, closes it and turns around. Sophie is standing in front of her, still wearing the clothes she arrived in the night before. Sophie flaps her hands impatiently, like a flustered policeman directing traffic. Keep doing exactly what she would usually do! Valérie gives a thumbs up, walks further into the apartment and tries to think what it is she usually does. But now she has a complete mental block. She cannot remember a thing. Despite the fact that Sophie made her repeat the list of actions several times, she can think of nothing. Pale as a ghost, Valérie stares at Sophie. She cannot move. Sophie places her hands on her friend's shoulders and sits her on the chair next to the door where she usually leaves her bag. A second later, Sophie is on her knees, has taken off Valérie's shoes and put them on herself. Now she moves about the apartment. She goes into the kitchen, opens and closes the fridge, goes into the bathroom, leaving the door open, waits for a moment, flushes the toilet, then goes into the bedroom. Valérie, meanwhile, has managed to regain her composure. She feels guilty. She is not equal to the task. Sophie reappears in the doorway. She gives her a nervous smile. Valérie closes her eyes, relieved. When she opens them again, Sophie is holding out the telephone and giving her a worried, quizzical look.

For Valérie this is a second chance. By the time she has dialled the number she is walking around the apartment herself. Be careful, Sophie has told her, nothing would be worse than overplaying things, so in a casual tone she says no, she doesn't fancy going out tonight, she has a deadline, she gives a little laugh, spends longer than usual listening then says her goodbyes, yes, yes, you too, O.K., see you soon, then she goes back into the bathroom, washes her hands and takes out her contact lenses. When she re-emerges, Sophie has her ear pressed to the front door, she is staring at the floor, her face rapt as though praying.

They have not exchanged a word.

When she came in, Valérie noticed a faint smell of urine in the apartment. The smell is more pungent now. While putting away her contact lenses she noticed that Sophie has peed in the bath. She gives her a questioning look, gesturing towards the bathroom. Sophie abandons her listening post for a second, gives Valérie a sad smile and spreads her hands helplessly. She was determined not to make the slightest noise all day and had no choice. Valérie smiles in turn and mimes taking a shower.

Over supper they are silent. Valérie has read the long document Sophie spent the day writing in longhand. From time to time, as she reads, she hands her a page and gives a dubious frown. Sophie picked up the pen and carefully wrote more words in the margin. Valérie read slowly, shaking her head again and again, it all seems insane to her. Sophie turned on the television, allowing them to talk in low voices beneath the sound. Valérie finds these precautions excessive and faintly ridiculous. Sophie squeezes her arm and looks her in the eye. Valérie swallows hard. In a barely audible whisper Sophie says, "Can you buy me a laptop, a little one?" Valérie rolls her eyes. What a question!

She gave Sophie everything she needed to change her bandages and watched as she did so. Sophie seemed thoughtful. She looked up for a moment and murmured:

"Are you still going out with that girl from the pharmacy?"

Valérie nodded. Sophie smiled.

"And she still can't say no to you?"

A little later Sophie yawns, she is so tired her eyes are watering. She smiles by way of apology. She does not want to sleep alone. Before she dozes off, she puts her arms around Valérie. She wants to say something, but the words will not come. She hugs harder.

Sophie is sleeping like a stone. Valérie holds her close. Every time she sees the bandages she feels her stomach lurch and a shudder run through her body. It is strange. For more than ten years, she would have given anything to have Sophie here in bed with her. "But it had to be now, like this," she thinks. It is enough to make her cry. She knows how much that desire played a part in her instinctive act of hugging Sophie when she showed up last night.

It had been almost 2.00 a.m. when Valérie was woken by the doorbell: Sophie had spent two hours making sure the building was not being watched. When she opened the door, Valérie immediately recognised that shadow of what was once Sophie in the woman standing in the doorway, arms dangling by her sides, wearing a black vinyl jacket. She looks like a smack addict, was Valérie's first thought. Sophie looked ten years older, her shoulders sagged, she had dark rings around eyes that spoke of utter desperation. Valérie took her in her arms.

Now she lies listening to her steady breathing. Without moving, she tries to see Sophie's face, but can make out only her forehead. She wants to turn her over, to kiss her. She feels tears welling. She opens her eyes wide, determined not to succumb to such facile temptation.

She has spent most of today turning over in her mind the information, the interpretations, the signs, the theories that Sophie rattled off when she arrived last night. Valérie remembers the countless telephone calls, the anguished e-mails Sophie sent her over several months. Months when she thought her friend was going mad. In the nightstand beside the bed, she can sense the presence of a passport photograph that is Sophie's most treasured possession, her spoils of war. It is not much: the sort of dreary photograph you realise looks awful the second it is spat out of the booth, but you think "It doesn't matter" because it is only for a travelcard and you find yourself having to stare at it for a whole year, dismayed by how ugly you look. In the photograph, which Sophie has carefully preserved with layers of Sellotape, she has a slightly inane expression, a forced smile. The flash makes her complexion deathly pale. But in spite of these flaws, this photograph is the one thing Sophie values above all others. She would give her life for that photograph, if she has not already done so.

Valérie imagines Sophie's bewilderment on the day she stumbled across it, imagines her turning it over and over in her hands. In that first instant, Sophie is too distraught to understand: she has slept for ten hours straight and woken with her brain more fogged than ever, her skull feels as though it is about to explode. But this discovery has such an effect on her that she drags herself to the bathroom, clambers into the bath, angles the shower nozzle above her head and, after a flicker of hesitation, grimly opens the cold tap. The jolt is such that the scream sticks in her throat. She almost faints, but steadies herself against the tiled partition, her pupils dilate, but still she stands in the freezing spray, her eyes wide open. A few minutes later, wrapped in Frantz's bathrobe, she is sitting at the kitchen table cradling a steaming bowl of tea and staring at the photograph. Though she has gone over and over it in her mind until her head aches, what she is staring at is literally impossible. She feels like throwing up. On a sheet of paper she jots down dates, reconstructs the logical timeline, correlates the events. She scrutinises the photograph, making a note of her haircut, of the jacket she was wearing when it was taken. But the conclusion is always the same: this is the photograph from the travelcard she kept in the handbag that was stolen in 2000 by a motorcyclist at the traffic lights on rue de Commerce.

Question: how can she have found it in Frantz's flight bag? It is *impossible* that Frantz could have found it among the affairs of Marianne Leblanc because it has been missing for more than three years.

She had been looking for a pair of old sneakers in the hall cupboard when she slipped her hand into the lining of one of Frantz's old travel bags and came out with a small photograph three centimetres square. She glances at the clock on the kitchen wall. Too late to start now. Tomorrow. Tomorrow.

The next day, and in the days that follow, Sophie scours the apartment from top to bottom, leaving no trace of her movements. She suffers vicious waves of nausea. Ever since she began to force herself to vomit up the various medications Frantz gives her (this one for migraine, this one to help her sleep, this one to keep her calm, "don't worry, they're just herbal remedies . . ."), she finds herself retching and just has time to run to the bathroom. Her insides are churned up. Despite all this, she searches, she probes, she turns the apartment upside down: nothing. Nothing but this solitary photograph, but that in itself is something major.

It leads her to other questions which date from much earlier. Sophie racks her brain for hours on end, looking for answers that never come. Sometimes she is literally blazing, as though truth is a flame she cannot quench, that burns her hands.

Then, without warning, it comes to her. It is not a revelation, more an intuition, a bolt from the blue. She stares at her mobile on the living-room table. Calmly she picks it up, removes the back, takes out the battery. With the point of a kitchen knife, she unscrews a circuit board and discovers a tiny orange microchip stuck on with double-sided tape. She removes it using tweezers. With a magnifying glass, she manages to make out a code, a string of letters, some numbers: SERV.0879, then: AH68-(REV 2.4).

A few minutes later, Google has led her to an American electronics website, to the page for the AH68 which it lists as a "G.P.S. Tracker".

"Where were you?" Frantz asks her, panicked. "Four hours! Can you believe it?" He says it over and over as though he himself does not believe it.

Four hours.

Just enough time for Sophie to leave the house, take the bus the eighteen kilometres to Villefranche, order a coffee in a café, hide her mobile in the toilets before leaving and going upstairs to the restaurant above the Marché Villiers, which offers panoramic views of the city, of the street, and of the café past which, less than an hour later, a cautious but plainly anxious Frantz rides slowly on his motorbike.

Of everything Sophie told Valérie last night, this is what she remembers most: the man she married in order to escape her nightmare is her torturer. This man she sleeps next to every night, who climbs on top of her. This time, Valérie's tears encounter no barrier, they trickle silently down her face and fall into Sophie's hair.

M. Auverney, wearing blue overalls and work gloves, is stripping the paint off his gate. For two days, Frantz has been watching his every move, monitoring his comings and goings, but he has nothing to compare them to, he cannot tell whether there has been any change in the man's routine. He has kept a close watch on the house for any sign of life when the man is away. Nothing stirs. The man seems to be alone. On a number of occasions Frantz followed him when he went out. Auverney drives a large, metallic grey Volkswagen. Yesterday he went to the supermarket, then filled up with petrol. This morning, he went to the post office and then spent about an hour at the *préfecture* before heading home via the garden centre, where he bought bags of compost which he has still not unloaded. The car is parked in front of a shed that serves as a garage. It has two very wide doors, one of which would offer more than enough space for the car to drive in. Frantz forces himself to ward off his nagging doubts: after two days, it seems pointless to carry on waiting and more than once he has considered changing tactics. But whichever way he looks at the problem, this is the only place where Sophie can be. At about 6.00 p.m., Auverney seals the tin of paint stripper and goes to wash his hands at the outside tap. He opens the boot of his car to unload the compost but, remembering their weight, he changes his mind and drives the car into the shed to unload them.

Frantz scans the sky. It is clear for the moment, and his hiding place is safe.

Once he had reversed into the shed and opened the car boot for the second time, Patrick Auverney looked at his daughter, who had been curled up behind the bags for the past five hours, and he came within a whisker of speaking to her. But Sophie has already raised her hand in warning and is staring at him authoritatively: he said nothing. When she crawled out, she did a few stretches to ease her aching limbs, but already she was scanning the shed. Then she turned to her father. She has always thought him handsome. He cannot bring himself to admit that she is scarcely recognisable. Haggard, drawn. There are purple rings around her glittering, feverish eyes. Her skin is the colour of parchment. He is upset, and she understands this. She pressed herself against him, closing her eyes and sobbing in silence. They stood like this for a moment. Then Sophie took a step back and, smiling through her tears, fumbled for a handkerchief. He offered her his. She has always thought he was strong. She took a sheet of paper from the back pocket of her jeans. Her father took his reading glasses from his shirt pocket and began to read attentively. From time to time, he pauses and looks up at her, shocked. He looks at the bandages on her wrists: it makes him feel ill. He shakes his head as if to say, "It's not possible." When he has finished reading, he makes the thumbs up sign mentioned in the document. They smile at each other. He puts away his glasses, straightens his clothes, takes a deep breath and leaves the shed to work in the garden.

When Auverney emerged from the shed, he moved the garden seat and the table into the shade, then he went into the house. Through the binoculars, Frantz saw him walking through the kitchen and into the living room. He re-emerged a few minutes later with his laptop and two cardboard folders stuffed with files, and settled himself at the garden table to work. He rarely consults his notes. He types quickly. From his vantage point, Frantz can see only his back. From time to time Auverney takes out a map, unfolds it, checks a figure, scribbles rapid calculations on the cover of the folder. Patrick Auverney is a serious man.

The scene is excruciatingly static. Any other sentry would be caught off guard, but not Frantz. No matter the time, he will not leave his post until long after the last light in the house has been turned off.

*

p.auverney@neuville.fr has just logged on
You there?

souris_verte@msn.fr has just logged on
Papa? I'm here.

Phew!

Pls don't forget: you need to look natural, check your notes, act like a professional …

I am a professional!

You're a professional Papa.

Are you alright????

Don't worry.

Are you kidding?

I mean: don't worry anymore. I'll be fine.

You gave me a hell of a fright.

I gave myself a hell of a fright. But stop worrying, everything will be alright now. U read my mail?

Reading it now. Open in another window. But first: I love you. I miss you so much. SO MUCH. I love you.

I love you too. It's so good to see you again, BUT STOP IT NOW PLS YOU'LL HAVE ME IN TEARS!!!

OK. I'll stop for now. Until afterwards … You sure there's a point to what we're doing right now, because otherwise we look like idiots …

Read my mail: I'm SURE he's here, he'll be watching you RIGHT NOW.

It feels like acting in an empty theatre.

If it makes you feel better you have an audience of ONE. And he's riveted.

If he's here …

I KNOW he's here.

And you think he monitors EVERYTHING?

I'm living proof that he monitors everything.

Makes you think …

What?

Nothing …

Hey?

…

You there, Papa?

Yes.

You had time to think yet?

Not really …

What U doing?

Pretending to work. Reading your mail.

OK.

It's completely insane but strangely it makes me feel much
better …

What?

Everything. Seeing you, knowing you're here. Alive.

Knowing I didn't do all that stuff, go on, admit it.

Yes, that too.

You had your doubts, didn't you?

…

Hey?

Sure, I had my doubts.

I don't mind, you know, even I believed it, so why wouldn't
you …

…

Hello?

Just finishing reading.

…

OK. Done. I'm speechless.

Any questions?

Too many.

Any doubts?

Look, this is hard enough as it is …

DOUBTS?

Yes, alright, of course I have fucking doubts.

That's why I love you. Let's start with the doubts.

This thing about the keys …

You're right, that's where it all starts. July 2000, a guy on a motorbike snatches my bag from my car at a traffic light. Two days later the police return the bag, long enough for him to get copies of all the keys: apartment, car … He could come in, take stuff, move things around, access e-mail, ANYTHING, absolutely ANYTHING.

And that's when your … problems started?

About then. At the time I was taking a herbal remedy to sleep. No idea what he put in it, but think it's what he's been giving me ever since. After Vincent's death I got the job with Mme Gervais. The cleaning lady lost her keys a couple of days after I started, looked for them everywhere, she was totally panicked and afraid to talk to Mme Gervais. Then miraculously they turn up over the weekend. Same set-up … I reckon he used them to come in and kill Léo.

Possible … And the guy on the motorbike?

GUYS on motorbikes, plural, there have been loads of them. The one who stole my bag, the guy who was following Vincent and me, the one Vincent knocked down who ran off, the one I tricked by hiding my phone in the toilet of the café in Villefranche …

OK, OK. The pieces fit, it all sounds plausible. Why haven't you gone to the police yet?

…

You've got proof, haven't you?

I'm not going to the police.

???? What more evidence do you need?

It's not enough.

??

Let's say it's not enough for me.

You're being stupid!

It's my life.

OK then, I'll call them.

Papa! I'm Sophie Duguet, I'm wanted for AT LEAST three murders!! If the police find me now, I'll be banged up. For life! You really think the cops will take my theories seriously unless I have HARD EVIDENCE??

But … you've got evidence …

No, everything I have is circumstantial, it all depends on the theory that it began with a minor incident, which won't count for much against three murders, including the murder of a six-year-old boy!

OK, fine. For the moment … Another thing: how can you know that this guy is YOUR Frantz?

He met me through a dating agency where I was registered as Marianne Leblanc (the name on the birth cert I bought).

He never knew me under any other name.

So ...?

So explain to me why, when I slit my wrists, he started screaming and calling me "Sophie"???

OK, I get it ... But why cut your wrists???????

Papa, I'd managed to escape once before and he caught me at the station. After that, he was with me day and night. When he went out, he locked me in. For days I managed not to take the stuff he was giving me and the migraines, the panic attacks, they all went away. What option did I have? I had to find a way out: a hospital was the one place he couldn't watch me twenty-four hours a day.

But it could have gone horribly wrong ...

No, it couldn't. The cuts I made looked serious, but they were minor. Not enough to kill someone. Besides, he would never have let me die. He wants to kill me himself. That's what he's always wanted.

...

You still there?

Yes, yes, I'm here. I'm trying to think straight but the problem is I'm so angry, so fucking furious. I can feel a terrible rage boiling up inside me.

Me too. But anger is no good against this guy. With him, it'll take something else.

What??

...

WHAT??!!

He's intelligent, it will take cunning …

?? What the hell are you planning to do now??

Not sure yet, but one way or the other, I have to go back.

Hang on, that's CRAZY!! There's no way I'm letting you go back there, it's OUT OF THE QUESTION!

I thought you'd say that …

You are not going back with him and that's that.

So you're saying I'm on my own again?

What?

I'm asking whether I'm going to be on my own again. Let's be clear: this is the help you're prepared to offer me? Your sympathy and your anger? DO YOU KNOW WHAT HE'S PUT ME THROUGH???? Have you any idea? Vincent is dead, Papa! He killed Vincent! He destroyed my life, he killed … everything. And you're saying I'm on my own again?

Listen, my little mouse …

Don't give me that little mouse shit! I'M RIGHT HERE! Are you going to fucking help me or not?

…

…

I love you. I'll help you.

Oh, Papa, I'm so tired …

Stay for a while, get some rest.

I have to go. And that's where you can help me, OK?

Of course … but that still leaves one major question …

??

Why has he done all this? Do you know this guy? Did you know him in the past?

No.

He's got the money, he's got the time, he's got a pathological determination … but why YOU?

That's why I'm here, Papa. You've still got maman's files, haven't you?

???

I think that's where the answer is, Maybe he was one of the patients maman treated. Him, or someone close to him. I don't know.

I've got a couple of folders, I think. In a box, somewhere … I never opened them.

Well, now might be the time.

Frantz slept in the rental car. Four hours in the supermarket car park the first night, four hours in the bus station car park the second. A thousand times he has regretted his strategy, a thousand times he has thought of turning back, but each time he has stuck it out. He needs to keep a cool head, that is all. Sophie has nowhere else to go. She is bound to come here. She is a wanted criminal, she cannot go to the police, she will go home or she will come here, she has no choice. But still. Sitting here watching a house where nothing happens can sap your morale, doubts make their way in. It takes four years of planning and conviction to keep them at bay.

At the end of the third day, Frantz does a round trip to his apartment. He takes a shower, changes his clothes, sleeps for four hours. While he is there, he picks up various things he needs (flask, camera, fleece jacket, Swiss army knife). By dawn, he is back at his post.

Auverney's house is a long, single-storey building like so many in the area. To the right is the laundry room and the shed in which he probably stores his garden furniture in winter. To the left, directly facing Frantz, is the large barn where he parks the car and keeps his impressive array of tools. It is a large building that could easily accommodate two more vehicles. When he is at home and intends to take the car out at some point, he leaves the right-hand door open.

This morning he appeared wearing a suit. He must have a meeting. He opened the doors to the hangar and brought out a tractor mower, the sort they use to cut grass on golf courses. It must be broken because he has to push it, and it looks as though it weighs a ton. He tucks an envelope under the seat. Someone is probably coming to pick it up during the day. Making use of the fact that both doors are open, Frantz studies the hangar – and takes several photographs. Half of it is taken up with piles of boxes, sacks of compost, battered suitcases sealed with packing tape. Auverney left the house at about 9.00 a.m. He has not come back since. It is now almost 2.00 in the afternoon. Nothing is stirring.

*

Clinical file

Sarah Berg, née Weis, born July 22, 1944.

Parents deported to Dachau, date unknown.

Marries Jonas Berg, December 4, 1964.

Gives birth to a son, Frantz, August 13, 1974.

1982 – diagnosed with Manic Depressive Psychosis (Type III: Melancholic
   depression) – Hôpital L. Pasteur

1985 – hospitalised at the Clinique du Parc (Dr Jean-Paul Roudier)

1987–88 – hospitalised at the Clinique des Rosiers (Dr Catherine Auverney)

1989 – hospitalised at the Clinique Armand Brussières (Dr Catherine
   Auverney)

June 4, 1989 – after an interview with Dr Auverney, Sarah Berg put on
   her wedding dress and threw herself from a fifth-floor window.
   Death instantaneous.

Even if he is made of stone, waiting can weaken any man. It has
now been three whole days since Sophie disappeared. Auverney
came home at 4.30. He glanced at the lawnmower and, with a hint
of resignation, picked up the envelope he had left there earlier.

At precisely that moment, Frantz's mobile rang.

At first there is a long silence. He said "Marianne . . .?" He
heard something that sounded like sobbing.

"Marianne, is that you?"

This time, there can be no doubt. Through the ragged sobs she
said:

"Frantz, where are you?"

She said:

"Come quickly."

Then, over and over, she repeated: "Where are you? Where are you?" as though not expecting a response.

I'm here, Frantz tried to say.

Then:

"I'm home," she said, her voice hoarse, exhausted. "I'm at home."

"O.K., stay where you are. Don't worry, I'm here, I'll be home soon."

"Frantz . . . Please, please come quickly."

"I'll be there in . . . about two hours. I'll leave my phone on. I'm here, Marianne, you don't have to be afraid anymore. If you start to feel scared, you call me, O.K.?"

Then, when she did not reply.

"O.K.?"

There was a long silence and then she said:

"Come quickly . . ."

And she started to cry again.

He snapped his mobile shut. He feels a huge wave of relief. She has not taken her medication for five days, but from her voice he can tell she is shattered, vulnerable. Fortunately, she does not seem to have regained her strength during her disappearance, the results of his work are intact. He needs to be vigilant, though. To find out where she has been. Frantz has already reached the fencing. He crawls under it, then breaks into a run. What if she leaves again before he gets there? He will call her every fifteen minutes on the way. He still feels vaguely worried, but mostly he feels an overwhelming relief.

Frantz races to the car, and then the floodgates burst. As he pulls away, he begins to weep like a child.

SOPHIE AND FRANTZ

When he opens the door, Sophie is sitting at the kitchen table. She looks as though she has been sitting there, motionless, for centuries. There is nothing on the table but for an overflowing ashtray; her hands are clasped and resting on the oilcloth. She is wearing clothes he has never seen before, crumpled, mismatched, they look as if they were bought in a charity shop. She turns to him very slowly, as though to do so requires a superhuman effort. He walks towards her. She tries to stand up, but cannot. She simply tilts her head to one side and says: "Frantz".

He takes her in his arms. She smells of cigarette smoke. He says:

"At least tell me you've had something to eat?"

She presses herself against him, he can feel her shake her head. He had promised himself he would not ask any questions just yet, but he cannot help himself:

"Where *were* you?"

Sophie shakes her head vaguely as she draws away from him, her eyes vacant.

"I don't know," she says, "hitching lifts here and there . . ."

"Nothing happened to you?"

She shakes her head.

Frantz pulls her to him and holds her for a long time. She has stopped crying, but she huddles in his arms like a frightened animal. Resting against him, she feels so slight. She is so thin.

He cannot help but wonder where she went, what she can have been doing all this time. She will tell him eventually, Sophie has no secrets from him. But his overriding feeling in these silent moments as they hold each other is how scared he was.

When he inherited his father's money, Frantz was convinced that he would be able to dedicate himself to dealing with Doctor Catherine Auverney, so the news that she had died some months earlier felt like a betrayal. Life itself seemed treacherous. But today, something new stirs him: the same relief he felt when he first learned of Sophie's existence and decided that she would take the place of Doctor Auverney. That she would die in her mother's stead. This is the consolation he all but lost these past days. He hugs her to him and feels a surge of happiness. He dips his head to inhale the scent of her hair. She draws back slightly, looks up at him. Her eyelids are swollen, her face grubby. But she is beautiful. Undeniably beautiful. He bends down and suddenly the truth is laid bare to him in all its simplicity: he loves her. It is not this that he finds most striking, he has long known that he loves her. No, what he finds profoundly affecting is the fact that, by dint of caring for her for so long, working, directing, guiding, moulding, her face now looks exactly like Sarah's. Towards the end of her life, Sarah had these sunken cheeks, the greyish lips, the vacant eyes, the bony shoulders, this evanescent thinness. Just as Sophie does today, Sarah would gaze at him lovingly as though he were the one and only answer to the troubles of this world, the single promise that one day she might find a glimmer of peace. This resemblance between the two women moves him deeply. Sophie is perfect. Sophie is an exorcism, she will die a beautiful death. Frantz will weep copious tears. He will miss her terribly. Terribly. And he will be genuinely desolate to be cured without her.

Sophie could go on looking up at Frantz through this gauzy veil of tears, but she knows that tears have only a temporary effect. It is difficult to know what is going on inside his mind. So she stays there, motionless, allows things to take their course. She waits. He holds her by the shoulders, pressing her against him and in that precise moment, she feels something in him weaken, crumble, melt, though she does not know what. He hugs her and she begins to feel afraid because his eyes are frozen in a strange, fixed stare. She can almost see the thoughts teeming in his brain. She does not take her eyes off him, as though attempting to paralyse him. She swallows hard and says, "Frantz . . ." She purses her lips and he bends down to meet them. The kiss is tense, restrained, though there is something voracious about his mouth. Something urgent. And something hard in his groin. Sophie concentrates. She wishes she could calculate without factoring in her fear, but it is impossible. She feels caught, captive. He is physically powerful. She is afraid of dying. So she hugs him to her, grinds her pelvis against him, feels him grow harder and this reassures her. She lays her cheek against him and stares at the ground. She can breathe. She relaxes each of her muscles, one by one, and her body gradually melts in Frantz's arms. He lifts her up. He carries her into the bedroom and lays her down. She could fall asleep now. She hears him move away, go into the kitchen, she briefly opens her eyes then closes them again. She hears the familiar sounds of a teaspoon knocking against a glass. Senses him looming over her again. He says: "You should get some sleep now, get some rest." He holds her head and slowly she swallows the liquid. He always adds a lot of sugar to mask the taste. He goes back into the kitchen. Immediately she rolls onto her side, pulls back the sheet and pushes two fingers down her throat. She retches, vomits up the liquid, feels her stomach lurch then draws the sheet over the stain and rolls back. He is there already. He runs his hand over her brow. "Sleep tight," he says in a whisper. He presses his mouth against her lips. He admires her beautiful face. He loves it now. This face is his possession. He has already begun to dread the moment when she is no longer here.

"The *gendarmes* came round."

Sophie did not think of this. The *gendarmes*. Her face immediately betrays her terror. Frantz knows how much the real Sophie has to fear from the police. Play his cards right.

"The clinic had to contact them, obviously," he says, "so they came here."

He revels for a moment in Sophie's panic, then takes her in his arms.

"I took care of everything, don't worry. I didn't want them out looking for you. I knew you would come back."

In all these months she has managed to have no contact with the police. Now, here, she is caught in the net. Sophie takes a deep breath, tries to gather her thoughts. Frantz will have to get her out of this. Their interests coincide. Play her cards right.

"You need to go in and sign some papers. Just to say that you're back . . . I told them you were in Besançon. With family. We should probably get it over with as soon as possible."

Sophie shakes her head, murmurs "no". Frantz hugs her a little harder.

The reception area of the police station is plastered with faded posters showing blown-up identity cards, offering safety advice, emergency numbers for every situation. The *gendarme* Jondrette looks at Sophie with good-natured detachment. He would like to have a wife like this. Sickly. It must make a husband feel useful. His gaze shifts from Sophie to Frantz. Then he taps the desk in front of him. His fat fingers draw their attention to a form.

"So you thought you'd run away from hospital."

This is his way of being tactful. In front of him is a woman who tried to kill herself and he can think of nothing else to say. Instinctively, Sophie realises that she needs to pander to his idea of masculine power. She lowers her eyes. Frantz puts an arm around her shoulder. A handsome couple.

"And you were in . . ."

"Besançon," Sophie says in a hushed whisper.

"That's right, Besançon. That's what your husband told me. With family."

Sophie changes tactics. She looks up and stares at Jondrette. He may be a little rustic, but he can sense things. And what he senses is that this Mme Berg is a character.

"A good thing, family," he says. "I mean, at times like this, it can be a good thing."

"I believe my wife is supposed to sign something?" Frantz's voice interrupts this rather oblique conversation and brings them back to earth. Jondrette snorts.

"Yes. Right here."

He turns the form around for Sophie. She looks for a pen.

Jondrette hands her a biro bearing the logo of a petrol station. Sophie signs. *Berg.*

"Everything will be alright now," Jondrette says.

Difficult to know whether this is a question or a statement.

"It'll be fine," Frantz says.

The good husband. Jondrette watches the couple, arm in arm, as they leave the station. Must be good, to have a wife like that. Then again it must come with a shitload of bother.

This is something she painstakingly learned, the even breathing of the sleeper. It demands great concentration, ceaseless attention, but she is now a skilled deceiver. So much so that twenty minutes later, when he comes to check on her, he is convinced. He caresses her through her clothing, lies on top of her and buries his face in the pillow. Her body utterly limp, she opens her eyes and stares at his shoulder, she feels him fumble with her clothes then penetrate her. She almost smiles.

Sophie has slipped into a phase of sleep that means he can allow himself a brief respite from his vigilance. This time, in the excitement of the moment, the joy of being reunited, he was a little heavy-handed with the sleeping pills: she is sleeping deeply in the bedroom. He watches over her for a long time, listens to her breathing, noting the fleeting expressions that flutter across her face, then he gets to his feet, leaves the apartment, locking the door behind him, and goes down to the cellar.

He considers the state of his plans and, realising that they will be of no use, he decides to erase the digital photographs of Sophie's father's house. He scans through them on his camera, deleting them as he goes. The house, close-ups of the windows, the car, Auverney coming out of the front door, leaving the envelope on the mower, Auverney working at the garden table, stripping paint from the gate, unloading the bags of compost. It is 2.00 a.m. He takes a U.S.B. cable and connects the camera to his computer so he can download some of the images and study one or two properly before deleting them. He chooses four. In the first, Auverney is walking in his garden. Frantz kept this one because Auverney's face is clearly visible. For a man of sixty, he is in fine fettle. Square jawed, spirited, keen-eyed. Frantz adjusts the resolution to 80%. Intelligent. To 100%. Cunning. The sort of man who could be a threat. It must be a genetic trait, since it is her cunning that has kept Sophie alive. The second photograph shows Auverney working at the garden table. He is in three-quarter profile. Frantz zooms in on a small section, the corner of the computer screen. The result is blurred. He launches his photo-editing software and applies a filter to sharpen the image. He can make out the tool bar of what seems to be a word-processing programme, but the text itself is a blur. He drags the image into the trash. The third photograph was taken on his last day. Auverney is wearing a suit, walking towards the tractor mower to leave the envelope probably intended for the repair man. It is impossible to decipher what is written on the envelope, but it is not important. The last picture was taken at the very end of his stake-out. Auverney had left the front door wide open. Frantz scans the interior which he has previously seen only through his binoculars: a large, round table with a low-hanging ceiling lamp, at the far end of the room a hi-fi is set into a shelving unit that holds an impressive number of C.D.s. Frantz drags the picture to the trash. As he is about to shut down the photo-editing software, one final thing occurs to him. He takes the photograph of the shed from the trash, reopens it and zooms in on an area in shadow: boxes, sacks of compost, gardening implements, tool boxes, suitcases. The door casts a shadow across the stack of boxes; those at the top are in darkness, while those at the bottom are still visible. Zoom 120%. 140%. Frantz tries to decipher what is scrawled on the side of a box in black marker pen. He applies a sharpening filter, adjusts the contrast, zooms in a little more. On the first line, an A, a V, and at the end an S. On the next line a word that begins with D, then a C, a O, then something that begins AUV, so obviously "Auverney". The last line clearly reads "H–L". The box is at the bottom of the stack. The one at the top is bisected by shadow. The lower part is legible, the upper part obscured. But what little he can see roots him to the spot. Frantz sits, dumbfounded, as he tries to process the significance of what is on the screen. He is looking at the case files of Doctor Auverney.

His mother's medical file is in one of those boxes.

The key turns in the front door. She is alone. Sophie immediately gets up from the bed and hurries to the wardrobe, stands on tiptoe, takes the spare key and unlocks the door, her every muscle tensed. She listens as Frantz's footsteps echo in the stairwell. She runs back to the window, but she does not see him emerge from the building. Unless he took the side exit past the rubbish bins. She slips on a pair of flat shoes, silently closes the door behind her, and pads down the stairs. There are no televisions blaring in this part of the building. Sophie controls her breathing, she pauses when she reaches the ground floor, glances around her. This is the only other door. She opens it slowly, praying that it will not creak. At the foot of the flight of steps she can just make out a faint glow.

She listens, but she can hear only her heart beating, her temples pounding. She creeps down the steps. The glow is coming from one of the cellars to her right. At the far end of the passageway, a door stands ajar. She does not need to go any further, in fact it would be dangerous. Frantz's keyring has three keys. This, then, is what the third key is for. Sophie noiselessly goes back up the stairs. She will wait for the right opportunity.

From the taste – much more bitter than usual – she can tell it is a massive dose. Fortunately, by now Sophie is organised. Next to the bed she leaves a pile of crumpled tissues into which she can spit out the medicine. She replenishes the tissues each time she goes to the toilet. It does not always work. Yesterday, Frantz lingered too long, refusing to leave her side even for a second. She felt the liquid insidiously slipping down her throat. Fearing it might make her cough – something he would certainly find suspicious – she decided she would have to swallow, turning as she did though sleeping fitfully. A few minutes later, she felt her limbs grow numb, her muscles become slack. It reminded her of the last moments before an operation when the anaesthetist asks you to count to five.

On that particular occasion, her strategy failed, but she has a sophisticated system and, in the right circumstances, all goes well. She has found a way to keep the medication in her mouth as she swallows saliva. If Frantz walks away in the minutes that follow, she rolls onto her side, takes the pile of tissues and spits the liquid out again. If she has to hold it in her mouth for too long, it is absorbed through the mucous membrane and mingles with her saliva. Even on those rare occasions when she is forced to swallow, there is always the possibility she can make herself throw up, though she has only minutes to spare before the effects take hold. This time, everything went well. A few minutes after spitting out the drug, she feigns the even breathing of deep sleep and when Frantz comes and bends over her, begins to stroke her, to whisper to her, she shakes her head as though to shake off his words. She moves restlessly, gently at first, then quickly becomes more agitated, thrashing and writhing, sometimes even jack-knifing her body when she wants to give the impression of convulsing in her nightmare. Frantz follows his own ritual. He begins by leaning over her, speaking softly, stroking her hair, trailing his fingers over her lips, her throat, but later all his passion is channelled through his words.

Frantz whispers to her, watches over her. What he says depends on whether he is trying to frighten or to calm her. But in all of his speeches, he summons up the dead. Tonight, it is Véronique Fabre. Sophie remembers it clearly: the sofa on which she was sprawled, the body of the young woman lying in a pool of blood. The kitchen knife Frantz must have placed in her hand.

"What happened, Sophie?" Frantz says, "A fit of rage? That's right, isn't it, a fit of rage . . ."

Sophie squirms as though trying to escape him.

"You can still see her, can't you? Picture her now. She is wearing a grey trouser suit, it's rather drab. All you can see is the white collar of her blouse, the base of her throat. Can you see her? Good. She is wearing flat shoes."

Frantz's voice is grave, he speaks unhurriedly.

"I was worried, you know, Sophie. You were at her place for almost two hours. I was waiting for you outside . . ."

Sophie gives a little moan, jerks her head fearfully. Her hands flutter over the sheet.

". . . then I see this woman running to the pharmacy down the street. I follow her inside and overhear her tell the pharmacists she's not feeling well . . . Surely you can imagine how worried I was, my angel?"

Sophie rolls over, trying to get away from the voice. Frantz walks around the bed, kneels and continues to whisper into her other ear.

"I didn't leave her time to help you. As soon as she went inside, I rang the bell. When she opened the door she was still holding the bag she'd got at the pharmacy. Behind her, I could see you, my angel, my Sophie, you were lying on the sofa, in such a deep, deep sleep, just like today. When I saw you, all my worry melted away. You were so pretty, you know. So pretty."

Frantz runs his index finger over Sophie's lips, she cannot help but flinch. To throw him off the scent she blinks rapidly, twitches her mouth.

"I did exactly what you would have done, my little Sophie. But first, I stunned her. Nothing savage, she fell to her knees just long enough for me to take the few steps to the table and pick up the kitchen knife. She looked surprised, and terrified, obviously. It's understandable, it was a lot for her to take in. Don't toss and turn like that, my angel. I'm here beside you, nothing can hurt you."

Sophie jerks her body again, rolls over. She brings up her hands as though to stop her ears, but she cannot remember how, her movements haphazard, futile.

"I did just as you would have done. You would have come close to her, wouldn't you? Do you remember her eyes? Those soulful eyes? You would have given her no time, you would have stared into those eyes and, with a powerful thrust, buried the knife in her belly. Can you feel it in your arm, Sophie? That wrench as you plunge the knife into her stomach. Let me show you . . ."

Frantz crouches over her and gently takes her wrist. She tries to resist, but he already has a firm grasp and as he says the words again, she feels a jerk as he forcibly tugs at her hand, slashing at the air until it meets a supple resistance.

"That's what it feels like, Sophie, you thrust the knife in, a single stab, and you twist it, deep in the wound."

Sophie opens her mouth to scream.

"See Véronique's face. See her suffer, see the pain you have caused her. Her whole belly is on fire, you see her eyes grow wide, her mouth gape in horror but still you push the knife deep into her belly. You are cold-blooded, Sophie. She screams. So, to shut her up, you remove the knife – slick with her blood now – and you plunge it in a second time. Sophie, you have to stop!"

But even as he says this, Frantz continues to force Sophie's hand to stab at the empty air. With her free hand Sophie grabs her wrist, but Frantz is too strong, she is howling now, thrashing and writhing, she tries to raise her knees but it is no good, it is like a child trying to grapple with an adult.

"Is there nothing that can stop you?" Frantz says. "Once, twice, and again and again and again, you slash at her stomach, again and again and in a little while you will wake up with the knife in your hand and Véronique lying in a pool of blood beside you. How can anyone do such a thing, Sophie? How can you go on living knowing you are capable of such things?"

For several days now, thanks to an explosive cocktail of vitamin C, caffeine and glucuronamide, Sophie has managed to sleep for only a few short hours. Frantz sleeps soundly. Sophie watches him. The man has a determined face and, even in sleep, he radiates a powerful, obdurate energy. His breathing, usually shallow and regular, is more erratic now. He moans in his sleep as though having trouble breathing. Sophie is naked, she feels a little cold. She folds her arms and looks at him. Dispassionately, she despises him. She goes into the kitchen where a door opens onto a small space that, for some inexplicable reason, people in the building refer to as an "airing cupboard". Less than two metres square, with a narrow vent – summer and winter it is cold in here – this is where people store their junk; it also houses the rubbish chute. Sophie carefully pulls out the drawer of the rubbish chute, reaches her hand into the shaft and pulls out a plastic bag which she swiftly opens. She sets a syringe and a small vial of colourless liquid on the table. She replaces the rest in the plastic bag and stows it back in the chute. Then, as a precaution, she takes a few steps towards the bedroom. Frantz is still asleep, snoring quietly. Sophie opens the fridge, takes out the four-pack of Frantz's probiotic yoghurt drinks. The needle slides easily through the pliant lids, leaving only a tiny hole in the foil. Having injected a dose into each one, Sophie shakes the pack to mix it in and replaces it in the fridge. A few minutes later, she has returned the plastic bag to its hiding place and is slipping into bed. The very touch of Frantz's body disgusts her intensely. She could cheerfully kill him in his sleep. With a kitchen knife, for example.

By his reckoning, Sophie should sleep for about ten hours. This will be more than long enough if all goes well. If it does not, he may have to try again later, but he is so excited by his plan that he does not contemplate the possibility of failure. In the dead of night, it takes two hours to drive to Neuville-Sainte-Marie.

Rain has been forecast. This makes it ideal. He parks the

motorbike at the edge of the woods, as close as he dares in other words. A few minutes later, two welcome discoveries greet him when he sees the Auverney house in darkness and hears the first raindrops splatter on the ground. He sets his sports bag at his feet, quickly peels off his leathers under which he is wearing a tracksuit. Having pulled on a pair of trainers and zipped up the bag, Frantz heads down the small hill that separates the woodland from Auverney's garden. He leaps over the railing. He knows there is no guard dog. Just as he comes to the door of the hangar, he sees a light go on in an upstairs room. It is Auverney's bedroom. He presses himself against the door. Unless he goes downstairs and comes outside, Auverney cannot possibly see him. Frantz checks his watch. It is almost 1.00 a.m. He has plenty of time, but he is also very impatient, precisely the state of mind that can lead to mistakes being made. He takes a deep breath. The bedroom window casts a rectangle of light that pierces the fine drizzle and falls onto the lawn. He sees a figure pass through it. On the nights Frantz was keeping watch, Auverney did not seem to suffer from insomnia, but you never know. Frantz folds his arms, stares at the rain streaking the darkness and prepares himself for a long wait.

When she was a child, she found nights when there was a storm exhilarating. She throws the windows wide and inhales the cool air that chills her lungs. She needs it. She did not manage to spit out all the medication Frantz gave her and is reeling a little, her head heavy. It will not last, but just now she is beginning to feel the soporific effects, and tonight the dose was particularly strong. That Frantz increased the dose must mean he is planning to be out for some time. He left at about 11 p.m. Sophie is sure he will not be back before 3.00 or 4.00 a.m. To be on the safe side she settles on 2.30. Steadying herself on the furniture, she makes her way to the bathroom and opens the door. It has become routine now. She pulls off her T-shirt, steps into the bath, takes a deep breath and turns the shower on cold. She lets out a hoarse, determined cry, forces herself to carry on breathing. A few seconds later, she is cold and rubbing herself down with a towel which she then hangs up in front of the vent in the airing cupboard. She makes herself a cup of strong tea (unlike coffee, it leaves no odour) and while she waits for it to infuse she exercises her arms, her legs, does a few press-ups to get her blood flowing and gradually feels her energy restored. She sips the scalding tea, then washes and dries the cup. She steps back and studies the kitchen to make sure she has left no trace of her presence. She stands on a chair, pushes up one of the ceiling tiles, and takes down a small, flat key. Before going down to the cellar, she changes her shoes and pulls on a pair of latex gloves. Gently closing the door behind her, she pads down the stairs.

The rain has not let up. In the distance, there is the muffled roar of trucks on the main road. Marking time here on these few square centimetres, Frantz is starting to feel the cold. It is just as he sneezes for the first time that the bedroom light goes out. It is precisely 1.44. Frantz gives himself twenty minutes. He returns to his lookout post and wonders whether he will need to go to a doctor. The first crash of thunder rumbles in the distance, a flash of lightning rips across the sky illuminating for a fleeting second the whole property.

At 2.05, Frantz leaves his post, walks slowly along the side of the building and tests the frame of a small window at head height through which, by the light of his torch, he can clearly see inside.

The window frame is ancient, the wood swollen from many winters. Frantz takes out his tool kit then places one hand in the centre of the glass to test the resistance, but hardly has he touched it than the window flies inwards and slams against the wall. In the deafening roar of the storm, it is not likely that the sound would be heard upstairs in the house. He snaps shut his tool kit and sets it carefully on the ledge, hoists himself onto the sill and drops lightly down on the other side. It is a dusty concrete floor. He takes his shoes off, careful to leave no footprints. A few seconds later, torch in hand, he is moving towards the stacks of boxes containing Doctor Auverney's case files. It takes less than five minutes to extricate the box marked "A–G". He cannot contain the excitement, it is causing him to lose his composure and he has to force himself to take long, slow breaths and allow his arms to hang limply by his sides.

The boxes are extremely heavy. Each is sealed with a length of packing tape. Frantz turns over the one he is interested in. The bottom is simply glued together. The blade of a Stanley knife carefully inserted is enough to unstick the four corrugated cardboard flaps. This done, he finds himself faced with a pile of folders. He picks one at random: Gravetier. The name is written in block capitals in blue marker. He puts it back in the box. He takes out a sheaf of files and he can feel his salvation fast approaching: Baland, Baruk, Benard, Belais, Berg! An orange file, the name inscribed in the same handwriting. It is very thin. Frantz opens it nervously. It contains only three documents. The first is a "Clinical Assessment" concerning Berg, Sarah. The second is a simple note containing official and administrative details, the third, a hand-written, largely illegible prescription detailing a regimen of medications. He takes out the clinical assessment, folds it and tucks it into his tracksuit. He puts the file back in the box, applies a few spots of extra-strong glue to the flaps, turns it over and leaves everything as he found it. Less than fifteen minutes later he is driving back along the *autoroute*, taking care to observe the speed limit.

The moment she stepped through the door, Sophie was shaken to the core. She has come to know Frantz well, but seeing what is in the cellar . . . it is like tumbling into his subconscious mind. The walls are plastered with photographs. She feels tears spring to her eyes. She feels devastated as she catches sight of the huge, close-up photographs of Vincent, his sad, handsome face. Four years of her life are here. Her walking (where is that?), enlargements of the snapshots taken in Greece that forced her to leave Percy's in such painfully humiliating circumstances. Her coming out of a supermarket – the photograph would have been taken in 2001. There is the house in the Oise. Sophie bites her lip. She would like to scream, would like to blow up this cellar, this building, the whole world. Once more she feels violated. In another photograph, Sophie is being manhandled by a supermarket security guard. Here she is entering the police station. There are several close-ups from a time when she was still pretty. In this one, she looks ugly. It was taken in the Oise, she is in the garden, walking arm in arm with Valérie. Already she looks sad. Here she is holding little Léo by the hand. Sophie begins to weep, she cannot help it, she cannot think, all she can do is sob, her head shaking as she stares at this panoramic collage of the catastrophe that is her life. She begins to whimper, ragged sobs rise in her throat, her tears wash away the images, the cellar, her whole life. Sophie sinks to her knees, she looks up and sees a photograph of Vincent, naked, lying on top of her. It can only have been taken through the window of their apartment – how was this possible? There are close-ups of her belongings, her wallet, her bag, her contraceptive pills. Here she is with Laure Dufresne. She wails, presses her forehead to the ground and continues to weep; Frantz could turn up at any minute, but it does not matter anymore, she is ready to die.

But Sophie does not die. Eventually, she lifts her head. A fierce anger drives out her grief. She gets to her feet, roughly wipes away her tears, her black fury undiminished. Frantz could turn up at any minute, but it does not matter anymore, she is ready to kill him.

Sophie is plastered all over the walls, except for the wall on the right which has only three images. Ten, twenty, thirty prints of the same three images, framed, colour, black and white, sepia, retouched, three pictures of the same woman. Sarah Berg. This is the first time Sophie has seen her. The resemblance to Frantz is staggering: the eyes, the mouth . . . In two of the pictures, she is young – thirty or thereabouts. Pretty. Beautiful, in fact. In the third picture she is sitting on a bench beside a lawn, a weeping willow in the background. Her eyes are vacant, her expression lifeless.

Sophie blows her nose, sits down at the desk, opens the laptop and presses the power button. A few seconds later, the password prompt appears. Sophie checks the time, gives herself forty-five minutes and starts with the most obvious: sophie, sarah, Maman, jonas, auverney, catherine . . .

Forty-five minutes later, she is forced to give up.

She closes the laptop and begins to rifle through the desk drawers. She finds various objects that belong to her, including many of those in the photographs on the wall. There are still a few minutes remaining of the time she has allowed herself. Just before she leaves, she opens a ruled notepad and begins to read:

May 3, 2000
I've just seen her for the first time. Her name is Sophie. She was coming out of her apartment block. I barely caught a glimpse. She's obviously a woman in a hurry. She got into a car and sped off so fast I had difficulty keeping up on my motorbike.

CONFIDENTIAL

Dr Catherine Auverney
Clinique Armand Brussières

Attn:
Dr Sylvain Lesgle
Clinical Director
Clinique Armand Brussières

Clinical Assessment

Patient:	Sarah Berg, née Weiss
Address:	(see attached)
Born:	July 22, 1944 in Paris (XI)
Profession:	none
Died:	June 4, 1989 in Meudon (dép. 92)

Mme Sarah Berg was first admitted to a psychiatric unit in September 1982 (Hôpital Pasteur). Her case notes for the period have not been forwarded. From what we have gathered, the admission was made on the instructions of her attending physician at the insistence of her husband, Jonas Berg, although with the consent of the patient. She does not appear to have been held beyond the period of the emergency section order.

Mme Sarah Berg was admitted for a second time in 1985 by Doctor Roudier (Clinique du Parc). The patient was suffering from chronic clinical depression, an ongoing condition, symptoms of which first became apparent in the 1960s. The compulsory committal, resulting from a suicide attempt in which the patient swallowed barbiturates, lasted from March 11 until October 26.

I personally treated Sarah Berg in June 1987, when she was hospitalised for the third time (she was discharged on February 24, 1988). I would later discover that the suicide attempt, the basis for this committal, had been preceded by two earlier attempts in 1985 and 1987. The approach to treating the previous attempts – essentially through medication – were, at the time, considered effective. The state of the patient upon admission required intensive treatment as the only efficacious preventive. As a result of the aforesaid treatment, it was not until July 1987 that it became possible to engage directly with the patient.

When we did so, we determined that Sarah Berg, then forty-three years old, was a woman of keen intelligence, with a rich, complex vocabulary and an unquestionable talent for hyperbole. Her life had been severely marked by the deportation and the subsequent death of her parents in Dachau soon after she was born. The first symptoms of depressive disorder, with attendant delirium, doubtless appeared at an early age and suggest a strong sense of guilt – not uncommon in such circumstances – and serious narcissistic haemorrhagia. During our sessions, Sarah talked about her parents and frequently raised the issue of historical validation (viz. why them?). This issue clearly masks more primordial psychological issues stemming from the loss of parental love and the loss of self-esteem. It should be emphasised that Sarah is a profoundly compassionate individual, often disarming – and sometimes excessive – in her willingness to question herself. Her account of the loss of her parents is profoundly moving, and her refusal to mourn – she diverts her pain through displacement activity, obsessively researching holocaust survivors – reveals Sarah to be a woman of painful sensitivity who is at once lucid and naïve. The key psychological factor influencing her childhood was survivor guilt and the feeling of unworthiness common to orphans who unconsciously construe the "departure" of their parents to be grounds for their low self-worth.

It is impossible to dismiss the possibility that genetic factors – which fall beyond the purview of this assessment – may have contributed to Sarah Berg's illness. As a result I would strongly recommend that any offspring of the patient be monitored closely for symptoms of marked depression, morbid fixation and obsessional behaviour [. . .]

*

Frantz came home in the middle of the night. Sophie woke up when she heard the door, but she at once feigned a deep sleep. From the sound of his brisk footsteps in the apartment and the way he closed the fridge door, she could tell he was excited, he who is usually so calm. She sensed his presence in the doorway. Then he came to the bed, knelt down and stroked her hair. Despite the fact that it was late, he did not come to bed. He went back to the living room and into the kitchen. She thought she could hear the sound of rustling paper, as though he were opening an envelope. Then, silence. He did not come to bed at all that night. In the morning she found him sitting at the kitchen table, staring into space. He looked so much like the photograph of Sarah, though more forlorn. As though he had aged ten years overnight. He said nothing but simply lifted his head and looked straight through her.

"Are you not well?" Sophie said.

She put on her dressing gown. Frantz did not answer. They stayed frozen like that for a long moment. Strangely, Sophie found herself thinking that this sudden, unexpected silence was the first time they had properly communicated since they first met. She could not have explained why. Sunlight streamed through the kitchen window, splashing Frantz's feet.

"Were you out?" Sophie asked.

He looked down at his mud-spattered shoes as though they did not belong to him.

"Yes . . . I mean, no."

Clearly something was wrong. Sophie moved closer and stroked the back of his neck. She found the simple act of touching him repellent, but she held firm.

She put the kettle on.

"Would you like some tea?"

"No. I mean, yes."

A curious atmosphere. As though she were emerging from the night just as he was entering it.

His face is pale. All he can say is "I feel a bit off colour." For two days he has scarcely eaten. She suggests dairy products to settle his stomach: he eats the three pots of yoghurt she brings him, drinks some tea. The rest of the time he sits at the kitchen table and broods. She finds it frightening, this sombre air. He sits for a long time, lost in thought. Then he begins to cry. Just that. There is no sign of sadness in his face, the tears trickle down and fall onto the oilcloth. For two days.

Awkwardly he wipes away his tears, then says, "I'm sick." His voice is tremulous, weak.

"Maybe it's flu?" Sophie says.

A foolish thing to say, his tears would hardly be a symptom of flu. But it is so extraordinary for him to cry.

"Have a lie-down," she says, "I'll make you a hot drink."

He murmurs something like, "O.K., that's good," but she cannot be sure. The atmosphere is strange and unsettling. He gets up, turns, walks into the bedroom and lies down, fully clothed. She makes him his tea. This is the perfect opportunity. She glances back to make sure he is still lying there, then opens the rubbish chute.

She does not smile, but feels an intense relief. The tables have been turned. Luck has been on her side, but that is the least she could expect of it. She had planned to take control at the first sign of weakness. Now, she vows to herself, she will not let go. Till death do them part.

When she goes into the bedroom he looks at her curiously, as though she were someone he was not expecting, as though he is about to say something. But no. He says nothing. He props himself up on one elbow.

"You really should get undressed," she says, bustling about.

She plumps the pillows, smoothes the sheets. Frantz gets up and slowly undresses. He seems completely worn out. She smiles: "You look dead on your feet." Before he lies down, he takes the tea she has made for him. "It will help you sleep." Frantz begins to drink and says, "I know."

*

[…] In 1964, Sarah Weiss married Jonas Berg (born 1933), eleven years her senior. Her choice confirms that she has been searching for a symbolic father figure who might – as far as possible – compensate for the absence of her biological parents. Jonas Berg is an outgoing, imaginative man, a diligent worker with an excellent instinct for business. In 1959, making the most of the opportunities afforded by the post-war boom, Jonas Berg had set up the first chain of mini-markets in France. Fifteen years later the franchise had expanded to more than four hundred outlets, accumulating for the Berg family a substantial fortune which the prudent M. Berg managed to safeguard throughout the crisis of the 1970s and indeed increase by the acquisition of real estate, principally residential properties. He died in 1999.

Jonas Berg's steadfast strength and his unconditional love would become the bedrock of his wife's security. The first years of the marriage seem to have been marked by the gradual, initially unobtrusive, escalation of Sarah Berg's symptoms which were progressively to deteriorate and become clinical depression.

In February 1973, Sarah falls pregnant for the first time. The young couple are delighted at the news. If Jonas Berg secretly longs for a son and heir, Sarah is hoping for a daughter (destined, evidently, to become the "ideal object of atonement" and the palliative which might stem the original narcissistic flaw). This hypothesis is confirmed by the happiness of the couple during the early months of the pregnancy, and the marked alleviation of Sarah's depressive symptoms.

The second pivotal event in Sarah's life (following the death of her parents) occurred in June 1973 when she gave birth, prematurely, to a stillborn daughter. The reopening of that initial gaping wound was to cause profound and lasting damage which her second pregnancy would make irreparable. [...]

*

When she is certain that he is asleep, Sophie goes down to the cellar and fetches the notepad containing his diary. She lights a cigarette, sets the book on the kitchen table and begins to read. From the first words, everything is there, almost exactly as she imagined it. Page after page, she feels her hatred swelling to become a tight knot in her stomach. The words in Frantz's diary corroborate the photographs on the walls of the cellar. After the portraits come the names: first Vincent and Valérie . . . From time to time, Sophie glances towards the window, stubs out a cigarette and lights another. Her hatred is such that, were Frantz to enter the room right now, she could plunge a knife into his belly without a qualm. She could stab him in his sleep, it would be so easy. But it is because she hates him that she does not do it. She has various solutions. She has yet to decide on one.

Sophie takes a blanket from the wardrobe and sleeps on the sofa.

Frantz comes into the living room having slept for twelve hours straight, although even now he does not seem awake. His movements are sluggish, his face is pale. He looks at the sofa where Sophie has left the blanket. He does not say anything. He simply looks at her.

"Would you like something to eat?" she says. "Do you want me to call a doctor?"

He shakes his head but she is not sure whether this refers to eating or to the doctor. Possibly both.

"If it's the flu, it will sort itself out," he says, his voice toneless.

He slumps rather than sits opposite her. He lays his hands on the table in front of him, like objects.

"You really should eat something," Sophie says.

Frantz shrugs. To signal he does not care.

He says, "Whatever you want . . ."

She gets up, goes into the kitchen, puts a frozen meal into the microwave and lights another cigarette while she waits for the timer. Frantz does not smoke, usually he finds the smell irritating, but he is so weak he does not even seem to notice that she is stubbing out cigarettes in the breakfast bowls. Usually he is extremely fastidious.

Frantz turns away from the kitchen. When the meal is ready, she spoons half of it onto a plate, checks that Frantz has not moved and then stirs the sleeping tablet into the tomato sauce.

Frantz tastes it, looks up at her. The silence makes her uncomfortable.

"It's nice," he says, eventually.

He eats the pasta, pauses for a second, then tastes the sauce.

"Is there any bread?" he says.

She gets up again and brings him a plastic bag containing a couple of slices. He starts to mop up the sauce. He eats the bread without savouring it, mechanically, conscientiously, until it is all gone.

"What exactly is wrong?" Sophie says. "Have you got a pain somewhere?"

He gestures vaguely towards his chest. His eyes are puffy.

"A hot drink will do you good."

She goes to the kitchen and makes the tea. When she comes back she can see that he is tearful again. He sips the tea, but after a while he gives up, sets down the cup and struggles to his feet. He goes to the bathroom, then back to bed. Leaning against the doorframe, Sophie watches him. It is 3.00 p.m.

"I'm just going to do some shopping," she says.

He has never allowed her to go out alone. But this time, Frantz opens his eyes, looks at her, his whole body seems overcome by fatigue. By the time Sophie has put her coat on, he is asleep.

*

[...] By February 1974, Sarah is pregnant again. Given the profound depression she suffered during this period, the pregnancy seems fraught

295

with symbolism since this second child is conceived exactly a year after the first. Sarah is plagued by baseless fears born of magical thinking ("This child has killed my daughter to take her place"), bouts of self-recrimination (she killed her daughter just as she killed her mother), and feelings of worthlessness (she considers herself an "unfit mother" and incapable of giving birth to a healthy child).

The pregnancy, which proves to be an ordeal for the couple, and for Sarah in particular a time of immense suffering, is punctuated by a number of incidents only some of which can be treated with therapy. Unbeknownst to her husband, Sarah attempted on several occasions to provoke a miscarriage. It is useful to compare Sarah's intense psychological need to abort the child to the self-harm she inflicts on herself at the time. The period is marked by two suicide attempts, symptoms of a refusal to accept the pregnancy on the part of a young woman who sees her unborn child – and she is convinced it is a boy – as an intruder, as "unrelated to her", a being she increasingly considers to be wicked, even diabolical. Miraculously, the pregnancy reaches full term, and on August 13, 1974 a son is born, whom they name Frantz.

As a symbolic substitute, the child will overshadow her grief for her parents and potentiate Sarah's violent hatred, which frequently manifests itself. The first such manifestation takes the form of a mausoleum which Sarah constructs during the first months of her son's life to the memory of her stillborn daughter. The occult, mystical nature of the "black masses" she purports to celebrate in secret during this period provides proof, if proof were needed, of the metaphorical aspect of her subconscious entreaty: by her own admission, she appeals to her "dead daughter who is in heaven" to cast her living son "into the flames of hell". [...]

*

For the first time in weeks, Sophie goes out to do the shopping. Before she leaves, she looks at herself in the mirror and thinks she looks ugly, but she enjoys being out in the street. She feels free. She could go away. And she will do just that, she thinks, when everything is settled. She carries the grocery bags upstairs. There is food enough for several days. But she knows she will not need it all.

He is asleep. Sophie sits on a chair by the bed. She looks at him. She does not read, or talk, she does not move. Their roles are reversed. It is hard to believe. Can it really be so easy? Why now? Why has Frantz crumbled all of a sudden? He seems a broken man. He has nightmares. He tosses in his sleep. She observes him as she might an insect. He sobs. Her hatred of him is so all-consuming that there are times when she can feel nothing else. At such moments, Frantz becomes an idea. A concept. She will kill him. She is killing him already.

Inexplicably, just as she is thinking this, Frantz opens his eyes. As though she had flicked a switch. He stares at Sophie. How can he be awake after the dose she has just given him? Perhaps she made a mistake. He reaches out, grasps her wrist firmly. She sits back in the chair. He continues to stare at her, to grip her hard, he has not said a word. Then he says, "Are you there?" She swallows hard. "Yes," she whispers. Then, as though this were simply a brief parenthesis, Frantz shuts his eyes again. But he is not asleep. He is crying. His eyes are closed, but tears trickle down his neck. Sophie waits a while longer. Frantz angrily turns to the wall. His shoulders are racked with sobs. A few minutes later, his breathing slows. He begins to snore.

She gets up, goes to sit at the table in the living room and reopens his notebook.

The gruesome key to all the mysteries. Frantz's diary describes his room in the building opposite the apartment where she lived with Vincent. Every page is a violation, every sentence a humiliation, every word a wound. Everything she has lost is here before her, everything that was stolen from her, her life, her love, her youth. She gets to her feet and goes to watch Frantz sleep. Standing over him, she smokes a cigarette. She has only ever killed once, a manager in a fast-food restaurant, something she remembers without pity or remorse. But that was nothing. When it comes to killing the man now sleeping in this bed . . .

The overweight figure of Andrée appears in Frantz's diary. A few pages later, Vincent's mother falls down the stairs of her suburban house while Sophie is lying in a comatose sleep. She dies instantly. Andrée is thrown out of a window. Even before now, Sophie has feared for her life. But she had no idea of the extent of the horrors he has perpetrated. It leaves her gasping for air. She closes the notebook.

*

[…] It is undoubtedly thanks to the self-possession of Jonas, to his emotional and physical strength and his unquestionably positive influence over his wife that Sarah's hatred for her son did not result in a fatal accident. It should, however, be noted that the child was subjected to subtle abuse, physical and psychological, by his mother: she confesses to pinching him, slapping him, twisting his limbs, burning him, etc. but is careful that his injuries are not going to attract attention. Sarah explains that it cost her every ounce of strength not to kill this child who now embodies all her bitterness.

The presence of his father, as I have said, doubtless offered the fundamental protection which meant that the boy could survive a potentially infanticidal mother. It is precisely this vigilance on the part of the father which leads Sarah to manifest symptoms of dissociative identity disorder. In effect, at great psychological cost to herself, she manages to play a double role, that of a loving, attentive mother to a child whom she secretly wishes were dead. This secret desire manifests itself in many of her dreams in which, for example, he is doomed to take the place of her parents in Dachau. In other dreams, the little boy is emasculated, eviscerated, even crucified, or is accidentally drowned, burned or crushed to death, more often than not suffering terrible pain in which the mother finds comfort and even liberation.

To deceive those around her, and indeed the child himself, requires tireless vigilance on the part of Sarah Berg. It may well be that the very care she takes to disguise, to hide, to suppress the hatred that she feels for her son is what saps her psychological strength and finally hastens the major depressive disorder she suffers in the late 1980s.

Paradoxically, it is her own son, her (unwitting) victim, who becomes her (unwitting) killer, since it is his very existence that acts as the trigger to his mother's death. [...]

*

Twenty hours later, Frantz wakes up. His eyes are puffy. He has cried a lot in his sleep. He appears in the doorway of the bedroom while Sophie is standing at the window smoking and staring at the sky. Given the drugs he has ingested, making it this far has been an act of sheer will. Sophie definitely has the upper hand. In the past twenty-four hours, she has won the molecular war they have been waging against each other. "You're a complete hero," Sophie says coldly while Frantz staggers down the corridor to the toilet. He shivers as he walks, powerful shudders that run the length of his body. Stabbing him here, now, would be a formality. She walks to the bathroom and looks at him, sitting there. He is so weak that smashing his head in with the first blunt instrument that comes to hand would be child's play. She takes a drag on her cigarette and stares at him evenly. He looks up.

"You're crying," she says, inhaling deeply.

He smiles an awkward smile by way of answer, then, steadying himself against the wall, he struggles to his feet, stumbles through the living room and back to the bedroom. They meet again in the doorway. He cocks his head hesitantly, clinging to the door frame. He looks at this woman with her icy stare and hesitates. Then he bows his head without a word, lies down on the bed, his arms flung wide. His eyes shut.

Sophie goes back to the kitchen and takes out his diary, which she keeps hidden in the bottom drawer. She picks up where she left off. She sees Vincent's accident, his death. Now she discovers how Frantz managed to get into the clinic, how, after dinner, he went and found Vincent, pushed his wheelchair past the deserted nurses' station, opened the emergency door leading to the stone staircase. For a fraction of a second, Sophie sees Vincent's terrified face, imagines his helpless body as though it were her own. It is at this moment that she decides she is not interested in reading the rest of the diary. She closes the cover, throws open the window: she is alive.

And she is ready.

*

This time Frantz sleeps for almost six hours. He has now gone for thirty hours without eating or drinking anything, drifting in and out of his comatose sleep. Sophie begins to think that he might die here, now. By accident. An overdose. He has already consumed a dose that would have killed a lesser man. He has had terrible nightmares, Sophie has heard him sobbing in his sleep. She slept on the sofa. She also opened a bottle of wine. She went out to buy cigarettes and to do some shopping. On her return, Frantz was sitting on the bed, his head, too heavy for him to support, lolling from side to side. Sophie looks at him and smiles.

"You're ready," she says.

He gives her a clumsy smile, but he cannot manage to open his eyes. She walks towards him, pushing him with the flat of her hand. It is as though she has knocked him with her shoulder. He grips the bed, manages to remain upright, though his whole body rocks, trying frantically to keep his balance.

"You're ready at last," she says.

She places her hand on his chest and effortlessly pushes him back. He lies down. Sophie leaves the apartment, carrying a large green rubbish bag.

This is the end. Her movements now are calm, precise, determined. One phase of her life is coming to its conclusion. For the last time she looks at the photographs, then one by one she rips them off the wall and stuffs them into the bag. It takes her almost an hour. Sometimes she stops for a moment to look at one in more detail, but it is no longer as painful as it was the first time. It is like a photograph album in which she might accidentally light upon a picture she has all but forgotten. Laure Dufresne laughing. Sophie remembers her hard, cold face as she laid out the poison pen letters

Frantz had made. She should want to proclaim the truth, to make amends, to purify herself, but this life seems so remote. Sophie is weary. Relieved and remote. Here is Valérie, her arm around Sophie's shoulders, whispering something in her ear and smiling seductively. Sophie had forgotten what Andrée looked like. The girl barely registered in her life before today. In this photograph she finds her simple and sincere. She refuses to think of this body falling from the window. After this, Sophie scarcely pauses for breath. She drops all the other objects into a second rubbish bag. Seeing them again is even more upsetting than the photographs: her watch, her bag, her keys, the notebook where she wrote her reminders . . . And when everything has been packed up, she puts the laptop into the last bag. This is the first thing she throws into the skip, tossing the bags filled with other items on top. She goes back down to the cellar, locks the door and takes the bag full of papers up to the apartment.

Frantz is still sleeping, but lightly now. Out on the balcony, she sets down a large, cast-iron pot in which she begins to burn the documents, ripping out fistfuls of pages from the diary. Next come the photographs. Sometimes the flames rise so high that she has to step back and wait before she can add more fuel. Then she pensively smokes a cigarette and watches the images twitch and writhe in the flames.

When she is done, she cleans the pot. She takes a shower and packs her travel bag. She is not going to take much. The bare minimum. She needs to leave everything behind her.

*

[…] Prostration, fixity of gaze, expressions of grief, fear, sometimes terror, intricate fantasies, resignation in the face of death, overwhelming feelings of guilt, magical thinking, desire for punishment – these are just some of the symptoms that appear in the clinical assessment of Sarah in 1989, when once again she is hospitalised.

Thankfully, the trust established between Sarah and I during her previous stay here make it possible to instil a positive atmosphere designed to allay – this being our primary objective – the feelings of aversion, disgust and hatred she secretly nurtures for her son, emotions that must be all the more exhausting to sustain since she has successfully managed to hide them, at least until the most recent suicide attempt which led to her being committed. By this point, hiding behind her pretence of being a loving mother, she has spent fifteen years repressing her feelings, her visceral, almost murderous feelings towards her son. […]

*

Sophie sets down her bag next to the front door. As though she is checking out of a hotel, she makes a last tour of the apartment, tidying things away, plumping the cushion on the sofa, running a cloth over the hideous tablecloth in the kitchen, putting away the dishes. Then she opens the cupboard, takes out a cardboard box and sets it on the table in the living room. From her travel bag, she takes a bottle of pale-blue gel capsules. From the box, she takes Sarah's wedding dress, goes into the bedroom where Frantz is still sound asleep and begins to undress him. It is a difficult task, his body is heavy, almost a dead weight. She has to roll him this way and that. Eventually he is naked. One by one she lifts his legs and slips them into the dress, rolls him onto his side while she pulls it over his hips. After this, it is more difficult; Frantz is too stocky for the dress to fit over his torso and shoulders.

"Never mind," Sophie says, smiling. "Don't worry."

It takes twenty minutes before she is satisfied with the results. She has had to unpick the stitching on both sides.

"You see," she whispers, "I told you not to worry."

She steps back to gauge the effect. Frantz, draped rather than dressed in the faded wedding dress, is sitting up in bed, his back against the wall, his head lolling to one side, unconscious. His chest hair peeks out of the scooped neckline. The effect is arresting and utterly pathetic.

Sophie lights one last cigarette and leans against the doorframe.

It is time to finish this. She goes in search of a bottle of mineral water, shakes the barbiturates into her hand and in twos and threes, pushes them into Frantz's mouth, making him swallow.

"'Makes the medicine go down ...'"

Frantz coughs, he retches, but in the end he always swallows. Sophie plans to give him twelve times the lethal dose.

"It may take a little time, but it will be worth the effort."

By the time she has finished the bed has been splashed with water, but Frantz has swallowed all the pills. Sophie stands back. She gazes at this tableau which truly looks like something out of a Fellini movie.

"Just one little thing missing . . ."

She goes to her travel bag and rummages until she finds a lipstick.

"It's not quite the right colour, but, well . . ."

She outlines his lips, drawing over the edges at the top, the bottom, the sides. She takes a step back to assess the result: a clown in a wedding dress.

"Perfect."

Frantz groans, struggles and manages to open his eyes. He tries to say something but gives up. He begins to gesture fretfully, then falls back.

Without another glance, Sophie fetches her bag and leaves the apartment.

*

[…] It is about her son that Sarah talks almost exclusively during the therapy sessions: the boy's physical appearance, his intelligence, his manner, his language, his tastes. Everything is used to bolster the loathing that she feels for him. It has become necessary to take time to plan the boy's visits to the clinic, with the help of his father, who has been scarred by the events of recent years.

Indeed, it is a visit from her son that eventually triggers her suicide on June 4, 1989. In the days leading up to the visit, she vigorously expresses her desire not "to be forced to be in the same room as Frantz". She claims that she is physically incapable of playing her role for even a second more. Only through a permanent separation, she claims, can she hope to survive. The unintentional pressures of being in an institution, her own feelings of guilt, and her husband's insistence persuade her to agree to the visit, but, in the moments after her son has left the room, channelling her rage and aggression against herself, Sarah puts on her wedding dress (a symbolic tribute to the husband, and to his unstinting support) and throws herself from the fifth-floor window.

The police report issued on June 4, 1989 at 2.53 p.m. by Brigadier J. Bellerive of the Meudon *gendarmerie* is appended to Sarah Berg's file, ref. JB-GM 1807.

Dr Catherine Auverney

Sophie realises that she has not thought about the weather in a long time. It is a beautiful day. She pushes open the glass door of the building and pauses for a moment on the top step. Only five more steps before she begins a new life. This one will be her last. She sets her bag down at her feet, lights a cigarette, then changes her mind and immediately stubs it out. Before her are some thirty metres of tarmac and, beyond that, the car park. She looks at the sky, picks up her bag, walks down the steps and away from the building. Her heart is beating fast. She has trouble catching her breath, as though she has narrowly avoided an accident.

She has walked about ten metres when she hears her name being called from far above.

"Sophie!"

She turns.

Frantz calls to her from the balcony of the fifth-floor window; he is wearing the wedding dress. He has climbed over the parapet and, clutching the balustrade with his left hand, he is leaning into the void.

He sways uncertainly. He looks at her, and in a soft voice he calls:

"Sophie."

Then, with a fierce determination, he leaps like a high-diver. He flings his arms wide, he does not scream, he comes to earth right beside Sophie. The sound is horrifying, ghastly.

*

NEWS ROUNDUP

A 31-year-old man leaped to his death from a fifth-floor balcony of the Résidence des Petits-Champs yesterday. Frantz Berg lived in the building. He died instantly.

He was wearing a wedding dress that had belonged to his mother who, by curious chance, met her death in similar circumstances in 1989.

The chronic depressive chose to end his life in full view of his wife, who was just setting off to spend the weekend with her father.

An autopsy revealed he had taken sleeping pills and a considerable quantity of barbiturates. How he acquired the drugs is not known.

His wife, thirty-year-old Marianne Berg, née Leblanc, is sole heir to the Berg family fortune, her late husband being the son of Jonas Berg, who founded the supermarket chain Pointe Fixe. The business was sold to an international consortium some years ago.

*

souris_verte@msn.fr is now online
Papa?

grand_manitou@neuville.fr is now online
Hello my little mouse . . . So, have you decided?

Yes, I didn't have much time to make up my mind, but I've decided to stay as Marianne Berg. This way I avoid the paperwork, the explanations, the interviews with the media. And I get to keep the money. I'm planning a whole new life.

Well, it's your decision.

Yes.

When will I see you?

I have to get the paperwork out of the way, which will take

a day or two. Shall we meet up in Normandy as planned?

OK. I'll go via Bordeaux, it's the safest route. Having a daughter who's wanted by the police makes for a lot of complications that are beyond me at my age.

Your age! You say that as though you really are old.

Don't try to flatter me.

It's the best way of making money, flattering people.

That's true.

Hey, Papa, one thing …

Yes?

Maman's case files. You gave me everything there was, didn't you?

Yes. I thought I already explained that.

Yes. And?

And … it's just that there was nothing except for that form, the admissions slip. The one I gave you … To tell you the truth, I didn't even know it was there.

Are you sure?

…

Papa?

Yes, I'm sure. In fact, it shouldn't even have been there: your mother was working from home a few days before she went into hospital. She left behind a small box of index cards she always carried with her. I should have given it back to the clinic but I just didn't think to at the time, and then I forgot all about it. Until you brought it up …

But her files, the REAL files, the notes from her sessions, where did they all go?

…

Papa, where did they go?

Well, after your mother died I thought they'd been left with her colleagues. I don't even know what these things look like. Why do you ask?

Because I found something weird among Frantz's things. A report written by Maman.

About what?

It's about Sarah Berg. It was pretty detailed. And strange. They weren't the notes from her therapy session, it was a report to someone called Sylvain Lesgle. It's dated late 1999. I don't know where Frantz got hold of it, but for him it must have been a pretty devastating read. And that's putting it mildly.

…

You sure you've never seen it, Papa?

Absolutely.

So why haven't you asked me what was in it?

You said it was about Sarah Berg, didn't you?

I get it. I have to say, it was very unlike anything Maman would have written.

??

I read it VERY carefully and I can tell you it was anything but professional. It was headed "Clinical Assessment" (have you ever heard of one?). Sounds professional if you skim through it quickly, in fact it's not badly written, but when you read it carefully, it's complete bullshit.

...?

It's supposed to be an account of Sarah Berg, but it's full of meaningless gibberish, psychiatric words and phrases lifted straight from an encyclopaedia or some popular science book. The patient's biographical notes, aside from the stuff you can find online about her husband, are so sketchy that they could have been written by someone who'd never met her. All you'd need is a couple of facts about her to throw together that pseudo-psychobabble shit.

Oh?

It's UTTER tosh, but if you don't know much about the subject, it's convincing enough ...

...

If you want my opinion (and I could be wrong) the whole thing was made up by someone.

...

What do you think, Papa dear?

...

Cat got your tongue?

Look, the thing is, I've never really understood the way shrinks talk ... Architecture and public works, that's more my thing.

Meaning?

…

HELLO?

Well, look, my little mouse, I did my best …

Oh, Papa!

OK, OK, I admit it was all a bit cobbled together.

Tell me more!

The few details we got from the admission slip told us most of the story: Frantz had obviously spent years planning to avenge his mother's death by murdering yours. And since he couldn't do that, he transferred his hatred to you.

Obviously.

I reckoned we could use that as leverage. Hence the idea of the Clinical Assessment. I thought it might be a chink in his armour. And you needed help …

But how did Frantz find it?

You were the one who told me he was watching us the whole time. I stacked up a load of boxes supposedly containing your mother's files. Then I left the door to the hangar open just long enough… It took a bit of time to create a bunch of other files for patients with names beginning with B, then I slipped this one in especially for him. I admit that the report itself was a bit, well, rudimentary.

Rudimentary, maybe … but VERY effective. The sort of report that would break the spirit of any son, especially one who adored his mother.

Let's just say it was logical.

I can't believe it … You wrote that?!

I know, it was wrong of me.

Papa …

So, what did you do with the thing? You didn't give it to the police?

No, Papa. I didn't even keep it. What do you think I am, crazy?

Pierre Lemaitre

IRÈNE

Translated from the French by Frank Wynne

THE NOVELIST KILLS BY THE BOOK

For Commandant Camille Verhœven life is beautiful: he is happily
married and soon to become a father

HE'S ALWAYS ONE CHAPTER AHEAD

But his blissful existence is punctured by a murder of unprecedented
savagery. When he discovers the killer has form – and each murder
is a homage to a classic crime novel – the Parisian press are quick to
coin a nickname . . .

AND HE HATES HAPPY ENDINGS

With the public eye fixed on both hunter and hunted, the case
develops into a personal duel, each hell-bent on outsmarting the other.
There can only be one winner – whoever has the least to lose . . .

BOOK ONE OF THE BRIGADE CRIMINELLE TRILOGY

MACLEHOSE PRESS

www.maclehosepress.com

Subscribe to our newsletter

Pierre Lemaitre

ALEX

Translated from the French by Frank Wynne

SHE'S RUNNING OUT OF TIME

Kidnapped, savagely beaten, suspended from the ceiling of an abandoned warehouse in a wooden cage, Alex Prévost is in no position to bargain. Her abductor's only wish is to watch her die.

HE ONLY WANTS ONE THING

Apart from a shaky police report, Commandant Camille Verhœven has nothing to go on: no suspect, no leads. If he's to find Alex, he'll have to get inside her head.

BUT ESCAPE IS JUST THE BEGINNING

Beautiful, tough, resourceful, always two steps ahead – Alex will keep Verhœven guessing till the bitter end. And before long, saving her life will be the least of his worries.

BOOK TWO OF THE BRIGADE CRIMINELLE TRILOGY

MACLEHOSE PRESS

www.maclehosepress.com

Subscribe to our newsletter

"Moves from **read-as-fast-as-you-can horror** to an intricately plotted race to a dark truth . . . *Alex* is about thrills. And as the novel barrels triumphantly towards its unexpected but satisfying conclusion, it's in this respect that it delivers"
ALISON FLOOD, *Observer*

"It is quickly apparent that **Lemaitre is worthy of all the fuss** . . . And Alex herself turns out to be the author's ace-in-the-hole. By page 200 you may believe that you're moving to a pulse-raising conclusion. But you will be wrong; **in some senses, the novel has only just begun**"
BARRY FORSHAW, *Independent*

"Unlike many novels of this type in which the promise of a sensational premise fizzles out, there is **a spectacular plot twist** and the tension, along with the body count, mounts ever higher – **an invigoratingly scary, one-sitting read**"
LAURA WILSON, *Guardian*

"**Harsh, fierce crime writing** with a Gauloise tinge. It would not be out of place filmed in black and white by the late, lamented François Truffaut"
GEOFFREY WANSELL, *Daily Mail*

"Pierre Lemaitre . . . **another master of crime fiction** destined to become a household name"
ADAM SAGE, *The Times*

Pierre Lemaitre

CAMILLE

Translated from the French by Frank Wynne

WITH NOTHING ELSE TO LOSE

Anne Forestier was in the wrong place at the wrong time. Beaten beyond recognition at a raid on a jeweller's, she is lucky to survive. But her ordeal has only just begun.

HE CAN BREAK ALL THE RULES

Lying helpless in her hospital bed, with her assailant still at large, Anne is in grave danger. Just one thing gives her hope: Commandant Camille Verhœven.

TO PROTECT THE WOMAN HE LOVES

For Verhœven it's a case of history repeating. He cannot lose Anne as he lost Irène. But this time his adversary's greatest strength appears to be Verhœven's own powers of intuition.

BOOK THREE OF THE BRIGADE CRIMINELLE TRILOGY

MACLEHOSE PRESS

www.maclehosepress.com

Subscribe to our newsletter

PIERRE LEMAITRE was born in Paris in 1951. He worked for many years as a teacher of literature and now writes novels and screenplays. In 2013 he was awarded the C.W.A. International Dagger for *Alex*, and again in 2015 for *Camille*, the second and third books in the crime trilogy featuring Commandant Camille Verhœven that began with *Irène*. In 2013 he was also the winner of the Prix Goncourt, France's most prestigious literary award, for his novel *Au revoir là-haut*, published in English in 2015 as *The Great Swindle*.

FRANK WYNNE is a translator from French and Spanish of works by Michel Houellebecq, Boualem Sansal, Antonin Varenne, Arturo Pérez-Reverte, Carlos Acosta and Hervé le Corre. He has been the winner of the Impac Prize, the *Independent* Foreign Fiction Prize, the Premio Valle-Inclán and the Scott Moncrieff Prize.